HOMICIDE HOST PRESENTS

A Collection of Original Mysteries
BY
Robert Randisi

Sandra Brewer

Margaret Lawrence

Marthayn Pelegrimas

Carol Caverly

Hugh Holton

Ann Blaine

Mark Zubro

John Lutz

Edward Hoch

Loren Estleman

Thomas Sullivan

Helen Olmsted

William Kienzle

Compiled by Helen Esper Olmsted

A Write Way Publishing Book

ACKNOWLEDGEMENTS

Many thanks to my son-in-law, Bob Wickenhiser, and my grandsons, Rob and Joey Lambert, whose invasion into my home (to install a computer and bully me into putting a whole book on this monstrous machine) was not unlike the Marine landing on Okinawa.

Also thanks to a dear friend, writer and computer expert, Sandra Brewer, who held my hand (when I'd given up in despair) while she guided my persistent husband, Don, as he put this book on a disk (bless him).

As there never would have been a book without the many authors who contributed to it, my gratitude goes out to them, and to my daughter, Janet Sandison, for the cover.

And last but not least, a special thanks to Dee Devlin and Dorrie O'Brien; Dee for suggesting I get this book compiled, and Dorrie whose patience is unlimited.

Without all, *Homicide Host Presents* would not have come about.

Write Way Publishing

10555 E. Dartmouth, Ste. 210

Aurora, CO 80014

First Edition; 1996

ISBN 1-885173-14-8

1 2 3 4 5 6 7 8 9 10

DEDICATION

To my wonderful husband, Don, my five children, and their equally wonderful spouses. Lots of love to my nine companionable grandchildren and the last of the train, Donnie, who is sometimes still loveable and huggable, but always my "Partner in Crime;" and finally my great-grandchildren, Christopher and Alexandria, who are still always loveable and huggable, as well as my "Happy Campers."

And in loving memory of my mother, Georgina Esper, whose first name I gave to my detective; and my father, Joseph Esper, whose beautiful flower gardens I am reminded of every spring.

TABLE OF CONTENTS

INTRODUCTION

by

Helen Esper Olmsted

The classics have always been of great enjoyment to mystery writers everywhere. But it has only been within the last fifty years that the mystery has fully come into its own. In this introduction, I will pay tribute to our earlier writers as well as those more recent, and the amazing number who are relatively new at the game.

Known as the "Master of Suspense," E.A. Poe's most popular works are probably in *The Crown Crime Companion* collection (1995): *Tales of Mystery and Imagination*. However, Poe's detective A. C. Dupin, introduced in *The Murders in the Rue Morgue* (1841), has gone down in the annals of famous fictional detectives of all time.

The Victorian Era in foggy olde London brought us Sir Arthur Conan Doyle, who began his career writing detective fiction for London's *Strand Magazine*. As Jack the Ripper stalked the ladies (*Harlots of White Chapel*), committing his never-to-be-solved heinous murders, Sir Arthur had already begun penning his stories about Sherlock Holmes, the gentleman detective, who only applied himself to those cases that presented a mental challenge, rather than monetary gain.

Doyle often used Holmes' sidekick, Dr. Watson, as Sherlock's sounding board ("Elementary, my Dear Watson"). Sir Arthur's career spanned the years of 1887 to 1927. But the Sherlockian Society, "The Baker Street Irregulars," and its scions are alive and well; as any good Sherlockian will tell you: "It's always eighteen ninety-five."

In 1923, Dame Agatha Christie, probably the greatest mystery plotter to date, published her first mystery, *The Mysterious Affair at Styles*. She went on to publish more than eighty mystery novels and a few stage plays (including the very popular *Mousetrap*, which Dame Agatha adapted from a radio script she had written for Queen Victoria's birthday).

Christie's most memorable detectives are Miss Marple, the old lady who eavesdrops on conversations (to help solve the crime) while knitting a baby sweater; and Hercule Poirot, the little man with the egg-shaped head who stands out in a crowd in his unforgettable apparel of bowler hat and patent leather shoes. He brags that his little gray cells will solve the crime and so they do. Dame Agatha was the first recipient of the coveted Grand Master awarded by the Mystery Writers of America in 1955.

When speaking of the greats in English detection, let's not forget Dorothy L. Sayers' debonair Lord Peter Whimsey and his man, Bunter. Lord Peter saved Harriet Vane, detective novelist, from the gallows in *Strong Poison* (1930); Lord Peter and Harriet have since married and now they do their sleuthing together.

Leaving our British counterparts, let's take a look at the new American Private Eye. Dashiel Hammett had Sam Spade, and Nick and Nora Charles (well remembered from television). *The Maltese Falcon* (1930) is considered his finest work.

Raymond Chandler's *The Big Sleep* (1939) was Chandler's introduction of the hard-boiled private eye, Phillip Marlowe, who—though he is tough as nails—lives by a strict moral code. It's not hard to figure that Humphrey Bogart depicted Marlowe in the movie of the same name or that Lauren Bacall was his co-star. Hammett and Chandler will always be idols of upcoming hard-boiled detective writers.

Also in 1939, Rex Stout brought out the soft-boiled detective, Nero Wolfe, who grew orchids and overindulged in good food and drink to the point where he became a mountain of a man, which led to Archie Goodwin, Wolfe's man of all trades, doing the sleuthing. Stout's first book, published in 1939, was *Fer de Lance*.

Around 1944 the world heard from Mickey Spillane and his detective Mike Hammer. Spillane has also created a comic strip, which will be written by Max Allan Collins and will probably be out by the time this collection is published.

In 1945, the mystery genre received a shot in the arm when a handful of writers started a national organization called Mystery Writers of America. Although it started small and the meetings were held only in New York City at the Stork Club, it now has close to 3,000 U.S. members (with some international members), and has had an office of its own for several decades. MWA's annual banquet is held in New York City every spring. They had their 50th birthday bash in April, 1995.

And, over the years, mystery writers noticed that their books were gradually being moved from the darkest recesses of the bookstores' shelves to the front where they now stand tall with the mainstream fiction; mystery books have hit the big time and are here to stay.

Latter-day mystery writers who started appearing in the late '60s, and '70s and beyond were: Dan J. Marlowe: *Earl Drake, The Man with Nobody's Face,* who worked undercover for the government; Mary Higgins Clark: *Where are the Children;* Donald Westlake (probably most famous for his Dortmunder gang): *Bank Shot;* John D. MacDonald (the color writer): *The Dreadful Lemon Sky;* Lawrence Block: *When the Sacred Gin Mill Closes;* Gregory McDonald: *Fletch;* Sue Grafton with her alphabet crimes: *A is for Alibi*; Tony Hillerman, most famous for his Navajo detective, Joe Leaphorn: *Coyote Waits*; Carol Higgins Clark (with her not-so-hard-boiled detective Regan Riley): *Decked*; D. C. Brod's medium-boiled detective, Quint McCauley: *Brothers in Blood*; Barbara D'Amato's investigative reporter Cat Marsala: *Hard Christmas*; Diane Mott Davidson and her catered murders: *Killer Pancakes*; Carolyn G. Hart and her two series, Annie Lawrence and hubby, Max Darling: *A Little Class in Murder*; Henry 0.: *Murder in Fair Haven*; and finally my favorite horror/mystery writers, Stephen King: *Carrie*; and Robert Wilson: *Crooked Tree*.

In 1982, Robert Randisi, one of the contributors to this collection and himself a best-selling private eye writer, founded the Private Eye Writers of America; the organization has thrived under his smooth administrative hand.

In 1986, Sarah Paretsky, and a handful of others, seeing the need for more recognition of women mystery writers, founded Sisters in Crime, which now boasts several brothers in crime as well. The organization has climbed from a few to over 3,000 members and has several national and international chapters.

For those who have aided and abetted in the commission of the felony, *Homicide Host Presents*, we have: **Ed Hoch**, author of over 700 short stories, has given us a story with quite a twist. **John Lutz**, author of the Carver and Nudger Series and a couple of psychological thrillers, *SWF Seeks Same* (aka on the silver screen: *Single White Female)*, has written a slightly different story for this collection. **Ann Blaine**, editor of *The Livingston County Literary Magazine*, gives us a cliff-hanging suspense story. **Carol Caverly**, one of the newest voices in mysteries, has taken on the keyboard as a clue. **Hugh Holton**, a commander in the Chicago Police Department whose *Windy City* flourished for several weeks on *The Chicago Tribune*'s Best Seller List, has let his imagination run wild in his tale of fantasy and murder. **Margaret Lawrence**, best noted for her Winston Sherman (Professor Sleuth), has also started a Victorian Series. She has contributed an exhilarating and delightful medieval story to this collection. **Robert Randisi**, a very prolific writer who writes two detective series, Miles Jacoby and Nick Delvecchio, is giving us a story about a most unusual horse and the girl who takes care of him. (Could be Bob's a track man!) **Sandra Brewer**, our computer specialist, takes on the meaning of justice. **William X. Kienzle**, creator of the Father Koesler series, has given us a different kind of priest who is almost too klutzy to believe. **Loren Estleman**, who has more than thirty published novels from western-historical to mystery, has stuck with his detective, Amos Walker, for which he is best known. **Mark Zubro**, author of *Why Isn't Becky Twitchell Dead?*, has given us a taste of just deserts. **Thomas Sullivan** has chosen to play mind games with us and **Marthayn Pelegrimas** has written the only horror story in the collection. As for yours truly, the story I have written is a preview to a series character, Georgi Raconni, which I have started and hope you'll see more of at a future date.

This completes the roster and I apologize profusely to the many talented writers I would have included had I not run out of space and energy. I think you know who you are.

As for the readers, all I can say is ENJOY!

Bob Randisi

ROBERT J. RANDISI has had over 260 books published since 1982. He has written in the mystery, western, men's adventure, fantasy, historical and spy genres, authoring both the Nick Delvecchio and Miles Jacoby series. He has edited and published fourteen anthologies. He is the founder and Executive Director of the Private Eye Writers of America, the creator of the Shamus Award; he is the co-founder of *Mystery Scene Magazine*, and of the American Crime Writer's League. His newest novel is *Alone With the Dead* (St. Martin's, 1995).

THE GIRL WHO TALKED TO HORSES

A Henry Po Story
by
Robert J. Randisi

The trainer's name was Carlucci and everybody said he had an edge. What was it? Well, they said he was a whiz with horses, but he liked them better than people, and that's why they performed for him.

I don't know how many people believed it, but Anthony Carlucci had been having a hell of a career in New York for the past four years, but if he had an edge it had run out today.

Today Carlucci was lying in a stall at Belmont Park, out on Elmont, Long Island, and he didn't have an edge anymore because he was dead.

When Carlucci's body had been discovered by his assistant trainer that morning, I'd been called in because I was in charge of security for the New York State Racing Club. That is, I was in charge when there was some investigating to be done. There were uniformed guards working the track who worked for another outfit. They didn't have to report to me, but we had an understanding.

So, to get the sequence of events right, the assistant trainer, Dick Dermott, found Carlucci's body when he arrived on the backstretch at five-thirty AM. He immediately called for a uniformed guard, who then called his boss, who then called me. Being the fair-minded man I am, since we were all up, I figured I might as well call my boss and wake him up, too.

"This better be good," J. Howard Biel said when I identified myself on the phone.

"Murder," I said.

"Murder?"

"Well," I said, "somebody's dead, let's put it that way. I don't know if it's murder, but—"

"Who's dead?"

"Apparently," I said, breaking it to him gently, "Anthony Carlucci."

"What?"

He had a right to be upset. One of the hottest young trainers to come down the pike had chosen the Belmont/Aqueduct/Saratoga/Staten Island Downs circuit to ply his trade. That was good, that was a feather in the N.Y.S.R.C.'s hat. Having him turn up dead was ... well, bad.

Biel agreed to meet me at the track, but I arrived before he did and identified myself to the guard on duty. His name tag identified him by his last name, Mattingly.

"Anybody call the cops yet?" I asked.

"I don't know," Mattingly said. "I called my boss, and he told me to stand guard and not let anyone in until you got here."

"Okay," I said. There was nobody else around. "Where's Mr. Dermott? You didn't let him leave, did you?"

"No, sir," the guard said. "He's in Mr. Carlucci's office."

"Good."

"Do you want me to get him, Mr Po?"

"No, no," I said, "leave him there. I'll take a look at the body first, and then talk to Dermott. Since we don't know if the police have been called, if they do show up let them in, all right?"

"Yes, sir."

"Also, Mr. Biel is on his way, so let him through, too."

"Yes, sir."

That settled, I went into the barn to take a look at Anthony Carlucci. He was lying on the floor of one of the stalls, and had obviously been kicked to death by a horse. His head was bleeding, and the blood had soaked into the straw and dirt around him. I went into the stall and bent over him, but there was nothing for me to do. I didn't touch him, or move him. I got out of there, feeling slightly sick. It's not every day you see somebody's brains scattered about.

Outside I asked the guard, "Who moved the horse?"

"Mr. Dermott."

"What horse was it?"

"I'm not sure, sir," the man said, "but it might have been Tobasco Boy."

That didn't surprise me. Tobasco Boy was the crown jewel of Carlucci's barn. He was supposed to run in the Kentucky Derby in three weeks. Last year's two-year-old champ, he was going into the Derby undefeated in five starts last year, and three starts as a three year old.

As brilliant as the horse was on the track, though, his comportment off the track was legendarily bad. He had taken a piece out of more people—his trainer, assistant trainer, groom, hot walker—than any other horse, and he made the newspapers for it. It would come as no surprise to any reader of any of the racing newspapers that he had stomped someone to death.

The question I had was, what was Carlucci doing alone in the stall of such a notorious horse?

"I'm going into the office to talk to Mr. Dermott now. Watch for the cops, and Mr. Biel."

"Yes, sir."

I walked to the end of the shed row and found Anthony Carlucci's office. I knocked and entered and found Dick Dermott sitting behind his boss' desk, like he belonged there.

There were photos on the walls, as well as various pieces of racing equipment, like whips and bridles, and, on one wall, a saddle. The office smelled of leather, and the creams used to soften and preserve it.

"Mr. Dermott?" I asked, even though I recognized him. I didn't know if he knew me, though.

"That's right."

He was in his mid-thirties, a bit younger than Carlucci himself, who I thought I recalled as being in his early forties. They were considered to be a good team, each a fine trainer in his own right, but the barn was Carlucci's and so was the reputation.

"My name is Henry Po," I said, "I work for the Board—"

"I know who you are, Mr. Po," Dermott said, cutting off my introduction. "I've seen you on the grounds. Are the police here?"

"No," I said. "Uh, did you call them?"

The man looked surprised. "No, I thought you had."

"I will, if I can use that phone," I said, "but afterward I'd like to ask you some questions."

"Shouldn't we wait for the police?" Dermott asked.

"We could," I said, "and we will, but we might as well talk while we're waiting, don't you think?"

"I don't know," Dermott said. I found his eyes and his state of mind remarkably clear for someone who had found his colleague, and for all I knew his friend, dead. This had never happened to me before, but I was suddenly very certain that he had something to do with Anthony Carlucci's death.

***

"Mr. Po?"

"Yes?"

"You wanted to use the phone?"

"Oh, yes, thank you."

That was when I knew I was staring at him, and maybe he did, too, because he was watching me, now, as I dialed 911 and reported the incident.

"It'll be a while before detectives get here," I said, as I hung up. "First they'll send a uniformed patrol, and then they'll send for a supervisor, and finally they'll call for the detectives."

"I see," Dermott said, "then this is going to go on for a while."

"Yes."

"I'd better let my people know."

His people? They were his people, already?

"Your staff, you mean?"

"Yes."

"Can you do that by phone?"

"Why?"

"Well ... I really can't let you leave the area, Mr. Dermott. After all, you did find the body, and ..."

"And I'm a suspect?" Dermott asked. "Is that what you mean?"

Suddenly, I felt like Columbo, playing cat-and-mouse games with a famous guest star, only I wasn't a brilliant-yet-rumpled cop, and Dermott was not a famous star.

"I thought it was an accident," I said. "At least, it looks like an accident."

Dermott surprised me by shaking his head, violently. "It couldn't be."

"Why not?"

"Tony would never have gone into Tobasco Boy's stall alone. I'm sure you're aware of the horse's violent nature."

"I've read about it, yes."

"Then you understand," Dermott said. "We agreed that no one would ever try to handle him alone."

"Who usually handled the horse?"

"His groom, and his hot walker."

"Who are they?"

"Oh, sorry," Dermott said. "The groom's name is Hennessy, and the hot walker is Amanda Ellis."

I didn't know either one of them, but then, there was no reason I should. I did spend time at the various tracks, but there was no way I could know the personnel of each individual stable, unless they had been there as long as I had, and Carlucci's Canyon Valley Stable had only been in New York four years.

"The police will want to talk to them."

"They're probably around," Dermott said. "They're usually here even before me and Tony."

There was only one guard outside, and I needed him to keep people out of the stable. I didn't have anyone to send looking for Hennessy or Ellis.

As if on cue, there was a knock at the door.

"May I?" I asked.

"Please."

I walked to the door and opened it. There was a girl standing there, about five-five, slender and attractive, wearing a sleeveless T-shirt, exposing the powerful forearms and upper arms of someone who worked with horses for a living. She was not muscle-bound, but well-toned, like Linda Hamilton was in *The Terminator II*. When your job was controlling an animal who weighed over a thousand pounds, you tended to be in shape. It was the case with jockeys, exercise riders, hot walkers and grooms.

Also, if you watch racing on television you've probably noticed how many of the people who hold these jobs—especially the hot walkers—are women, and attractive young women. I don't mean that they could be models, but they're usually wearing T-shirts and jeans, and they're almost always in fabulous shape, as this woman was. She appeared to be in her early twenties.

"What's going on?" she demanded. "Who are you? Why can't I get into the stable? Where are—"

I held up my hand and said, "I can answer your questions, Miss, but they have to come one at a time."

"Amanda?"

She looked past me to Dermott, who had called her name.

"Dick? What's going on?"

"Mr. Po, that's Amanda Ellis. Would you let her in please?"

"Of course," I said, backing away. "Miss Ellis?"

She came in, giving me a sideways glance, and walked right to the desk.

"Dick?"

"There's been an accident," Dermott said, without standing up. I thought he looked extremely comfortable behind the desk.

"What kind of accident?" she asked. "One of the horses?"

"Not exactly," Dermott said. "It's Tony. He's dead."

"What?" Her back was to me, so I couldn't see her face, but she lifted her hands to her mouth.

"Tobasco Boy stomped him to death this morning."

"What?" This time her tone was more strident. "What will they do to him?"

Dermott shook his head and shrugged helplessly.

"I don't know," he said. "This is Mr. Po. He works for the Board—"

She turned quickly to stare at me. She was not the most beautiful woman I had ever seen, but at that moment she was certainly the most attractive. She was magnificent, muscles tense, nostrils flaring ... why did I think she was more concerned about the horse than the poor, dead trainer?

***

I answered honestly.

"I have no idea what will happen to the horse," I said, "*if* he did, in fact, stomp Mr. Carlucci to death."

"If?" she asked. She turned on Dermott. "You said he did it."

"Mr. Dermott," I said, "found Mr. Carlucci in the stall this morning, dead."

Dermott nodded.

"Tobasco Boy's stall, and the horse was standing over him."

"So then you don't know for sure that Toby did it?" she asked.

"Toby?" I asked.

"My nickname for Tobasco Boy."

"We don't know for sure that the horse did it," I said, "no. The police are on their way, Miss Ellis. They'll want to talk to you."

"About what?"

"About the horse, about Mr. Carlucci—"

"Does Sam know?"

"Sam?"

"Hennessy," Dermott said. "I told you about him."

"The groom."

"Does he know?"

"Not yet."

"Someone has to tell him."

"Why don't you do that, if you don't mind?" I asked.

"No," she said, "I don't mind. I—I'd like to tell him."

"Fine," I said, "you can also tell him the police will want to talk to him, too."

"Are you some sort of a detective?" she asked.

"As a matter of fact, I am," I said. "I have a private detective's license, but I work primarily for the racing board. I report directly to Howard Biel."

She looked impressed. "Does he know about this?"

"Yes," I said, "in fact, it's a toss-up as to who will get here first, him or the police."

"I'll want to talk to him."

"About what?"

"Toby—Tobasco Boy," she said. "If he did it he'll need someone to plead his case, won't he?"

"Probably," I said, "but who will plead Tony Carlucci's?"

She and Dermott exchanged a glance and then she left, promising to get Hennessy and stay around.

"Why do I get the feeling she and Carlucci didn't get along?"

"They didn't."

"Why not?"

Dermott shrugged. "Who knows?"

I turned and faced him squarely. "I think you do." In fact, I thought he knew a lot more than he was saying.

"All right," he said, "Tony was something of a chauvinist. He treated Amanda like he'd treat a girl, woman ... do you know what I mean?"

"I think I do."

"He'd pat her on the ass, send her on menial errands, like getting coffee, you know. She finally had enough one day and told him off. Since then ..." He shrugged.

"Why'd she stay?" I asked. "Why didn't he fire her?"

"For the same reason."

"Which was?"

"She was the only one who could handle Tobasco Boy."

"I thought nobody could handle him."

"Except Amanda," Dermott said. "She's uncanny with horses. She—well, this will sound silly ..."

"Go ahead."

"She claims that the horses talk to her."

"I'm sorry?"

"She says that she can communicate with the horses," Dermott explained. "It sounds odd, I know, but she gets along with them like no one I've ever seen. Often she's able to figure out what's wrong with them when they're not training right in the morning, or not running right in the afternoon."

"How?"

"She says that ... they tell her."

"And you believed her?" I asked. "You and Carlucci?"

"We didn't care," he said. "She worked wonders with them and we didn't care if she was goddamned Doctor Dolittle, as long as she was right."

"Great," I said, "maybe she can get Tobasco Boy to tell us what happened here this morning."

"Who knows?" Dermott asked. "Maybe she can, at that."

***

The next few hours were hectic, and confused. Howard Biel arrived just ahead of the police. As I'd predicted, we ended up with cops, supervisors and then plainclothes detectives. Not only that, but the man who was in charge of the uni-formed guards at the track, Patrick Lukas, also arrived, ready to kick some ass. He regarded the "incident" as a black mark against himself and his crew.

The detective in charge of the case was a man named Zeke Tomachek, a tall, gray-bearded, dignified-looking man who stood over six feet tall, but seemed to stoop a bit to hide it.

Biel had a talk with Tomachek first thing and managed to arrange for me to remain on the scene as his representative.

"Henry," he said to me, "I have to go to my office and make some calls. I've got to try to keep the lid on this. Keep an eye on things, all right?"

"All right, Howard."

Tomachek asked that Carlucci's "employees," Dermott, Hennessy and Amanda Ellis, wait in the office to be questioned. Dermott agreed to do so, but complained about being called Carlucci's employee.

"I'm sorry," Tomachek said, "I'm not up on my racetrack terminology. What is it you do, Mr. Dermott?"

"I'm the assistant trainer."

"Very well," Tomachek said, "I'll refer to you that way from now on."

"Thank you."

As Dermott walked away, Tomachek asked me, "Who paid his salary?"

"Carlucci."

He nodded. "That's what I thought: He worked for the guy."

"Right."

"Then why does it upset him to hear it?"

"Because he liked to think he worked *with* Carlucci, not *for* him."

"Hmm," Tomachek said, "looks to me like somebody's not satisfied with his lot in life."

Tomachek also had an altercation with Lukas about his

men. He wanted the private security people off the premises—
except for me.

"My men belong here, Detective," Lukas complained.

Lukas was ex-military. You could tell it by looking at him.
He might also have been an ex-mercenary. His demeanor ex-
hibited all of the worst attributes of both.

In other words, he was an asshole.

"Mr. Lukas," Tomachek said, "I've asked you nicely to remove yourself and your men from the scene. They are free to
maintain their posts in another area of the track, but I want
them—and you—gone from here."

"But—"

"Please leave willingly; don't make me have you removed."

They stared at each other and, in the end, Lukas blinked.

He and his men were gone by the time the coroner and his
men arrived, or else we would have really had a crowd. I never
heard the coroner's name. They only called him "Doctor."

Tomachek and I entered the stable area with the coroner
and watched while he examined Carlucci's body.

"What do you say, Doctor?" Tomachek asked.

The doctor—in his fifties, with steel-gray hair and goatee—
crouched next to the body and shook his head.

"What a mess."

"Is that your professional opinion?" Tomachek asked.

The man ignored Tomachek's attempt at humor, the first
indication that he had no sense of humor—or maybe he just
didn't have one when it came to death.

"This man has been bludgeoned about the head, very possibly beaten to death. I won't say more until the autopsy."

"Just tell me this, Doctor," Tomachek said. "Did the horse
do it?"

The doctor stood up and scowled. "How could I possibly say that with a certainty?"

"Then just tell me if it *could* have done it. I just want to know if I can rule it out or not."

"Of course you can't rule it out," the doctor said, "not until I've autopsied the body—and if I can get out of here, I can do that."

"All right," Tomachek said, wearily, "take him away." He turned to me and asked, "I don't suppose there's someplace we can get some coffee."

"There's a backstretch cafe," I said. "I can have somebody— wait, you chased all the track security away."

"I'll have an officer get it," Tomachek said, "Just give him directions—"

"All right."

"—and tell him what you want."

He brought a man over and I did as he asked, asking for a black coffee for myself.

We watched as the coroner's men bagged the body and removed it. That left the stall empty, except of blood. The coroner's people had also picked up whatever minute pieces of bone and brain matter might have been left behind.

"Where's the horse?" Tomachek asked me.

"He's in a stall farther down."

"Who moved him?"

"Dermott."

"I thought one person couldn't handle him?"

"The first guard on the scene, Mattingly, helped him. He, uh, just followed Dermott's instructions and they got Tobasco Boy moved."

"I don't know anything about racing," Tomachek said. "Is this a good horse?"

"One of the best in training."

"Too bad."

"Why?"

"If he did it," Tomachek said, "what will happen to him?"

"I'm not sure."

"If it was a dog they'd put him to sleep."

"A thoroughbred is not a dog," I said. "There are investors, and insurance premiums ..."

"Hmm," Tomachek said, "insurance ..."

We walked into the stall together.

"Did you examine him?" Tomachek asked.

"I didn't touch him," I said. "I just wanted to be sure he was dead."

He started moving bloody straw around with his foot, whether idly or with purpose, I didn't know, but I saw something.

"Wait," I said, "don't move."

"What?" he asked, freezing.

"Just back away a minute."

He did. I stepped outside the stall and looked around until I found a pitchfork. I came back in the stall and used the tool to move the straw until I had cleared it away.

"See?"

He stepped forward and looked down.

"I see," he said, and we both stared at the twin marks in the ground that could only have been made by the bootheels of a man being dragged.

"Look here," I said, pointing to the front of the stall. "There were marks, but they were wiped out."

"We've got a murder here," Tomachek said.

"And the killer missed the bootheel marks that were hidden by the straw."

"Now the question is," Tomachek said, "was he dead when he was dragged in, or was he unconscious and helpless while the horse stomped him to death?"

"Maybe," I said, "we should ask the horse."

Naturally, I had to explain that.

***

Tomachek didn't know whether or not to take me seriously. Frankly, I didn't know either.

"Do you believe this stuff?" he asked.

"I don't know," I said, "but Dermott believes it, and that may be what's important."

"What do you mean?"

Tomachek and I were inside, while everyone else was outside. I decided to tell him what I'd been thinking.

"Have you had many feelings like this in the past?" he asked when I was done.

"No."

"Worked on many murders?"

"No."

He regarded me curiously.

"Why should I go along with this?"

I shrugged. "What have you got to lose?" I asked.

"Okay," he said, "then tell me how you see it."

"I see it done all of a sudden," I said. "It's too sloppy to have been planned. Those heel marks showing that he'd been dragged into the stall, that's amateur stuff."

"So you're saying it's a crime of passion?" Tomachek asked. "He was killed by someone he knew?"

"I'm just telling you what I feel," I said, "and what I think. I think that horse stomped an already-dead man. Maybe the coroner can tell the difference between a hoof print and some other kind of blow, but maybe he hasn't got enough skill to be able to. If this happened the way I think then the murder weapon is still around."

Tomachek regarded me for a few more moments and then said, "I'll have a thorough search done. Meanwhile, what do you want to do?"

"I want to talk to Amanda Ellis."

"What if she's the murderer?"

"Then she'll jump at the chance to implicate someone else, won't she?"

"Maybe."

"Again," I asked, "what have you got to lose? Maybe you've got a chance to solve this thing before another hour goes by. What'll that do to your statistics?"

I was talking about the statistic that said if a murder wasn't solved in the first forty-eight hours—or twenty-four, or seventy-two, whatever it was—then it wouldn't be solved at all.

"It would knock it to hell," Tomachek said. "Okay, I'm gonna go along with you on this, only because I don't have any feeling at all for the people, and you seem to."

I didn't bother telling him that I had only just met these people about an hour ago myself—but he was right about one thing. I had a feeling, and he didn't.

"I'll get the girl and have her brought in here," Tomachek said.

"Thanks."

While he went to arrange for the search and to have Amanda Ellis join me, I studied Tobasco Boy in his new stall. He stood very still, seemingly totally relaxed, and stared at me balefully.

"What have you got to say about all this, Toby?" I asked. "Are you getting a bum rap here?"

He didn't bother answering me. Maybe he'd tell Amanda Ellis.

***

When Amanda Ellis appeared she approached me tentatively. "Miss Ellis," I said. "Would you like to see Tobasco Boy? " She brightened and quickened her step. "Yes, I would." "Here he is."

I stepped aside as she approached the stall and reached her hand out to him. He came over to her immediately and nuzzled her hand.

"That's amazing," I said. "That horse is supposed to be to be as ornery as—"

"He's not ornery with me," she said.

"Because you can communicate with him?"

She turned and looked at me. "You're not like the others."

"In what way?"

"You refer to the horse as 'him' and not 'it,' like most of the others do."

"Like Dermott?"

She snorted. "Him, especially. I suppose he told you about me talking to the animals?"

"He mentioned it."

"Did he make the Doctor Dolittle reference?"

"He did."

"Asshole."

"*Can* you talk to the horses?"

"I don't exactly talk to them," she said, "but they are able to make their feelings known to me. There is a woman, though, out in California who says she can actually talk back and forth with the horses."

"How do the people around here feel about what you can do?"

"Most of them don't believe it," she said, "but they do listen when I tell them when a change of diet, or training regimen, might improve the horse's performance."

"And then it does?"

"Most of the time, yes."

"Amanda—may I call you Amanda?"

"Sure."

"Can you tell if Tobasco Boy, uh, stomped Mr. Carlucci?"

"I can look at his hooves."

"Would you do that for me?" I asked. "You're not afraid to go into the stall with him, are you?"

"Of course not."

She opened the door, slipped in and closed it behind her. She talked gently to the horse while lifting his hooves and examining them, then rubbed his neck lovingly and came back out.

"Well?"

"He's got blood on his hooves."

"He could have walked in the blood, though," I said. "He didn't have to stomp Carlucci to get the blood on him."

"You don't believe he did it?"

"No, I don't," I said. "Even if he did stomp the man, I think he was already dead."

"Who do you think killed him?"

"I was hoping you'd be able to tell me that."

"Me? How?"

"By asking the horse."

"What are you talking about?" she demanded, annoyed. "I just told you I can't really *talk* to the horses."

"But there are people who think you can," I said.

She frowned. "What are you asking me to do?"

***

When Detective Tomachek returned he was shaking his head.

"What?"

"No murder weapon," he said, "but we'll keep looking."

"It's got to be here."

"If it happened like you figure," Tomachek reminded me, "on the spur of the moment." He looked at Amanda. "Is Miss Ellis being helpful?"

"Very."

Tomachek gave her a long look.

"Am I under suspicion?" she asked him.

"At this point," he said, "everyone is. That's standard procedure."

"I'd like to talk to the others now, Detective," I said.

Tomachek showed me a warning finger. "I'm only going to give you so much leeway, Mr. Po," he said. "If your plan is not working I'm going to call it quits."

"Fine," I said "if that happens it will fall to you, anyway. I'll be out of it."

"Agreed."

We left the stable and went to Carlucci's office, where a uniformed policeman was at his post outside the door.

"Are they inside?" Tomachek asked.

"Yes, sir."

Tomachek knocked, then entered. Dermott was still behind the desk. Another man who I assumed to be Sam Hennessy was sitting in another chair, shoulders slumped. He must have been a jockey at one time, given his size and make-up. He looked to be in his late forties.

"It's about time," Dermott said. "How long are we going to be kept here? We've got work to do, you know."

"What sort of work, Mr. Dermott?" I asked.

Dermott looked from me to Tomachek in some confusion, then settled on me. "We've got a stable to run," he said. "The horses have to be tended to."

"You expect to continue to run the stable?"

"The owners will expect it," he said, "and who else will do it?"

"Well, I'd expect at least one day of mourning ..." I said, letting it trail off.

"Don't think for one minute that we won't mourn Tony, Mr. Po," Dermott said, "but as a trainer, not as a person."

"He wasn't a ... nice man, then?"

Hennessy snorted.

"Mr. Hennessy, is it?"

"That's right."

"You didn't like Mr. Carlucci?"

"Nobody did," Hennessy said, "not even the horses. I'm not surprised one of them killed him."

"Oh, Mr. Carlucci wasn't killed by the horse, Mr. Hennessy."

The smaller man looked confused, and tossed Dermott a long glance, which I found interesting.

"What do you mean?" he asked. "Mr. Dermott said—"

"Mr. Dermott said a lot of things," I said, looking at the assistant trainer.

"What are you talking about?" Dermott demanded. He looked at Tomachek. "Aren't you in charge?"

"Mr. Po has the floor right now, Mr. Dermott."

"You claim you found Carlucci in the stall," I said to Dermott. "You didn't."

"How dare you—"

"He was dragged into the stall," I continued. "The softer ground inside the stall still shows the drag marks made by his heels. You neglected to wipe out the marks beneath the straw."

This time it was Dermott who threw Hennessy a look. Things were becoming clearer.

"Let's get right to it, Mr. Dermott," I said. "On top of everything else, you're a bad actor."

"What ... what do you mean, everything else?"

"The coroner's report will show that Mr. Carlucci was not killed by blows from the horse, but that he was already dead when the horse stomped him. You killed him, then put him in the stall and agitated the horse so he would stomp the dead body. Then you hid the murder weapon, which will be found, eventually."

"Y-you can't prove any of this."

"No," I said, "I can't, but the horse can."

Now Dermott looked confused and, for the first time, shaken. "What?"

"Yes," I said, "you were right about Miss Ellis being able to communicate with the horses."

"What?" he said, again.

"The horse didn't do it, Mr. Dermott," I said. "He told Miss Ellis he didn't do it."

Dermott stared at Amanda for a few moments and she kept quiet. I'd asked her to play along, and she was, silently.

"Th-that's impossible."

"No, it's not," I said. "Every living thing can communicate, Mr. Dermott. Maybe the horse doesn't talk to Miss Ellis, but he communicates with her, and what he communicated was that he didn't kill Carlucci—you did."

Dermott looked at Tomachek for help. "This is preposterous," he said. "You can't honestly believe—"

"Mr. Dermott," Tomachek said, playing his part, "I think we better go downtown."

"Am I under a-arrest?"

"I think we'll just hold onto you until we get the coroner's report," Tomachek said. "At that time I'd say yes, you will be under arrest."

"But, I didn't—"

"Yes?"

Dermott looked at Hennessy, who was looking around the room, as if seeking an avenue of escape.

"What's wrong, Mr. Hennessy?" I asked.

"Huh? Nothin's wrong ... I just ..."

"Do you believe that Mr. Dermott killed Carlucci?" I asked.

"I—I don't know—I—"

"What was your part, Hennessy?"

"What?"

"Did you kill him, or just help drag him into the stall?" I asked.

"Po—" Tomachek said. He was confused now, but the looks Hennessy and Dermott had been passing back and forth were—for me, anyway—remarkably easy to read.

"They both did it, Tomachek," I said. "Both of them."

They looked at each other again.

"I didn't—" Hennessy finally said.

"Shut up!" Dermott shouted.

"Hennessy?" I said. "You want to wait until Dermott goes downtown and gives you up?"

"I didn't kill him!" Hennessy shouted. "He did. He got into an argument and ... and hit him."

"He wasn't dead!" Dermott said. "I—I hit him, but it was your idea to put him into the stall with the horse, your idea to let Tobasco Boy finish him." Dermott looked at us. "He helped me drag him into the stall." Then he looked at Hennessy again. "You were suppose to clean away the heel marks!"

"I did!"

"Not good enough," I said. "Detective?"

Tomachek went to the door, opened it and called in the uniformed officer. "I'm going to need your cuffs," he said.

***

Later, Amanda Ellis came with me to Howard Biel's office. She was upset, and I told her we'd talk, but I had to check in with my boss first. She stayed in the outer office while I went inside.

"So who killed him?" Biel asked, after I relayed the story to him. "Was it them? Or the horse? Did the horse stomp a dead man?"

"They killed him, all right," I said. "Whether or not he was dead when they dragged him in there, they're responsible for his death."

"But if the horse—"

"If the horse did it he was their weapon, Howard," I said. "Their other weapon, aside from the one Dermott hit him with, which still hasn't been found. To tell you the truth. I don't think they even know if he was dead when they dragged him into the stall or not. The coroner will have to come up with that answer."

Biel frowned. "What do we do with the horse?" he asked. "Can we let it continue to race if ... if it killed a man?"

"Howard," I said, "even if he did put the finishing touches on Carlucci, how can you blame the animal?"

"I'll ... have to talk to some people—think about this very carefully."

"I've got Amanda Ellis outside," I said. "She's real upset, and I told her we'd talk a while."

"Tell me something."

"What?"

"Did you ever suspect her?"

I hesitated, then said, "Briefly."

"What changed your mind?"

"Oh, I still think she could have killed Carlucci," I said. "She didn't like him, and maybe hated him."

"So why ..."

"The horse," I said.

"What about it?"

"She loves him, Howard," I said. "Even if she'd killed him, or been in on it with Dermott and Hennessy, she never would have tried to frame Tobasco Boy for it."

Sandra L. Brewer

SANDRA L. BREWER currently owns and runs her own computer consulting and training business in Michigan, where she has lived her entire life—other than a brief period in southern Illinois. She is a member of Sisters in Crime, can't remember a time when she didn't write or read, and is delighted to be a part of *Homicide Host Presents*. She has had one other short story, "The Wall," published in a literary magazine.

A CONFLICT
OF LAW & JUSTICE
by
Sandra L. Brewer

"Have you ever noticed that the foam on Coke is darker than the foam on Diet Coke?"

Daniel Lincoln Thorpe, sheriff of Brennen County and the man generally assumed to be the love of my life, did not look impressed by my observation.

He opened his mouth to respond, but was interrupted by an irritating buzzing noise. We'd just been beeped.

Now, I'm all for updating the sheriff's department. Their lack of computers has been a particular bitch of mine recently. But a beeper? Dan carries it everywhere and I have to resort to hiding it at night to prevent Rachel from tracking him down. Rachel is the sheriff's department dispatcher—better known as the Dispatcher From Hell: She never sleeps, never leaves her switchboard, and always, always knows when contacting the sheriff is going to set my teeth on edge. Personally,

I think she beeps him in the middle of the night just to irritate me. And, the gods forbid, if I do something that irritates her, she manages to make my life a living hell by refusing to let me talk to anyone, let alone Dan, at the sheriff's department. Actually that's incorrect; what she does is hang up the minute she hears my voice.

This particular beeper moment occurred during dinner. The first time in two weeks that I'd gotten to have dinner alone with the man and his beeper goes off. I'm going to have to do something fatal to either it or Rachel.

Dan left to find a phone as Elise delivered our meal.

"Rhi?" she questioned.

"You'd better wrap it up," I told her, sure Rachel would have some reason why we couldn't have a quiet, peaceful dinner. The wrapped food arrived as Dan returned to the table.

"I'll drop you off at the house," he said, eyeing the bag with apprehension.

"What does she want you to do now?"

Dan sighed and picked up the bag. "Come on."

I raised my eyebrows and followed as he exited the Gypsy Witch Cafe. Obviously, whatever Rachel had called about was too sensitive to discuss in public. I had every faith and confidence, however, that he would tell me what was going on once we got in the Blazer. Especially if he knew what was good for him.

"Well?" I asked, even before I buckled my seat belt.

"I have to investigate an apparent suicide."

I frowned. "Apparent?"

"That was Doc on the phone. He got called to Norman Michaels' house tonight. Michaels is dead and there's something wrong with what they found when they arrived. He wouldn't discuss it over the phone; he wants me to come over."

"I'd better come with you."

"Rhiannon ..."

I stopped his protest with an upraised hand. "Kathy Michaels has eight children under the age of ten and they live in a three-bedroom trailer."

"Good point," Dan conceded, starting the truck.

As he wound his way through town, I wondered how much of the local gossip concerning the Michaelses had reached the sheriff's department. I didn't think there had ever been a formal complaint.

I put a hand on his wrist as he stopped the truck in front of the dilapidated trailer. "Dan?"

He paused with his hand on the door. "Yes?"

"I think I'd better fill you in on a couple things before we go in."

He examined my face for a moment, then settled back into his seat and waited for my explanation.

"Kathy and the kids visit the hospital quite a bit."

"For?" I could see from the look on his face that he knew where I was headed.

"Emergency, usually. From what I understand, she has herself or one of the kids there a couple of times a month. And while she claims the injuries are accidents, no one at the hospital is convinced that's true. The going consensus is he beats the crap out of all of them."

"Has it been reported?"

I stared out at the pattern of lights flowing across the side of the trailer. "Not really. She and the kids have been asked about it repeatedly both at the hospital and at school, but they all stand by their stories. Perfectly normal childhood accidents and Kathy is just klutzy. My best guess is that no one wanted to get the sheriff's department or protective services involved because it would just make things worse for her."

"Calling the sheriff's department isn't going to ..." Dan stopped and sighed. "No, never mind, if we had gone over, after we left or after he got out of jail, he'd make her life a living hell—because it wouldn't matter whether she called or someone else called, it would still be her fault."

"You've got it," I agreed.

"Wonderful," Dan said. "Let's go see what's going on."

I followed him toward the trailer, veering away to join Kathy at the picnic table where she sat, dry-eyed, clinging tightly to her three eldest children.

"Kathy?" I gingerly sat beside her on the bench.

She turned to look at me. "He's dead."

"I know," I said. "Are you and the kids okay?"

Kathy Michaels graduated a year behind me and looked ten years older. A black eye, a swollen lip and a removable cast on one wrist, all several days old, did little to lessen the image of a haggard older woman. Her hair swung forward as she leaned over to kiss her oldest on top of the head. She pulled the children tighter within the circle of her arms. "We're okay," she mumbled.

"Where are the little ones?"

She glanced over my shoulder toward a neighbor's trailer. "Asleep in the car. It's over there." She jerked her head in the direction of an old station wagon.

"Rhiannon?"

I looked up to find Sergeant Eric Davidson standing next to me.

"Yes?"

"We're going to seal the trailer. Can you find Kathy and the kids a place to stay for a couple of nights?"

"I'll take care of it. Eric?"

He raised an eyebrow and waited for my question.

"Can you take Kathy in and help her get some things for her and the girls?"

"Send her in when she's ready and one of us will help her."

"Thanks, Eric."

He nodded and disappeared into the trailer.

"Kathy?" I reached over and touched her arm.

She flinched, then looked at me with apology in her eyes. "We need to leave?"

I nodded. "Can you go in and get some things for you and the girls while I go over to the truck and make the arrangements?"

I watched in amazement as Kathy's demeanor changed. Her chin came up, her face firmed with determination and her voice became serene. "We can do that."

With her arms still around the girls (one of Norman Michaels' perpetual bitches around town was that Kathy had given him only daughters—biology not being one of his strong points), she stood, holding them for a long moment before sending them over toward the station wagon. I watched Kathy disappear into the trailer and the girls into the car before heading for the Blazer.

Dan joined me as I hung up his cellular phone. "Have you found a place for them to stay?"

I nodded. "One of our rental houses is vacant. Indeg and Erin are over there getting it ready as we speak. It'll do for now."

"Good."

"What was Doc's problem?"

"Doc's problem is that this isn't a suicide."

"What happened?"

"Kathy Michaels called and said she and the kids had just gotten home from the junior high carnival and found the door locked, with towels lying on the floor, which made it difficult to open. When she did get the door open, she saw Norman with his head in the oven. She smelled gas and immediately left with the kids and called us from next door."

"So what's the problem?"

"The problem, my dear ..." Exasperation made his tone a little sharper than he'd intended and my eyebrows shot up. "Sorry. The problem is that you can't kill yourself like that."

"You can't?"

"No, Rhi, you can't. Natural gas replaced illuminating gas in nineteen fifty-two. Illumination gas was a favorite form of suicide for a number of years. But the gas companies changed to natural gas and it just isn't poisonous. It'll blow up like a son of a bitch, but you can't inhale enough of it to kill yourself. No carbon monoxide. Generally, when you find a carbon monoxide killing, the victim is in a car or garage."

"But there aren't any garages ..."

"Nearby," Dan finished for me. "Exactly."

"How do you know carbon monoxide killed him?"

"His skin is cherry pink."

"Oh." I considered his observations for a moment. "You don't think Kathy had anything to do with this, do you?"

He ran an agitated hand through his hair. "She's the logical suspect."

"Come on, Dan, it's just as likely that one of his drinking buddies found him dead in his truck and put him in the house."

He shook his head. "The odds are against it, Rhi. This kind of thing is almost always someone in the family."

"That kind of attitude is a sure way to railroad someone," I snapped.

"I don't intend to railroad anyone," he said stiffly. "I'm just trying to point out that statistically a member of the family is the most likely suspect in this type of death."

I took a deep breath, about to refute the lack of logic in some aspects of his police procedure, when Kathy stepped out of the trailer, Eric close behind her, both of them loaded with bags.

I frowned dauntingly in Eric's direction. My intention, when I asked him to help Kathy had been just that—to help her. In the face of Dan's revelations, I was sure every single thing she'd packed had been closely scrutinized by the representative of the law currently weighed down by teddy bears and Barbie dolls.

I was also sure that their motives in helping Kathy and me load the bags into the back of the station wagon were governed by their need to examine the interior of the car. Under my watchful eye, neither one of them actually searched her vehicle, but they did have ample opportunity to give it a thorough visual going-over. At least as thorough as it could get with eight sleepy children sprawled across the seats.

It was after Kathy followed me to their new home and after I unbuckled the baby and her car seat that I found the bag. A touch told me what the contents were and with the children out of the vehicle, a slight odor of exhaust teased my sense of smell. I stared off into space for several minutes, the baby on one hip, her car seat on the ground and my fingers rubbing softly across the silkiness of the paper and the lumpiness of its contents. My decision came quicker and easier than I'd anticipated. Nodding grimly to myself, I gathered the bag, baby and car seat into my arms and headed for the house.

***

Several days later, Daniel and I joined Tangwen, county prosecutor for Brennen County, in her office. We arrived separately and sat on opposite sides of the room.

Tangwen looked from one of us to the other before speaking. "Before we get into any discussions about what we're going to do with this case, I'd like the facts laid out. We'll deal with speculation later."

"Fine," Dan said, pulling his ever-present notebook from his pocket as well as retrieving a file from his briefcase.

I settled myself deeper into the chair as he began, speaking to Tangwen as if she were the only other person in the room.

"Kathy Michaels called the sheriff's department at nine forty-five p.m. last Thursday evening. She told Rachel that she and the kids had just gotten home from the carnival at the junior high school and found the door to their trailer almost wedged shut and when she finally got it open, she could smell gas. Before she even got the door all the way open, she saw her husband, Norman, sitting on the floor in the kitchen slumped over the open oven door." He looked up at Tangwen.

"You can see the oven from the doorway. Wisely, she took herself and the kids next door and called us.

"Eric swung by and picked up Doc at the hospital and they arrived at the Michaelses trailer at two minutes after ten. Eric entered the premises and shut off the gas. It was an older stove and there wasn't any safety on it. Then he opened all the windows while Doc examined Norman and declared him DOA.

"It was at that point ..." Dan paused as the door to Tangwen's office opened and my father, mayor of Sevyrn, and Rhan, Tangwen's husband and one of our county commissioners, joined us.

Dan looked resigned. Being the small northern Michigan community that we are and considering the number of Beltenes living here and the length of time we've been here, it's inevitable that a large percentage of the local government offices are held by my family. It is also inevitable that they choose to involve themselves in issues that aren't generally considered part of their domain.

"It was at that point," Dan repeated himself, "that Doc informed Eric that it was a suspicious death and had him beep me. Rhiannon and I arrived at ten twenty-five p.m. The body was still in place and Kathy Michaels was sitting with three of her children at the picnic table near the door to their trailer; I joined the officers in the trailer, Rhi joined Kathy. Her intent, as I understood it, was to assist Kathy in dealing with the children and she did, in fact, locate a place for them to stay while the trailer was sealed.

"Doc showed the body to me, explaining why it wasn't a suicide." Dan stopped and corrected himself. "At least, that it wasn't a suicide as they found it. Not by the natural gas that operated the stove. At that time he put forward the supposition that the body appeared to have expired due to carbon monoxide poisoning and had been removed from the location of the poisoning *to* the kitchen.

"The autopsy verified these conclusions. If he had died lying across the stove door there should've been signs of lividity in his arms and chest, maybe even in his face, but there wasn't, it was all in his feet, the backs of his thighs and buttocks. There also didn't appear to be any post-death trauma to suggest how he was moved. Doc has put the time of death between seven and eight p.m. based on the onsite examination, the autopsy, and the fact that Norman was seen at a bar in Marquette at six-twenty."

"Cause of death was carbon monoxide poisoning?" my father asked.

"Yes."

Tangwen pursed her lips. "Were you able to locate where the poisoning occurred?"

"Yeah. His truck. The interior reeked that night when we checked it. He always parked his truck between the trailer and the woods. They were the last trailer on the street. The neighbors also confirmed that it wasn't unusual for him to come home and sit, with the engine running, and drink. One neighbor said he thought he heard the truck running that evening, but couldn't be sure.

"The inside of the tailpipe was streaky, like there'd been a towel or something stuffed inside it. But there weren't any fingerprints on the tailpipe, nor did we find anything that looked like it had been stuffed up it.

"There were, on the other hand, thousands of little fingerprints all over the truck and house. The neighbors said that while the kids were never allowed to ride in the truck, when their dad finally passed out in it, their job was to get their grandmother's old wheelchair and take it out to the truck. They'd get it wedged next to the open door, drag and push their dad into the wheelchair, then take him into the house and put him to bed."

Tangwen choked on the sip of tea she'd just taken.

"Exactly," Dan said.

Even Rhan and my dad looked taken aback by the implications of what Dan had just revealed. I was probably the only one in the room who wasn't surprised. I was leery. The friction that had arisen between Dan and me over the last couple of days had arisen not over what had actually happened, but over Dan's concept of the law and my concept of justice. I wasn't sure even yet which one would win out.

"You mean to tell me," Rhan sputtered, "that you think those beautiful little girls of Kathy Michaels killed their father?"

"That's exactly what I think."

"Impossible," my father stated.

Dan shook his head. "I believe the three oldest girls found their father passed out in his truck before they went to the school that evening. I think they stuffed a garden hose and a towel into the exhaust pipe and put the other end in through the window of his truck. And then went blithely off to the carnival."

"How and when did they get him into the house?" Rhan asked.

"Their trailer park butts up to the woods behind the school. They're barely a thousand feet from home. I think they snuck out at some point during the carnival, came home, moved his body and returned to the school."

"Why?" Rhan's frustration was becoming more apparent.

I decided to add my two cents. "Kathy was at the hospital the week before. Roseanne said it was the worst shape she'd ever seen her in. Broken wrist, cracked ribs, concussion, bruises, and a severe wound that was probably from a knife."

Rhan shook his head. "You mean these children—ten, nine and eight—had the presence of mind to not only wait until they had an opportunity to kill their father, but to clean up their fingerprints, get rid of any evidence and try to make it look like a suicide?"

Dan shrugged. "We haven't found the hose or whatever was used to keep it in the exhaust."

"Television does give children a thorough grounding in

what cops look for at a crime scene," Tangwen added thoughtfully, turning to look out her window.

"Have you found anyone who noticed the children were missing from the school?" Dad asked.

"No one who'll admit it."

This was the crux of the matter. The women of the community had chosen to close ranks and refused to give weight to the police's notion that the children were responsible.

My problem was that I saw how Norman's own upbringing was responsible for his actions against his family. Everything I'd heard about his father led me to assume that Norman himself had been severely abused as a child. And abused children often become abusers themselves. Not all, but some. And I did understand that murdering your father was a crime, but I also failed to see what purpose would be served by turning three young girls over to an unreliable court system. Even in Brennen County, where I'd known the judges all my life, they were still obligated to follow the laws of the land—and in this case, I found those laws to be highly suspect.

I crossed my arms and stared silently toward our county sheriff.

"Do you have any evidence at all that implicates the girls?" Tangwen asked.

"Nope." Dan matched me stare for stare.

"Do you believe you'll find any evidence?" she continued.

"Nope."

Well, at least he was realistic. He wasn't going to find any evidence. The furnaces at Beltene Metalworks and Woodcarving incinerated things quite well. There was no evidence to find.

"And?" Tangwen prompted.

"And we let it go."

For the first time since we'd entered the office, I relaxed. The girls had already had two joint sessions with my Uncle Morgan, our local parish priest who also happens to have a degree in psychology, so their explanations, reasons and guilt were under both the seal of the confessional and the confidentiality of the psychologist.

Morgan, Kathy and I were the only ones, other than the girls, who actually knew what had transpired the evening Kathy had gotten injured. And the girls' solution was a great deal more compassionate and painless than the one I would have chosen.

Kathy had taken the five youngest ones over to her mother's so they could spend the night with their grandma and had arrived home to find her husband indulging in a little sexual bondage with their three eldest daughters. Her injuries had come when she *interfered* with his game. And, until the night of his death, he hadn't been near the trailer since he'd stormed out, leaving an injured wife to untie their daughters and get herself to the hospital. He'd been staying with one of his drinking buddies in Marquette.

I understood the reasons why Kathy chose not to report the abuse to the authorities. The papers are full of cases that are reported. Too many of the cases are prosecuted at the expense of the child and far too many are ignored completely, the system sending the child back into the care of an abusive parent.

The meeting at an end, Dan stood and held out a hand to assist me out of my chair. That it was a conciliatory gesture as well didn't escape me. As I came to my feet, he pulled me against him and held me tightly.

Norman Michaels' death may not have been within the letter of the law, but it was most certainly justice.

Margaret Lawrence

MARGARET LAWRENCE is the author of five previous novels. She has written for off-Broadway, the regional stage, and for the CBS television series, "The Equalizer." In addition to a new play, "The King of the Golden West," she has recently completed a novel, *Hearts and Bones,* to be published by Avon in the fall of 1996, set in a post-Revolutionary War village on the Maine coast in 1786, and centered on the character of Hannah Trevor, a midwife whose obligatory attendance at autopsies leads her into the unravelling of mysteries.

Her short story, *Holy Dying,* reflects a long-standing interest in medieval studies—the subject of her doctoral thesis way back when—and most especially her fascination with the character of King Henry II of England, about whose "less-than-holy dying" she hopes will soon to be the subject of a film.

Ms. Lawrence has three other novels in various stages of completion and marketing: *The Steadfast Soldier, The Very Dead of Winter,* and *The Woman Who Rose From the Dead.*

HOLY DYING
by
Margaret Lawrence

"*Pater noster, qui es in coilis: sanctificetur nomen tuum: adveniat regnum tuum: fiat voluntas tua.*"

The seven Fleming *routiers* Ifor and I have ridden with since Oxford have slipped, now, down off their horses to kneel in the dim, smoky woods. There is a grating sound that comes from them, the steel links of their hauberks, rusty from seven months of English damp, crying out like old men's bones in the late September chill.

Their captain, Guilbert de Muisson, has pale Saxon eyes like mine, though his hair is walnut brown instead of stubble-colored. But for that and my wicked Irish tongue that mangles the French, we might be brothers, he and I.

Something else, too, with Guilbert. A thing in him—as in myself—I cannot put a name to, a hidden thing that takes no joy in what he does, but does it anyway. When they pull some village girl from hiding in the straw of a barn and fall on her, slam inside her again and again, taking their turns until she is only a bloody hole in the burnt dark with screams coming out of it, Guilbert does not move to stop them, mind you. But if you could see how his pale eyes grow clear as cold water and his mouth narrows and sets, white teeth biting his lower lip, then you would know the half of me, too, that is with men, but never of them, and does not want to be.

For Guilbert does not rape, nor even watch.

Nor do I. Though sometimes Ifor and I come in the dark

and bury the girl, and speak some words in Welsh or in Irish. For singing, as I would have done at home, there is no time, and anyway the small harp in my scrip is missing two strings and sounds bitter, and the dark dead have enough of bitterness to bear.

So Ifor and I come plodding back to camp, and there is Guilbert watching the night fire for us, waking his secret dead.

As for the rest of these Flemings, if they have names we do not know them, nor care to. They are wolves, the common folk say. Under the steel helmets, their faces are only eyes that glance up and catch the small light fading through the trees and then sink away deep, deep into the cave of skull. To kill as they kill, for any master with the silver to buy you, you must hollow yourself away, and learn to be nothing.

They are what England is, now, what all the world is, maybe, and will be from now on, worse and worse. If we live, it is how you and I will be, too, then. Dead as a whore's heart, and our pockets weighed down with silver.

Wolves.

"Et ne nos inducas in tentationem. Sed libera nos a malo ..."

It is only Guilbert who knows the Latin. The others murmur along like ignorant monks, pretending, their voices rising and falling like the thick, sour smoke that drifts into our copse of bare maples and bronzing oak trees, thins away, then fills the lungs and darkens the sky again above the road southwest toward the Plantagenet stronghold at Devizes.

Between here and the far-off edge of Salisbury Plain, these few low boughs that hide us and our mounts are the only trees still standing. All the other forests King Stephen's troops have burnt, under his son Eustace's orders.

Oh, robbed the manors and the small towns first, of course,

of what little was left after fifteen years' madness, after the freebooters of a dozen petty barons and one or two great pirates like Geoffrey de Mandeville had already picked the whole of England clean as a marrowbone.

They say Christ and his saints are sleeping and cannot hear the cries of the poor. I say they hear us well enough, and do not listen.

And now, when the law is gone and there is little left but sticks and pickings, the wolves have come again, and this time it is worse. This time it is the King himself has burnt the stacks in the fields, the grain in the barns, burnt the very barns and the peasant girls and little boys and the old men who hide in them, burnt monks in their abbeys and their books with them, and burnt even the white nuns of Tidenham and set them wandering the roads until some *routier* ropes them together and marches them off east to sell for whores or bond slaves.

Oh, yes, we are such things, we modern men, and there is more outside the law than in it in our year 1149. When monks rape little boys and half-wits sit on thrones and the tooth of a man but two days dead is said to clear the mind of madness, what wonder will it be if kings themselves burn their own thrones from under them?

Besides, that is what you do when you are losing, as Stephen is. You leave the winner cold ruins to gain. When you are losing, hope is all you have left to kill.

It will ride this way soon, that is what many in England would tell you. Hope is always a bold, proud boy on a fine horse. From out of the smoke and the autumn fog and the falling dark, he will come pounding, Henry Fitzempress, son of the old king's daughter, Maud the Empress. If she had been a man, the barons would have had her on the throne the day after her father's burying, and said it was her true-born right. But she is a woman, and so they chose her cousin, Stephen, who is brave and sometimes kind, but mostly a hot-headed fool with a son worse than he is. No, I tell you, the hope is with Lord Henry of Anjou and Normandy, who is winning the great barons away from Stephen by the packs now, and who will soon enough be king.

But only if Eustace's plans do not take shape and Henry slips past us here on the roadside. Only if I let him live, and do not aim true.

***

Now I must tell you all of it. That is why these few trees have been left standing on the road to Devizes, where he will be coming before nightfall. You need trees to lay a proper ambush for a boy who will be king.

I will bring his horse down and him down, and Guilbert and his men will hack him to pieces and Ifor will take his head by its thick russet hair, first to Stephen and then to the Empress, his mother, who is waiting across the Channel in Falaise.

The short bow, drawn at waist level and fired upwards, from horseback or afoot—that is my weapon. It will shoot true for a hundred yards and more, fifteen arrows to the slow count of sixty, and sudden, before a man with a sword or a mace can ride close enough to strike. The Flemings think themselves too grand for anything but swords. Only now the Lord Henry is running and a sword cannot stop a horse at full gallop.

But I can. I can make sure he goes no farther toward the throne than this place on the roadside. That is why Guilbert de Muisson bought me and my bow for twelve silver marks in the tavern at Oxford.

But there, I have not said you my name yet. It is Aidan

Godwinson. And for the sake of my father and my grandfather and my great-grandfather Godwin, and my own proud mother, Grania, whose great-uncle was a prince in Ireland, and for myself, I am ashamed.

For I am to kill whatever ragged hope they have not burned. And it is not a good thing to kill the last of anything.

I am seven-and-twenty, now, and should have been a master weaver of Carrickfergus by now, with a fat wife and two or three sons trailing after me. But I have never any sons and no wife anymore, and my hands are for the bow and the harp, not for the loom. So I will kill him, then, and after, then I will sing him into the dark for my own forgiveness.

In the old days in Ireland, before the monks and before writing, I have heard from my Uncle Colm that my mother's people used to dip their arrow points in a poison made from flowers. That is what put the sorrow in our songs.

"What did our Guilbert give you to skewer Fitzempress, *brawd*?" mutters Ifor. He speaks no Irish and no French, and his English has a sweet Welsh singsong. "Twenty marks, is it? Or did he buy you cheap?"

The voice comes from a tangle of wild black beard, and to it the leavings of Ifor ap Caradoc's supper of buckwheat gruel are still clinging. He is big for a Welshman, almost six feet, and built hard, like a wrestler.

Brawd, he calls me. It means brother, and so I am slower to anger than I might be, for, like a fool, I have grown fond of the old bear.

"Guilbert only offered me ten *deniers*," I tell him. "But I bargained him up to twelve, Ifor *dubh*. Good English silver, too. I had it weighed at the Jew's before we left Oxford."

"There is a plain fool, you are, Aidan. Even Judas got thirty."

"Judas, is it?" I am still laughing, but now my hand is on the knife at my saddlebow. "Half of me's Saxon and the other half Irish, and why should I care what comes to some little Norman prince who'd grind me under his boot in a minute?"

Black Ifor growls. "Not to care is one thing. Plain murder's another."

"This is war, and no murder!"

"War is not falling on lone boys out of ambush! Sixteen, he is, Fitzempress, and riding for his life, like you when you came outlawed away from Ireland, and did you think you had justice because they called it war? War is not nine bought villains with swords and daggers to one fuzzcheeked boy! For that is all he is, see, whether he calls himself duke or king or what. Well, there is a fool, is Ifor. I thought it would make some difference to you. I thought you were not like that lot by there."

Ifor spits in the direction of the Flemings. They kneel, still, on the thin bed of fallen maple leaves, swords in their scabbards sticking out behind them like perverse tails, heads bent and hands on the hilts of their daggers, lips kissing the ground at the *Amen.*

"*Libera nos, quaesumus, Domine, ab omnibus malis, paeteritis praesentibus, et futuris: et intercedente beata, et gloriosa semper Virgine Dei Genitrice Maris cum beatis Apostolis ...*"

"And why did you come, then, if you didn't come to kill?" I hiss the words at him in English, which the Flemings do not understand.

"I came to fight, is what I came for, boy, not to murder from behind trees!" Ifor digs in the scrip at his waist and comes up with five silver coins that lie gleaming in his rough palm. "Look you, now. That's all they gave me, but then I'm not so good with a bow. Not much, is it? But I am worth more than you are, see. I don't kill like a thief from behind."

He throws the coins down and they clank against the rusty skirt of Guilbert de Muisson's hauberk. The pale eyes glance up from their prayers, puzzled but not yet alarmed.

"De propitius pacem in diebus nostris," he murmurs. *Mercifully grant peace in our days.*

"Where will you go, Ifor?" I ask him. But I know the answer: Fitzempress.

Without another word, he digs his heels into his sturdy Welsh pony and they lunge into the open where the narrow road from Swindon is just visible through the heavy cloud of reeking smoke. My sorrel rears, wanting to race, and then Guilbert is beside me, on his feet now, quick and cold, his sword point denting my Adam's apple.

"Go after him and put an arrow in him, now," he says quietly, "before he betrays us all. There's three hours yet, until dark, and Henry won't come before nightfall. We'll wait here for you. Be quick."

"And how if I don't come back?"

"I'll find you, then, Aidan Godwinson," says Guilbert, staring out against the smoke. "And see you hanged and quartered." Then he smiles. "But I promise to pray for your soul."

I ride southeast, into the worst of the smoke.

Sometime late in the second day it begins to rain, cold and fine and slanting from the east, and I am half a day's ride from Devizes when I pass through an empty village the fires have somehow missed. It is strange, here, and silent, only the rain and no dogs barking. At the edge of the place is a white smear in the mud, a flock of geese trampled down by a half dozen horses and nothing left of them but the dark blood and a few spent feathers.

Farther on, a brown dog with his back broken. I had a

good dog in Ireland, called Rua, because he was red. I wonder who has him now, and whether his back is broken in the rain.

There is a light wind, and it lifts the loose thatches of three or four cottages as I ride in, bangs the door of the smithy, rises into the crossbeamed tower of the village church and blows the hook that must have held the parish bell. The bell is gone, now, stolen to be sold for someone's treasury, but the iron hook clanks in the wind and I look in its direction.

And that is when I see him, soaked with the small rain and kneeling over the stripped and mangled bodies of two women in the mud of the cottage yard.

He is square-built and not tall, broad in the shoulders, with short, strong arms, and he looks more like five-and-twenty than sixteen. He wears no hauberk, only a woolen robe over his soaked linen *chainse* and plain brown *chausse*s, and a short, dark blue cloak to keep off the rain. In spite of it, almost every inch of him is splashed with mud and his thick cap of red hair, hatless and hoodless, is plastered to his high, pale forehead. He is too young for much beard yet, but he has not been shaved for some days and there is a red-blond blush along the obstinate, squarish jaw. When he turns to look up at me, one broad freckled hand still laid on the dead woman's shoulder, the smooth circle of his face, too, is flooded with freckles and his grey eyes are wide and bold, though there are rings of weariness dark as bruises underneath them, and a deep cut in one temple that is fresh and still bleeds a bit.

I know him at once, for I have heard him often enough pictured to me by de Muisson, in case we should meet him by chance and I have a shot at him. And mostly, I know him by the sweet cold along my backbone, like fine music.

He is Henry Fitzempress, who will be king.

But I am no fool. Even boy-kings can kill, and by now I have a good arrow seated low at my hip and aimed at his heart. "Where is your sword and your dagger?" I ask him, as though he is just another boy. "Throw them down and step away!"

He does not answer, only studies me a moment more and then turns back again to the two dead women. They have been raped many times and beaten before they were killed, and there are gashes on their breasts and their swollen bellies and half their hair is torn out. One is hardly more than a child, twelve or thirteen, but the other, her mother, maybe, is older, my age or thereabouts, and she was slim and long and sweet in her body and she had black hair in a tangle of curls that fell to her shoulders when her *coif* was off.

And then, as I look at her, whatever keeps me living crashes down, stops dead, and my feet move me forward until I can see her face, the dark woman. There is no Fitzempress anymore and no bow in my hand and no rain and no England. There is Ireland and horses' hooves on the dark stones of Antrim, and blood in my eyes that nine years have not washed away.

"Maighread?" I say to her dead body softly. But when I look at her face, it is not my wife.

Most Normans would shove these two dead ones aside with a boot, because they are women, partly, but mostly because they are poor. But Lord Henry puts the fingers of his right hand to his lips, then touches the fingers to the forehead of each woman in turn and makes the cross over them as if he were a priest.

Then he stands up to face me and again my bow is ready. He unclasps his cloak so I can see he is not armed, then lays it lightly over the bodies. I unseat the arrow and sling the bow over my back, where it always rides.

"You're of Ireland?" he says. He speaks English with a Norman French accent, but he does speak it, and that is more than most.

"By my mother, I am Irish. By my father, Saxon English."

"You wear no badge. Of whose party are you? King or Empress?"

"Neither."

"Or do you mean either?" He smiles. "And your name?"

"Aidan of Highcombe. Aidan Godwinson."

"Godwin? The great earl?"

"It's a common enough name among exiles' children. Many named Godwin went to Ireland and Flanders after the Conquest, my lord."

"Oh, I'm no lord!" Suddenly he is a boy, playing make-believe. "I am—only Miles. Miles Bassett. Merchant of Glastonbury. Wool. Hides."

I nod. "You're young. For a merchant."

"I ride on my—my uncle's business. I'm his clerk."

His young voice escapes him and cracks on the words and he almost laughs. But then he meets my eyes and is sober again, his hand absently looking for a sword belt to rest on and finding none. The rain is coming harder now, and a wind with it from the northeast. Henry motions to the little village church, mud-walled and straw-roofed.

"I see God's left His own hovel standing, and it's better shelter than this—though not much." He pauses, studying my face. I work hard to make it show him nothing. "Tell me, Aidan. Why do you think they've left this one village standing, out of a dozen like it burnt to ashes from here to York and back?"

I shrug. "Maybe they had to ride for their own lives before they'd finished taking these."

His voice lifts and roars above the wind, no hint of the boy in it now. "Or maybe they had another use for the place." He smiles as he says the words. "It's a sweet place for an ambush, don't you think?"

***

The wooden door to the church hangs by one leather hinge, sagging so heavy a single man cannot open it alone, but together we manage to block it open. A family of rats run up the mud-packed walls to hide themselves in the thatch as Henry, walking ahead of me faster than wise, moves into the dim, cross-shaped nave, and when he stops too fast I crash into him, hard.

When I am close, I can feel his body sway and hear his breath coming, short and quick and heavy, and there is a strange stiffness to the movements of his arms and legs, as if he no longer controls them. When I step level with him, I see that his freckled face is flushed dark red; the corner of his mouth drags down and spittle oozes from it, and the grey eyes stare upward and straight ahead.

I cannot tell for a minute if it is sickness or fear or rage that takes him, but then I see.

Six feet ahead of us, three men are hanging by their feet from the rafters. Two of them have been dead some time and their bodies are bloated and white as chalk. They are naked, and have been castrated before they were hanged, great bloody holes beneath their bellies, gaping like graves. One has the simple tonsure of a parish priest, the other the fire-blackened hands of a farrier, the owner of the smithy next door.

The third man I can put a name to. No, it is not Ifor *dubh*. It is the Flemish captain, Guilbert de Muisson.

He has not been long dead, only a matter of an hour or two, for his limbs are still supple and the mud on his soft leather boots is not yet fully dry. He is whole, not savaged like the others, and still wearing his rusty hauberk and the surcote with Stephen's badge on it, though his sword is gone, and his dagger. No torture was used on him, but I cannot support his pale blue eyes staring at me, and I brush my hand across his face to close them, then smooth his dark brown hair. His tall, well-built body moves gently of its own weight as I climb up to cut him down.

Whatever he was or was not, I regret him.

Below me, Henry turns the body by the shoulders to take it from me and I hear a soft cry from him. In the middle of Guilbert's back, where some of the links of his hauberk have rusted the worst and are weak enough to break through, there is a dagger, buried up to the jewelled hilt.

I am down, now, and I kneel beside Guilbert and hold him on my lap while Henry pulls out the knife. It is hard work and the boy's breathing is worse. But it is Guilbert I think of, as though he is still pained by the blade.

"This is plain murder, my lord," I tell Fitzempress, "and nothing to do with war! It needs justice, if it could be had."

What did I say two days ago to Ifor? *Why should I care what comes to some Norman bastard?* In the scrip at my belt the twelve silver *deniers* lie heavy, and my voice is thick with anger at them and at myself.

"He's not long dead." I tell the boy. "You must've ridden in soon after this was done. Do you know him, my lord Henry? Did he ride with you?"

No use anymore these games with him of merchants' clerks riding on mares. But he barely notices that I have unmasked him.

"I know n-nothing of him," he says, wiping away the trickle of spittle from his mouth with a rough wool sleeve. His speech is slurred and his tongue is stumbling. Whatever the fit is, he is trying to fight it off, but his eyes are still staring and his hand shakes like palsy as he lowers it from his mouth. "No, I don't know the man. But I know that d-dagger well enough."

My mind is a tangle. How Guilbert came here before me I can't think, unless he knew exactly where he was riding these two days and took a straight road, and I have been going in circles to keep away from the troops.

"His name was Guilbert de Muisson," I tell my lord. "And he didn't deserve a death from behind. If we can find the owner of the knife, some bastard ought to pay the price of this death. But whose dagger is it, then?"

"Mine," says Fitzempress quietly, and the last of the rats goes scuttling as he slumps like a dead man to the floor.

***

"Has he devils?" says a low, deep woman's voice from the dark near the open door as I bend over the boy.

She speaks more bemused than afraid of any devils, and when I turn to look at her I am expecting a bold thing, perhaps a young beauty. But she is none. As to her features, she is fair enough, round-eyed and paleskinned in the light of the torch she carries. But she has one humped shoulder and when she walks toward me her left foot drags over, twisted as some are by the hags who birth them badly and call it a curse of God and see them beaten half their lives for it. I can see that her nose has been broken, and more than once.

As to her age, she is older than me, and maybe past thirty.

"I didn't know he was so young," she whispers, and kneels beside him.

Henry's grey eyes are wide open and they follow her, though I do not think his mind sees her at all. His handsome face is drawn into a frown, a twitch like earthquake that runs from the left eye to the base of his neck. His hands jerk and flail and his body writhes so wild the woman cannot get near without help from me.

I hold the torch for her as she lays her head on his chest and listens to his heart, touches his face and neck with her thin fingertips. She strokes his eyelids shut and lays her hands on them, but when she takes her hands away, Henry's eyes open again, staring as before.

If I am to die here, say the grey eyes, *I will watch it coming.*

"He must've felt the fit on him and stopped here to wait it out." Why else would a hunted boy stop in a place where he suspected ambush? Plain enough he had no choice. "What is it ails him?"

"I can't put a clear name to it," she says. "With luck, he'll get no worse before he gets better, and then he'll sleep, long and heavy. But we must take him to my cottage, that's where my medicines are. If the wolves haven't smashed them all."

"Flemings? "

"They had the King's badge, like he has."

She glances at the slumped shape of Guilbert de Muisson, the great bloody gash in his back and Lord Henry's dagger on the dirt floor beside him. I am busy now, cutting down the other two, the priest and the blacksmith, and covering their ruins with my own cloak as best I can.

Foolish, maybe, to rob the living for the sake of the dead. But it is an old cloak, anyway, and they have paid more than its price.

"I'll need something strong to steep the woundwort in, for a drink to soothe his fit," she says. "Have you wine with you?"

"Only half a skin of mead. Will that do?"

I turn with the torch to get my saddlebags, and I see them, then, eyes gleaming in the dark. They have come in without a sound, one by one, and now they come closer: an old fellow, a woman, two scrawny men and one strong one, and a gangling boy of nine or ten.

"Have you any food there, friend?" says the old man, his voice croaking from a dry throat. "They took all we had."

I keep out the mead from my sack and toss the rest to them, and they fall on it. Not much, it is, some cold potatoes and half a monk's loaf and a bit of bacon and hard yellow cheese. They eat the bacon raw.

***

When I carry Fitzempress to the farthest of the crude cottages clustered inside a half-circle of rough woven paling, they all come with us, half-afraid and crouching in the shadows near the whitewashed clay walls of the small, square main room. There is something in the hunchbacked woman that keeps them, and they don't want to leave it yet, cannot keep strong without it, though they only stare at her and do not speak.

"That weedy fellow's Walter," she says, moving heavily around the shambles of the room, lame foot dragging. "He's a decent cobbler, and the old one next is his father, Lambert Blunt, who is our potter, and the best hereabouts. The woman is Hawisa, and that one her husband, Ailward Mason. They don't like me, and she's cried me a witch more than once in the church, but nobody heeds her because when her guts are wrenching she'll take my draughts soon enough herself, and Ailward, too. The strapping one's Godric. He eats regular, as he's woodward for Rannulf Paynell, who holds the honor of this land 'round here, and owns the village. The boy is named Stannard. Bastard of the dark-haired one you found in the yard, got by another troop that rode through here ten years ago. She was Donica, Godric Woodward's wife. And the girl their daughter, Edeva. When she lived."

The woman falls silent, busying herself with the herbs while I make a better blaze of turfs in the fire pit under the smoke hole in the thatch. In this small place, a torch will set the thatch blazing in a minute, and with the door shut against the rain, there is no other light than my fire and a rush-candle in a bit of broken crock. She sets it on a low stool near where the sick boy is lying, to get another look at him.

"You're not soldiers," she says at last. "You have a dagger and a bow, but no sword and no badge. And this young one has nothing."

"I am Aidan," I tell her softly, "and that is badge enough. But you have not named yourself to me."

"I'm called Haldis, when they call me no worse."

She bends over young Henry, who is tossing on a straw mattress near the fire, lifts his head and gives him more of the drink she has been steeping. Whether it is the medicine or the touch of her, calm and steady, the fit is easing, and when he has drunk, the wide eyes flicker and go shut, as if he is sleeping—though I wouldn't put it past him to feign, not even now.

I begin to pace the small square of the cottage. "The Flemings were long gone, for those poor souls in the church are three days dead at the least. Who else came today to drive you all back into hiding? Was it a big man on a Welsh pony?"

"How should any of us have seen him, big or little?" growls Ailward Mason. He has food in his belly, now, and has found his sour tongue. "We were all in the hole, every one of us!"

"We saw nothing and nobody," snaps his wife, Hawisa, "So take your boy and his devils, and leave us in peace!"

A true wedding, they are, bitter and sour shaken up in a jar.

"What is this hole you talk about? Show it me," I say.

"I'll go, Haldis," offers the boy Stannard, and slips out the door, glad to be shut of them all.

***

But old Lambert Blunt comes trotting along with us, squinting out of the one eye the cataract has spared him, as Stannard leads the way to a cottage smaller than the rest and butted against the west wall of the church.

"It's under the priest's house," says Lambert. "Haldis and Father Osmund between them thought of making us all a hiding place to run to, if the need came again. Stannard was too young to remember, but Godric and Eadwin Smith and my boy Walter and I did the digging, and it's served us well enough. When we could, we kept it stocked with food and clean water. But there's no food to spare for storing now."

Stannard holds open the door and we go into the dim, chill little room. The priest's clothes chest has been shoved aside from the wall, and near beside it is the way down. They have put a thin wooden trap over the hole and plastered the board with mud and clay to match the floor of the house, and then spread straw to hide the join and the handle, which is a thong of braided straw. A clever job that speaks of Haldis. The steps are carefully packed dirt and clay, and they open to a narrow space the width of a half dozen coffins, barely high enough to crawl through, and thick dark. But light, a bare crack of it, is coming from behind me, and I crane my neck to find the source of it.

"You see? It wasn't true what Ailward told you," says the boy. "He only wanted you to go away."

"The boy's right," Lambert chimes in. "We could look out plain enough, into the square."

At one end of the hole where we crouch is a slit cut in the earth, shored up with thick stakes and masked by a clump of dry weeds. Through them I can see where the two women's bodies still lie under Henry's blue cloak.

"What about your mother, Stannard, and your sister? Why didn't they come down here with you and hide?"

The boy has no tears in him, but his eyes stare at the peephole, remembering what he saw. "We were all at our work. Some of us had time to run here. Some didn't."

"Name me everyone you can think of, now, as truly as you can, and where they were. It matters."

I could not have told him exactly why, but so it did. Death mattered, and the way it came to you. Ifor was right. No woman deserves to die as those did. No man deserves a knife in the back. Or an arrow from ambush. I cannot punish wolves, maybe, but one villain with a knife is different.

"Eadwin Smith was in his forge, there, next to the church," says old Lambert. "He and the priest always stayed last, to close off the trap door above and help any who needed it. They stayed too long to save themselves."

"My mother and Edeva were picking the last apples from Father Oswin's trees, by the brook. Too far to run, and they were snatched up halfway through the meadow and dragged here, and—" Stannard stops, and old Lambert lays a hand on his shoulder. The boy goes on. "My father—I mean, Godric— had ridden on business to Fareham. That's my lord Paynell's manor. He came back only today, just before we found you."

"He was three days away? I shouldn't think there was much for a woodward to do, with all the forests burnt from here to Devizes and hardly a stick for a poor man to steal from his lord if he wanted to."

I wait for a reason. But Stannard only looks.

***

Outside, the rain has stopped falling. I say nothing more, and the three of us crawl back up again, into what is left of the gloomy afternoon light, slanting, now, from the west, where there is smoke again. The Flemings have found some other village to burn.

"Who is the one with the knife in him?" asks Lambert softly. "Your friend? Otherwise, where so many are dead, what does it matter how one dies, and who kills him?"

"I owe him a debt. That's enough reason."

"Where he's gone, money will serve him poor, my friend."

"Then I'll pay him in justice. Did you see him ride in?"

"I did." Stannard stares at the shapes of his mother and sister, now less than ten yards from us. "It was just after noon, I think. With all the smoke, it's hard to see where the sun is, and you lose the sense of time. "

"Did he come alone?"

"He did," says Lambert. "And never left again. We came up in the night and meant to bury our dead this morning, and maybe find some scrap of food they'd missed out. But a troop rode by too close for comfort. We ran for our rabbit hole again."

Guilbert's men, I am thinking, and he set them a task somewhere else and rode back. If I could ask him, I am sure he could tell me why the place was spared and not burnt. Did he reason the same as me, that Lord Henry would double back and ride this way to Devizes and scorn the road? Did he intend another ambush here? But if so, the troop would have been with him, not sent on ahead.

"His sword and dagger are missing," I say to Lambert. "Was he wearing them when he came?"

"Indeed he was," the old man replies, his one milky eye fixed straight ahead, and the other one, bright hazel, watching me like a cat with a rabbit, to see how I will jump next.

"A fine sword, and a dagger at his belt. He went into the church. That's all we could see of him, until we came and found you," says young Stannard, "and the other one. Is he Fitzempress, then, or not?"

"If he is," I tell him, an arm around his shoulder, "we're both better off not knowing it. When did he ride in?"

"Not a quarter hour after the other one," says old Lambert. "Looked sick already, all he could do to sit the horse. Took his mare straight into the smithy and didn't come out for some time, an hour or more. We thought he must be sleeping. There's good straw there, and they didn't burn it. Then he came out and went to the women in the yard."

"Could you see if he wore a dagger?"

"I could, surely. It was windy, and it caught his cloak and blew it back as he dismounted. No. I saw no dagger, unless he wore it hidden."

"And I expect not one of you saw the Fleming's horse vanish into thin air from out of the yard? Nor his sword and dagger walk past on their own two legs and disappear?"

They stare at me and wet their dry lips, but I am not finished yet with questions. I pull back the cloak over the body of Donica and lift one of her eyelids with my finger's tip, to see the color of her eyes. They are black, like her hair. Black, like Maighread's.

"Everyone but Godric was there in the hole, and nobody came away until you found us in the church with de Muisson's body?"

"Nobody," says the old man. But he blinks, dim-eyed, and the boy looks away. It is a lie, and they know I know it.

"Stannard!" I shout, and he turns and stares at me. His eyes are pale Saxon blue.

***

"Where did you lose your dagger, my lord?"

Henry Fitzempress is up, now, and pacing Haldis' cottage like a cat in a box.

"Lose it?" he roars, suddenly angry, the red hair flying as he turns on me. "God's bones, you think I lose Damascus steel like a pissing squire? I first rode into this country to claim it when I was nine years old and I first picked up a sword when I was four. A good dagger's worth more than most men, and ..."

The great voice falls, and he laughs softly, realizing he's given himself away to more than myself.

"Well, then. I didn't lose it, Aidan. I hid it in the top of my boot, as I always do when I'm feigning. I had it when I came here. I dismounted, went into the smithy—"

"And then the first of the fits struck you, and you fell down on the straw in the stalls." This is Haldis, sitting by her fire on a joint-stool, her eyes on the castles of ash under the grate. "And when the fit passed over you, then you slept, heavy, as you did just now. And anybody could have taken anything from you, then."

He stops pacing, and the grey eyes stick into her like another knife. "It's true," he says softly. It is the one thing he is afraid of, his own body's treason.

Henry sits down crosslegged at Haldis' feet, his fingers stroking her hands that lie folded in her lap. Does he not notice the hump and the bad foot, or does he even know what woman he is touching?

Perhaps he is like me. For me, every woman is Maighread, until I wake and am sorry.

Outside the rain has stopped and there is the sound of digging in the squelching mud. Godric and Walter and the boy Stannard are burying the dead in the little graveyard beyond the church.

All but Guilbert. With him, I am not finished.

Henry comes with me to the church, and we turn over the body of Guilbert de Muisson and pull away the hauberk and chainse to see better where the dagger went in, and how.

"He can't have been standing," says Henry. "See how the path of the blade lies?"

"He was a tall man, yet the blade struck downward, as though he were kneeling, and drove some of the rusty links with it. See here?"

"Killed at prayer?" Henry shudders slightly, and for a minute I think the fit is coming back.

"You were kneeling when I saw you first, but not at prayer, I think. Guilbert de Muisson did nothing without a reason, any more than you, lord. I think he knew this place, and these people. I think he sent his troop away and put it out that he went looking for me, to kill me, and came here instead."

"Kill you?" He is restless as always, moving about the small, dim church, thinking, planning. "And here you are puzzling out the name of a murderer who rid you of a threat against your own life? Do you care so much for dead Flemings?"

"No, my lord. Only I think there is enough of easy killing and no answer made to any law for it."

"An Irishman who believes in law?"

I gave him, then, a speaking of Cormac MacArt. "'Do not deride the old, though you are young; nor the poor, though you are rich; nor the lame, though you are swift; nor the blind, though you are given sight.' We have had written law in Ireland since three hundred years after Jesus."

"It sings, Aidan," he says, softly.

He is quiet for a little more, the light of the torch we have brought with us throwing shadows like caverns onto the bones of his young face. Then at last he looks up. "So, then. Justice for your Fleming. While I slept in the smithy, someone stole in and took my dagger from my boot and killed Guilbert as he knelt by the women. How and why?"

"How is not so hard to tell. The yard is mud, and soft underfoot, and whoever did it was small and probably lightfooted. He would have heard nothing 'til it was too late to run or fight."

"Not Godric, then. He's got a belly on him, and flat-footed to boot."

"And he's strong, and tall enough to have struck when Guilbert was on his feet. Unless it was done in the wild grief of a moment, thinking Guilbert the one who had taken his wife and daughter and killed them ..."

"But in the heat of passion, a man doesn't drag his victim into a church and hang him by his heels. That was strangely done."

"Unless the killer meant to make it seem like all these other deaths, done by the *routiers*."

"But why not pull my dagger out of his back, then? That's a fine amethyst in the hilt, and it's worth money at any shop in London. No *routier* would leave a knife like that behind."

"Perhaps the one who did it could not pull it out again. It taxed your own strength when you did it."

"I was ill then. But you're right. The blade was wedged tight between the links of the hauberk, and the point lodged in bone. As though his dead weight might have fallen on the knife."

"If the one who killed him was small, he may have dropped the body, dragging it into the church, here."

"But none of them is strong enough to drag a dead man's weight alone and truss him up as we found him. Talk sense, Irish."

Henry frowns, and sinks down before what is left of the small altar. They have left the cross above it, a fine carved one with a long-faced Christ such as Ifor told me he saw in Byzantium.

"I'll wager that whoever did it took Guilbert's sword from him and his dagger, too," I go on, "and led his horse away. Likely Godric has the use of one of his lord's nags, stabled to hide it from Stephen's sergeants. And wherever that horse is, de Muisson's *destrier* is with it. A good grey, it was, half Arab."

"You think he was killed for the horse and the weapons?"

"Here, then," cries a deep voice, "Have back his sword, and his dagger, too, and be damned!"

Godric Woodward throws down the fine weapons and they fall with a clatter on the hard dirt floor of the church.

"You'll find the horse," he says, "with my lord's bay gelding in the stabling beyond the first ford. It seemed to me we were owed, all of us, and so I took them."

"Not as if he'd have divided the price with the rest of us! Any profit Godric Woodward makes, he keeps."

This is from Hawisa. They are all coming, now, half in the dark as before, and watching. All except Haldis.

"But I didn't kill him for it! He was dead already, and God save the one who did it." Godric makes the cross over his breast. "You saw what the likes of him did to my wife and my girl. If I *had* killed him, who had better cause? I've nothing left but an empty house, now."

"You still have the boy." Henry speaks to him, but he looks to the others, eyes never still, nor body either. He thinks in his sleep, this one. "You still have your wife's son."

The big bald head droops. "My wife was a good wife," says the big man heavily. "She was true to me, and did well by our girl."

"But she had no bastard son." Henry's breath smokes in the chill and damp and he moves close to them, eye to eye. "Donica had no bastard son."

"She did! Not that it was blame to her." Old Lambert is jittering, feet tapping the hard earth floor. "But it's just as Haldis told you. Nine years ago, a troop of Flemings rode through and forced whatever women they could find—"

"As Haldis told me, yes," I say. "Because it was Haldis they found, not Donica. A hunchbacked girl with a bad foot who couldn't run fast enough to get away. But they didn't savage her to death. Somebody stopped them."

"And took her for himself. A captain's privilege." Henry stops pacing and looks down at the body on the floor at his feet. "Guilbert de Muisson. "

"He took no easy pleasure with women," I tell them. "To some men it comes cheap and doesn't matter, but he was a man half absent from himself. I think he had left the best of him here, in this small place, and he never found it again."

"And came back to look for it today." Henry's voice is sharp and sudden, and cuts like a sword between them. "Which of you killed him? Or was it all of you together? Surely you all helped to drag his body here and hang him, and that was shamefully done. But which one struck him down in the yard?"

He reaches down to his boot and takes out the dagger, the amethyst in its hilt glittering in the gloomy church. He lifts it with both hands, high above his head as his arms will reach, and strikes it deep into the thick oak of a low *prie-dieu* before the altar rail.

"Pull it out, boy," he commands.

Stannard comes forward, takes the dagger hilt in his two hands and pulls, and though he is not yet ten years old he is strong as the poor are strong. The dagger sticks only a minute, and then comes away.

Henry slams it down into the wood again, in another part of the prayer desk. "You, old man."

Old Lambert shuffles up to the rail and takes the knife in his hands, and though it costs him a little effort and some rocking the blade back and forward, at last it comes free.

"Now you," says Henry. "Ailward Mason."

If Ailward were born in a litter of piglets, he would've been last to the teat and first for the roasting spit. He takes the dagger hilt bravely enough, but he cannot pull it out. He tries again, fails, tries again. His knees give and he sinks down and makes the cross in front of him, his arm shaking and sweat running from his face in the cold.

"Guilty!" cries Lord Henry, and I know he is feigning. But when he lifts the knife over Ailward's breast, so set and absent is his face that I wonder myself if he will plunge it down. For that is the work of knives in the hands of men, to drive the hearts from the best of them.

"She did it!" shouts Hawisa suddenly. "Haldis! Ask them, ask Walter and the old man! Ask her bastard! She put the knife in the Fleming while he was praying in the yard! How could we pull it out of him, my lord, with you asleep in the stall? But it was her!"

"Hush, you bitch! When did you ever have a good word to say for her? If Haldis were a monk, my lord, and knew the healing in plants and how to use them, they'd make a saint of her. But as she's a woman, and crooked, Hawisa would have her a witch. This dead man here did her great wrong, and she has taken her own justice on him when there was no other," says little Walter Blunt, the cobbler, and his old father, leaning on his arm, nods his approval as he chimes in.

"We watched her do it, all of us, from the look-out in the hiding hole. She'd have left him there in the yard, only he fell upon Donica's body and that she would not have, nor would Stannard, neither. She tried to drag him off and couldn't, so we went up to help her. But we promised, all of us, to keep shut about it and tell no one. She's been good to us and had little enough return from some." Lambert frowns in the direction of thick-necked Hawisa, kneeling wild-eyed by her scrawny man.

"Should I have let Ailward pay for her evil?" she cries. "Take her, now, my lord, and hang her, and let her not be thought of."

"What is your Irish law, my friend?" says Lord Henry softly. "How shall we execute justice on those who do unto others who have long ago done unto them?"

"There is a saying of Cormac, my lord," I tell him. "'If you be too soon harsh, you will be too soon broken.'"

"There is a saying of mine, Aidan. 'If you be too tender, you will be tenderly dead.'"

***

When we find Haldis, she is crosslegged on the ground at the southeast corner of her cottage, looking out toward the dim autumn green of the water meadow and the Avon beyond. A few swallows, encouraged by the unburnt grass, swoop over the meadow in the fading light.

Haldis hears us come, but she does not get up, only goes on picking the ferny leaves from a plant beside her and breaking off its spent heads of white blossom. Now and then she nibbles a leaf or two. "The frost will take everything soon," she says. "It's time for gathering."

Henry goes down on the ground before her but I keep a little distance, watching, my hand on my bow. But who I am ready to fight for, that I do not know.

"Did you ever know his name, Haldis?" says Lord Henry gently. "He was called Guilbert de Muisson. The man you killed today. The man who fathered your boy."

She swallows the sweet green leaves, the last of the season. "We were picking cresses by the river when they found us," she says. Her voice is low and calm and afraid of nothing. "My sister, Auberta, and I. She was just fifteen. Perfect, she was. And the cresses were good that year."

Her eyes close and she might almost be asleep, except that her voice goes on as if it is no part of her at all. Henry's hand is on her shoe and lies there kindly, giving what courage it can.

"They rode on us out of the trees and tore her to pieces," says Haldis's voice. "Seven of them on top of her, and the blue-eyed one that I killed, watching."

"Guilbert."

"He took no part, not with Auberta, but he did nothing to stop them. Some of them would have turned on me, but they saw what I was and didn't want me. Then I thought they would kill me, and I prayed for it. Berta was dying and blood everywhere. I prayed for it for myself. But he stopped them. Said something to them. I have no French. Stripped me instead, and took me. I think they dared him to, and they stared at my body and laughed when he did it, and watched and made jokes because I was crooked. I knew what they laughed at. Enough men have laughed at me, and I know the sound. I am not a fool, if I am a woman."

Her eyes come open and her hand reaches for another of the still-succulent, fern-like leaves of the herb she is gathering. She chews another of the leaves and swallows it before she speaks. "When he had finished, he stroked me. As though he wanted to be loved. As though I was a dog he could kick and still I would love him for it."

"Enough, now," says Henry gently, and he takes her two hands in his own. "Let be."

Again Haldis's eyes close and she sways a little, leans back against the rough wall of the cottage. She goes on as though she hasn't heard him. "When I lay there, naked, with all their eyes on me and his seed smeared on my belly, I thought, 'Where is God, who put me here and broke me while they laughed?' Then I slipped away for a minute, no more than a blink. And when I came to myself, he was praying. On his knees beside me, and praying himself clean!"

Then a great cry comes from her, as though something has fallen on her chest and crushed the sound from her. "No other man ever wanted me, or ever touched my body. The only touch I ever had was his. How did he dare to pray for himself? How did he dare to take God from me, and leave me with no scrap of hope?"

Her body slumps, then, and I think she has fainted. But she straightens again. "I gave the boy to Donica, because she wanted a son. I couldn't love him. How could I?"

"So when you saw Guilbert ride into the yard this afternoon and bend over Donica's body—"

"He was praying again. So I killed him, praying. As he killed me. But I was kinder." She half-smiles. "I've heard the priest say that, no matter what he's done, a man who dies praying goes straight to the arms of God. But I am a woman," says Haldis, her low voice almost a whisper, now. "Besides, I doubt God has much use for crooked prayers."

She crumples, then, and Henry takes her against him. He feels for her heart in the side of her neck where the big vein pounds, but there is nothing. He sits holding her body to him, his eyes closed and his cheek against her hair, and I think that if he is king, he will be a kind of king England has not had since Arthur.

I remember, also, the words he spoke me: If you be too tender, you will be tenderly dead.

Then, fool that I am, I bend over the basket of plants she has been gathering and I would taste one of the leaves, but Walter Blunt is suddenly there, out from where he has been watching and listening. He tears the leaf from my hand.

"It's a strong poison," he says. "We called it winter fern, but Haldis called it hemlock. Even bad weeds can do good, that's what she said. My old mother was dying of canker, and when she could not live and could not die and was nothing but pain, Haldis gave her these leaves in wine to drink. She died quiet, then, in her sleep. Like Haldis."

The little grey-bearded cobbler is crying, but there are no tears and no sound comes from him.

"Christ. I wanted her, crooked and all. But she could not," he says softly, and hides himself in her hair.

"Well, Irishman," says Lord Henry, a voice so low I almost cannot hear. "How does justice taste to you?"

"Sour, my lord," I tell him. "But better food than lies."

**

I walk to the burying ground and take the twelve pieces of silver from my scrip and throw them onto the new-dug earth of Guilbert's grave, and I make the sign of Christ's cross over me, that I have not made since I left Ireland.

And behind me I hear the soft boy's voice of Fitzempress.

"Pater noster, qui es in coilis: sanctificetur nomen tuum: adveniat regnum tuum: fiat voluntas tua—"

Marthayn Pelegrimas

MARTHAYN PELEGRIMAS's work has appeared in such anthologies as *Borderlands 3* and *Best of the Midwest II*. "The Living Donor" was nominated for Year's Best by the Horror Writers of America (HWA). She is the author of the one-act comedy, "Good Golly, It's Holly!," which was produced in Omaha and Kansas City. Her humorous pieces have appeared in Penthouse's *Forum* and *Hot Talk* magazines. Two of her horror stories have been scripted and performed on the public radio program, "Teknicolour Radio." And finally, an award-winning poet, she has had over 200 poems published.

Under the pseudonym Christine Matthews, she has recently started writing mysteries. Her stories have already appeared in *Deadly Allies II, Lethal Ladies, For Crime Out Loud* and *The Ellery Queen Mystery Magazine*. She is also scheduled for future publication in *Vengeance is Hers: A Mickey Spillane Anthology*.

She is currently working on her first novel.

THE DIRT EATERS

by
Marthayn Pelegrimas

Desperate gasps echo within the great bellows that are his lungs. I sit beside him, keeping vigil, knowing his time will soon come. Shame does not enter my heart nor guilt, as my father lies dying. For it is because of me that the old man now grunts his last breaths. A candle winks, knowingly, as I shift my weight. The hours go on and on, insanely slow. Surely I will lose my mind if Elza's promise is not kept. I watch the eyelids covering his vicious gaze; thank God, he does not see me, pierce through the act of loving concern. Soon. Soon it will be over. Our household released from his savage grasp.

Ramona will marry me when she sees the man I have become.

Mama sits in her room reading. I remember how Papa shouted when he found out his wife was carrying another baby. I can still hear the sound of his hand slapping Mama's cheek, how she pleaded for him to stop hurting her, please *stop*. He threw her from their room, tossing her clothing in a furious whirlwind. Since just before the stillbirth, Mama sleeps alone, every night.

I move downstairs into my tiny room off the kitchen. I fear Papa will take out his rage on Mama as well as me should complaints of any inconvenience reach his ears.

I see the moon brightening behind dismal clouds. Rain will come tomorrow. Musty dampness filters through the lace curtains; Papa's breathing snags. I slowly release a sigh, wait, then scratch behind my ear where Elza cut the hair.

Somehow she knew, even before I existed, this day would come, this night filled with gloom leftover from the murky afternoon. For eighteen years she has waited until I grew strong enough to depose the tyrant so feared by our village. The night I went searching for help, frantic to put an end to Papa's brutality, Elza was in the field.

***

Snagging a rock, her wooden rake poised while she bent to toss the intruder. Pulling the crude tool through row after row, she clawed the ground. Lunar glow streaked her long hair and illuminated the midnight field as well. "You will be ready soon." She whispered, but I caught the words. "I can wait," she laughed. "I can wait."

I approached her. Fearful. She told me ancestral methods cultivated patience as well as her reputation. Dirt caked her jagged nails; she licked the mud with a gourmet's enthusiasm. A bit more compost. Sifting through clay, the procedure defined her being: raking, weeding, fertilizing—she performed each step artfully.

I told her I wanted my father dead. She smiled, all the while raking. Surprise never displayed itself in her manner or words. Then she started to chant. Her incantation wove into the moldy air.

"Chills and ills. Pains and banes. Dust to dirt. All life sustains."

She took an old knife from a burlap sack tied to her belt and grabbed—almost ripped the hair from my scalp. I was too afraid to object, too old to back off in pain. "It shall be done, young Thomas. Yes. It shall be done. There will come a time, however, when repayment is expected. Are you man enough to make good your debt?"

I told her, "Yes. I will pay anything you ask."

"Anything? This is not a child's game we play."

"This night, I shed my childhood. My request has destroyed any thought of retrieving past innocence."

"Good. Now, go. Soon your father will be struck down. Very soon."

Returning home, I carried her spell with me, "Chills and ills. Pains and banes. Dust to dirt. All life sustains."

Within the week, Papa took to his bed with fever, falling unconscious.

***

My hands are so cold, I rub them, trying to warm the aching joints. Yes, a storm approaches. I stand to latch the window.

Papa gasps; his eyes spring open as I turn. He knows. I can read hatred in those black eyes: they accuse me. Clutching his throat, he shouts, "You! You are not my son! Get away from me!" He collapses onto the pillow.

I freeze, waiting for him to revive. Holding my breath, for the first time aware of the wooden clock in the hall ticking, ticking, tick, tick. My legs refuse to move, my hands hang like icicles at my sides and still the clock ticks, ticks.

Suddenly, I'm startled, afraid. I scream, "Mama! Come! Papa, he is not breathing!" Dashing across the bare floor, down the narrow hallway, I shout, "Papa is not breathing!"

She throws aside her book, praying as we run the short steps to his room. He looks like Father Time captured in a life-size paraffin figure. "Husband." Mama puts her ear to his frozen chest.

"Quickly, Thomas. Get the midwife. Tell her Papa is very sick. Tell her please to hurry. Run!"

I run and cry, hating the ogre, wishing him dead. My tattered shoes flap their soles against the trail. "Hurry–hurry, hurry–hurry," they taunt.

I see through the open door. "Sophia! It's Papa! Mama says he is very sick, for you to please hurry. Come quickly!" But I know the truth, Papa will soon be gone forever; there is nothing anyone can do. Not tonight.

The midwife ties ragged ends of a shawl across her broad shoulders. "I'm coming," I hear her call as I turn homeward.

Mama sits beside Papa, unaware of my return. "Just a chill. You will see, my husband. You will soon be well." Is she trying to console him or herself? He is not listening; he is not even breathing. But very stubborn, notorious for his unyielding determination. She holds his hand, patting reassurance. "You will be fine. Fine." I cough, announcing my presence.

"Was she at home?" Mama asks. "Is Sophia coming?"

"Yes. She will be here; I ran ahead."

Silence bundles the drafty room as we sit together, both staring at the man beneath hand-embroidered sheets, both afraid to move for fear of disturbing the master of our household.

"Marta," Sophia calls, entering the room, "What is the ..." unable to finish her question. Even in the fluttering candle-light, it is obvious Carl Rimkis is dead.

"Sophia, please. I know you are for the babies, but surely you can help, in some way. Please. I am so frightened."

Sophia reaches to comfort her friend, avoiding the body stiffening on the bed between them. "There is nothing I can do now. Come, we will call together the women to prepare him."

"No!" Mama stands. "He is not dead. Look closer," she coaxes. "There must be something to do."

Hurry, God, I silently beg. Allow the devil to steal Papa's

soul. He was never happy with Mama, certainly never knew a moment of pleasure within the circle of his family.

To appease the hysterical woman, Sophia feels Papa's forehead. Lifting the bedclothes, she shows us a dark pool seeping into the feather mattress. She takes a cracked mirror from the bureau, holds it beneath Papa's nose. No foggy signs of life—no air exhaled onto the glass.

"He is dead. Marta, I am sorry. I will summon the others. You go rest. Thomas, take your Mama to her room." Gently she puts her arm around my quivering shoulder. "Then you go lay down. Rest while you can; the coming days will bring much sadness and difficulty."

I nod, leading Mama from Papa's bedside. Sophia pulls the blanket over his head. Strange. I swear I hear the midwife curse as we leave the room. I know she hissed "Bastard" at Papa. Just a few drops of satisfaction leak into my heart. My legs cramp from the cold. I want to dissolve into Ramona's arms, be shielded by her love. Mama slumps onto her soft bed; I draw the quilt, bend to kiss her cheek, then leave.

Elza's words thread through my head and out my lips. I enter my room chanting compulsively. I fear what Elza requires of me. Maybe I am not man enough to make good my part of the bargain.

***

They come to personally validate Papa's death. I understand their need to see, in the brightness of day, with their own eyes. Mama throws herself on top of the oak casket. She cries, "Don't go! Carl, don't leave me!" Poor Mama. I will take extra care with her now that I am man of our house. She will soon thank me for her freedom.

Sophia counsels Mama, "Come away. Do not make such a display in front of your people."

Ramona stands alone, silent, beautiful. Staring, I will her to face me. She turns, a smile starts across her pink lips but stops itself, vanishing into a grim look of concern. She asks, with her eyes, if I am well. I nod my appreciation for her concern. How I yearn to touch her velvet sleeve.

I watch the coffin being lowered into the ground and pray my gratitude. At long last I am free of Papa's beatings. Free from the threats he wielded over me solely because Mama and I come from the Other Side. Nights will now hold sweet dreams for my mother, not painful awakenings. The corners of my mouth are forced downward into a solemn line, concealing a grin.

Rain assaults our villagers, compelling them to run back into town. Mama folds her cloak around her, shouting to me against the cold wind, "We go home now."

I turn to follow and catch sight of a billowing shroud behind the dead maple. I know it is Elza; she has come to remind me of my promise. Papa has only been dead two days. Surely, she will give me more time. She points a twisted finger at me, beckoning. Her determined spirit insures business will be conducted between cracks of lightning. My heart leaps with each BANG!

"Boy," more chilling than slivers of rain beating against my bony frame. Her voice shrieks, "It must be done. My promise has been kept. Repayment is expected. Now!"

"So soon?"

"Before the full moon of Earth Feast, you must bring his little finger. This I demand from you."

"Whose finger?" Our bargain sealed with good faith and desperation allowed unlimited terms. But this? I am afraid to argue—afraid to agree.

The crone laughs, "*Whose* finger? Are you so stupid, boy? Your Papa's little finger. It must be taken from he who has perished, from his left hand."

I consider the great powers of Elza. God will surely frown on such desecration. I ask myself who presents immediate harm, the greatest threat to my escape, and answer, "I will do as you ask. But now, I must go comfort my mother." I do not look back to see if Elza remains.

***

It is forbidden for the widow to leave her home; she must observe thirty days of mourning before being allowed back on the public streets. I now assume duties requiring any journey beyond our gate.

"Did you get everything?" Mama asks, wiping her hands on a dusty apron.

"Yes. Vendor Laucas sends his sympathy."

"How kind." She empties the cloth sack into a ceramic container swirled with vermilion and ocher; the pot sits on a top shelf.

"How your Papa craved his daily spoonful, especially when Elza's crop came in. Remember?"

"Yes." My mind conjures the image of mud dribbling between a yellowed gap dividing Papa's front teeth. His mouth would water, mixing drool with the grit, causing his tongue to coat. He would crunch strong molars as he chewed. Mama tells me the story, many times, of how Papa introduced her to the pleasures of Elza's prime harvest. It was difficult at first—Mama, from the Other Side, a widow with a five-year-old son. But after moving to this village, she found an appetite for the moist dirt.

"Son, please to bring some water for supper."

I go to the back yard, bend for the bucket. "Thomas," Elza calls me.

"What?" I stare into her raven eyes. She is so close I smell her tainted breath.

"Your payment is needed tonight. I will meet you at the cemetery. Come when your Mama falls into sleep."

"How?"

"Shhh," she waves my question away. "I will wait for you. Do not make me come back to this house. Do as I say, and do it with gratitude in your soul."

I am glad Papa is dead. Only Elza knows to what extent I will go to prove my appreciation. After Mama retires to her room, when the house settles with night-time quiet, I will sneak to the cemetery.

Easing the wooden gate open, I hush its creak and slip out, onto the path. The crisp air cools my anxious skin, also bringing the smoky fragrance of burnt leaves. I tremble with the thought of seeing Papa again. I must remind myself of his cruelties, poke at memories of his perverted brutality. I recall his callused fingers stroking my bottom when Mama entrusted me to his care. Fury builds. By the time I reach the iron gate encircling the graveyard, I sense I am not alone. "Elza?"

"Here. Thomas, come to me." She stands affixed to the spot she occupied after Papa's funeral. Her cape enfolds her like bat wings. She holds no candle yet seems to emit her own illumination. I see her clearly, each hair blowing about her crinkled face. Her eyes are the colors baked into our dirt pot, swirling, forever changing intensity. Now mustard, now copper, finally a murky gray. I am entranced.

"Did you bring a knife?" she asks as we approach his marker.

I dig in my coat pocket, pulling out a kitchen utensil for her inspection. "Will this do?"

She examines my offering, smoothing the blade between her claw-like fingers. "It is fine. Now, you must dig. The soil has been damp for days; it should be an easy task."

"Will you help?"

"No, this must be done by the one whose wish has been fulfilled. You must exhume your father. You alone must cut the finger from his left hand." She drops a shovel at my feet.

I pick up the ancient spade and start scooping mud from near my father's headstone. Elza is correct; the digging goes quickly. Soon I strike the casket. We look to each other. "You are almost there, young Thomas, almost there."

Lowering myself into the grave, I hurry before purpose and resolve cloud over with hesitation. The coffin lid is divided into two separate portions. I kneel on the lower half, pry open the upper part. It comes unfastened easily.

"Now!" Elza lights a candle, lowers it below ground. Papa's face is inches from my own. I gasp in surprise at his rigid features. She squats above me, demanding, "The finger."

Reaching into the coffin, I yank Papa's hand from its poised clasp atop his chest. It is cold and stiff with death. I pull to separate the little finger from the others, bend it back until I hear a sickening crunch. The knife saws through the joint and with one final jerk, I have the dead appendage in my hand.

"Here, take it." I reach up to Elza. Slamming the lid, I claw my way out of the grave and quickly shovel dirt back over the old man.

"You are indeed worthy." Elza watches, almost admires.

I am sick, ashamed, burying Papa at a quickened pace. I want to run for home. I am a boy—a frightened, terrible, sinful boy, no better than his heartless step-father. I deserved all those years of torture.

"What will you do with it? The finger?" I ask after a long silence.

"Feed my compost pile. Magic grows beneath rotting leaves, decay begets fertility."

Elza's powers have always been the ribbons lacing my bedtime stories together. Papa believed it was because of Elza's dirt that his cows stayed healthy, giving the sweetest milk, losing fewer calves to disease.

The grave at last covered over, the wind ceases, allowing our candle to highlight spots left unfilled. Fat, lazy worms burrow back into the graveyard soil. "I must return home before I am missed."

"Your Mama sleeps well tonight. I guarantee dreams filled with only visions of contentment."

"You guarantee dreams?"

She laughs.

I drop the shovel and run, wanting desperately to get very far from her. The pitch of darkness brings insight: Elza is the heart of our village, controller and supreme manipulator. I must convince Mama to leave—return to her own village. Had not Elza admired my act? Said I was worthy? Surely someone with courage such as I possess can outsmart an old woman versed in ancient ways.

***

A summertime remnant flits through the fragrant air as we walk in sunshine to the field. Mama wears her widow's black; Sophia chatters gossip into her friend's ear. I walk solemnly behind.

"Thomas, do not be like the snail. Come." Mama is exuberant. This is her first outing since Papa's death.

"Oh, let the man of the household take all the time he requires," Sophia jokes.

I am suddenly aware of Mama's stature; she looks almost like a giant walking next to the midwife. I remember Mama and I were taller even than Papa. Could that have been at the core of his resentment? Having a wife more commanding, a step-son more deserving of respect than himself? Our size had been predetermined, on the Other Side, before joining the tradition of the Dirt Eaters.

We gather with the others in Elza's field. Legend tells us this place was once barren, sifted over with powdery dust. Now, for more years than have been recorded, her field is rich, velvet black, plucked naked of anything green. Elza made it so. She appears in front of our group, the descending sun casts her shadow, marking our time like a sundial.

"Family. Great descendants of my father's father's father. We gather to bless our harvest this great day marking Earth Feast."

I search the faces behind me for Ramona. She must be closer to the elders.

"Shall we repeat the prayer as we have done every year since the Great Plowman shared his riches with our humble people?"

"Yes! Oh, yes!" the united agreement comes.

In unison we recite words taught in school. There is no one who hesitates. "Soil spread soil. Dirt quench and maladies disappear. Sickness is destroyed. Be gone now. Whoever disturbs this ground be gone, be gone forever. False, evil once are there; like this water may they disappear."

On cue, Elza sprinkles symbolically from the tin watering can handed her by Father Norkus. "Thank you, Father," she speaks loud enough for all to hear.

"You are the Mother of us all, oh Elza."

"We obey and serve only you, Mother Elza," villagers chant the customary reply.

A crow flaps overhead; I follow his descent with my eyes. He finally lands on the other side of the road, behind the cemetery fence. I recognize Elza's charms attached to sticks poking out in all directions, like a huge porcupine, from her compost pile. The curious bird pecks a tiny bell, it clinks a response. My attention suddenly returns a reflex, I repeat, "We obey and serve only you, Mother Elza."

Father Norkus speaks in eloquent tones, "There is a special one among us who will have the first taste, deemed worthy by Mother Elza. He came from the Other Side, but was raised in the honored tradition of the Dirt Eaters. Today we recognize his manhood, show our respect for his position as head of his household."

Mama grabs my hand. "It is you he speaks of, Thomas. I am so proud."

The crowd turns toward my family. Father Norkus points, "Thomas Rinkis, come to Mother Elza. Come take this sacred offering. Stand proudly in front of your people and claim what today is yours alone."

Apprehensive, I slowly walk, searching for my darling Ramona. I stand while others kneel, looking to me for direction. Bringing a pinch of dirt to my mouth, mixing it with saliva, I swallow, making myself one with ancient ground. The taste lingers; I smell grass, the fresh promise of new growth.

My people chant, "Earth Feast begins, ground now broken. Protect all gathered, receive our token."

Elza tosses a handful of her delectable crop into the air. I feel the powder settle into my hair, sift against my face. "Earth Feast begins, ground now broken. Protect all gathered ..."

Tears wash away my doubts. With Elza's help, I am now a man. I take another taste. The texture is smooth, almost a delicacy, the consistency of chocolate. Delicious.

As I make my way back home with Mama, Ramona lingers by the road. "Tonight," she whispers. "Please, tonight." Her ivory fingers caress my cheek. I wonder if the burning flush I feel beneath my skin is detected by her cool touch.

"Yes. There is much I need to discuss with you. Where?"

"Behind the schoolhouse, by the pond. I love you, Thomas."

She runs away from me, embarrassed; her long skirt sweeps a dusty trail. She loves me. She has said it. I hold myself to the spot we shared; surprise restrains me. I cannot allow haste to destroy my plans for escape.

***

Ramona's scent is in the wind. It permeates my body, seeps into my soul. The schoolhouse appears as a guidepost; I push aside tall grass and make my way down to the pond. Like heavy raindrops, frogs splash, leap across the water's surface. Ramona sits on a flowered blanket, dipping her fingers in the green water. She turns as I approach.

"Thomas," she remains seated, holds out her arms, offering me refuge against her beautiful heart.

I fall to my knees, wrap her close to me and inhale the leafy aroma of her long dark hair. "Ramona, I love you. So very much. Please, come away with me."

"Away? But why?"

"We do not belong here. There is so much more beyond. I know it. I have read of such glorious things. I will seek employment, make you a home, we can ..."

"Thomas, Thomas, be still. Kiss me. Hold me."

Her mouth touches mine and desire ignites. I burn for her. Tiny pearl buttons give way to my desperate tug. My mouth bites her neck, her shoulder; I want to devour her. Lust overrides all intellect. I rip the dress from her body, tossing it into the weeds. She will want no other ... ever. Elza has deemed me worthy. We lay coupled and listen to the crickets sing. An orange haze outlines the half moon. Thousands of stars, in the lapis sky, shine for us. I understand now. Only I can protect Ramona and Mama. There is no other but me to guide them.

***

"You? You tell me to leave my friends? To leave this way of life? You are not my husband, Thomas." Mama is angry.

"I want to marry Ramona. She loves me."

"This is good. She can come share our home. A marriage will be good."

I try convincing her we belong on the Other Side. "No. Not here. Let us return to the life we were born to. We are not of this culture, Mama. Our very bodies are shaped differently from these people. I do not want my children to grow up in fear as I have. Mother Elza has greater powers than even you can know. Evil powers. Please, believe me."

"She is the Mother of us all. It is through her crop we come to be one with the village, this sacred ground. Thomas, are you not ashamed to speak ill of Elza?" she asks, convinced of my answer.

"I am ashamed of much, Mama. But defying Elza is something I think of with pride." I turn to leave. "If you will not come with me, then stay, but Ramona and I must begin our life together outside the boundaries of this village."

"No! I will not let you go." She runs behind me, grabs my shoulders with her large hands. "You will stay and remain one of us."

"I cannot." We struggle; I raise my hand and bring it flatly to Mama's cheek. She backs away; I strike her again, feeling an unknown power rush through my arms.

Mama screams, "I will tell Elza of your plans; she will stop you, make you see the true place you belong."

Her threats assault my ears. I swallow back the bitter truth of my step-father's cruelty. I hurry down the path. Ramona must go with me. We will start our own tradition. We do not need the Dirt Eaters.

I see her, sitting on the stone wall. She waves and I run. "Ramona!" I shout.

The sky is void of clouds. Her hair shimmers. I am close enough to see lashes thicken, brush across green, now golden eyes. She hunches beneath her cape. Elza waves from the spot Ramona occupied a second before.

"Hurry, my love," she cackles. "We must begin our journey."

Now close enough to suffer her putrid breath, I stop, shocked. "Where is Ramona?"

"Why here," she points to her heart, "inside here. Did not you tell your Mama that I possess powers even she can never imagine? Why, young girls are the easiest form to assume. How passionate you can become, my sweet Thomas."

"Ramona. She never lived? My Ramona was never real?"

"Of course she was and still is. If it will please you, have your Ramona now."

Before I can hide my face, Ramona peeks out from beneath fringed bangs and blows a kiss. "I love you," she whispers.

"You tricked me." I refrain from shouting and speak in a deliberate tone. "You lied and cheated me."

"I needed your help," she replies, almost apologetically.

"*My* help? But you are the Mother of us all, Elza."

"A woman is much like an unplowed field. She may be fertile but until the seed is sown, nothing will grow."

"I still do not understand." I do not want to understand. Staring into the green eyes of my beloved, I feel only terror.

"Your father's finger. I needed it to enrich my compost pile, and later, to fertilize my field."

"And I gave it to you; I did as you asked. Will you not let me leave?"

"Of course you did what was asked of you. Such a strong man, so like your father." She laughs at me. Taunts. "So like a true Dirt Eater."

"I am of the Other Side; he was not my birth father. I could never be like him." Rage bursts inside my head as I grab Ramona's soft neck. I see Elza laugh at me while I shake the beauty from her form. She feels no effect of my attack.

"See, you are becoming more like him every day. The secret has always been in the dirt, Thomas. The dirt you tasted on Earth Feast. Remember? The special crop blended with bits of your Papa. You are your father now. One and the other, father and son. Soon his life will make you one."

Her crooked finger stretches to hook a curl of my hair. "I did love him, you know. My one weakness. If only he had been stronger, had fought off the temptation to leave his people. And I do have responsibilities to the village ... my village. He did return, after I convinced him his place was here. And he brought you. And you, in turn, brought me ..." She pats her stomach.

"Maybe you are not all powerful as you would have us believe." I spit in her horrid face.

"Oh, have no doubts, dear one. I just had to wait for the right season. I told you once I have great patience. And he grew indifferent, old, fat, mean ... meaner than even I. I knew his son could offer me the chance."

"I am not his son. You know I am not of his blood."

"You are now more of his blood than a natural born child could be. His body rejuvenates as we speak. Within your heart, his heart beats, dictates the flow of your blood. His lungs revive within your chest and push the air throughout your body. He uses you to live again."

"What good will this do you? I shall leave, never return."

"But what about your child? It will be a boy; I know that without question."

She circles her hand across her stomach. "I needed your seed, Thomas, or shall we call you Carl now? Carl, my love. Carl, my own. Carl ... sweet, dear Carl."

"A boy?" What have I done?

She enfolds me inside her dirty robe as I cry my agony.

"Tomorrow you shall feel better. The day after and the day after that one, you shall feel stronger, vital again. You will marry Ramona and live with your dear Mama. Your son shall thrive and continue the tradition of the Dirt Eaters. He will learn my secrets for blending a special crop. You will be proud, Carl. Our son will make you proud."

I whimper as she begins to chant, "Chills and ills. Pains and banes. Dust to dirt. All life sustains."

CAROL CAVERLY

CAROL A. CAVERLY is one of the bright new voices in the mystery field. Her first mystery novel, *All the Old Lions*, debuted to rave reviews across the country. Her sequel, *Frogskin and Muttonfat* was published this August, by Write Way Publishing.

Ms. Caverly's stories have appeared in several different publications. She presently lives in Colorado Springs, Colorado, and works at the Aurora Public Library as the children's book collection librarian.

MY GAL MONDAY
by
Carol Caverly

Vonnie Meechum sat by the window at her IBM Selectric, Twinkies close at hand. Her heavy body overpowered the tiny typing chair, but it was comfortable enough. She was used to it. Her pudgy fingers flew over the keys, their rhythm altering to match the country-western tunes that flowed, one after another, from the radio. Now and then, her eyes shifted from copy to window, checking for action in the alley.

She hated working Saturdays. The place was dead. At least on weekdays she got to see the garbage men and the guys who delivered to the Dim Sum ptomaine shack at the far end of the shopette. They always waved to her, which was more than could be said for the snot who drove the print shop van, or hoity-toity Mr. Pinstripes.

She was surprised to see that he worked on Saturday. She would have thought he was too highfalutin' for that. But there he was, just like every other morning. Parked his car at nine, and never looked to the left or right, just clutched his briefcase and scurried through the back door of Carlyle Investments.

Well, she would work this Saturday, but no more.

She focused on the copy, picking up speed. She was good, close to a hundred words per minute when she really concentrated. She liked the IBM. None of the bimbos she worked with would touch it. They whined all day if they didn't get to use the fancy word processor. Her fingers slackened for George Jones' mournful rendition of "He Stopped Loving Her Today."

"Shee-it," she said, "story of my life."

Vonnie heaved a sigh, stretched, and got up. Twisting her faded red sweat pants back into line, she went out and got a Pepsi from the machine on the covered sidewalk. She pushed back through the frosted glass door marked My Gal Monday. Stupid name, she thought, not for the first time. Ought to be called the Vonnie Meechum Typing Service; old Prissy Pants was never there, anyway. "Hold down the fort, Vonnie," she always said after a couple hours' work. "I'm gonna go drum up some business." Vonnie snorted and plunked down on her inadequate chair. Scouting out nooners was more like it. She set her Pepsi down, opened the Twinkies, took a big bite out of one cake and began to type.

Stupid technical manuals, she thought. Who reads this crap, anyway? Her eyes shifted to the window as a car drove slowly up the alley, turned, headed back toward her and pulled into a Carlyle parking spot. One of them off-brand foreign jobs. Had a lucky plate, though—good poker hand—still, it was a wimpy little thing. She was saving up for a Chevy truck. Her eyes flicked from text to window and back again, fingers slowing a bit, but never losing the beat.

Nor did her eyes miss a thing. A man wearing a gray jacket and dark leather gloves stepped out and slammed shut the car door. He glanced up. Vonnie nodded and smiled, but he turned, expressionless, and disappeared into the back entrance of Carlyle Investments.

"So don't smile, turkey, who cares," Vonnie muttered, eyes back on her work. She picked up the tempo for a Charlie Daniels barn burner. She was on a roll. Another heading. Fourteen more to go. XII. TASK CONFIG ... the frosted glass door swung wide. Vonnie's mouth dropped open when she saw the long dark snout of the silenced gun, but her fingers continued automatically, even as the first bullet tore through her throat. A second pierced her forehead, and another the soft, billowy mass of her bosom. Her body slumped across the keyboard. Blood streaked the paper and trickled through the typewriter.

The man in the gray jacket picked up the spent shells with trembling fingers. He stepped to the desk, glanced at the last jumbled sentence on the paper in the typewriter, then stood for a moment, staring at the body. Satisfied there were no signs of life, he left the office, touching nothing.

Four hours later a print shop van drove in the back lot with a delivery for Carlyle Investments. Within minutes the seedy shopette was brought to life with the sound of whooping sirens and a dizzying kaleidoscope of flashing red and blue lights. The alley filled magically with eager-eyed spectators. Vonnie Meechum would have loved it.

***

Patrol Officer Sally McIntosh led the excited delivery boy out of the crowded investment office and into the alley. She was pleased that the detective in charge had asked her and her partner to stay to interview witnesses. She hated missing a chance to work with the crime team. It wasn't always possible, even if you were first on the scene, but it was a slow day and Detective Claborne was a good guy. She had worked with him a couple of times before, and he knew she liked to see things through.

She stopped outside the alley door and away from the knot of gawkers. The glazed look of shock had begun to recede from the delivery boy's eyes. She checked her notes and listened patiently as he told his story for the third time.

"Like I told ya, I just come in here like always, you know? I got two reams of paper and four boxes of number ten envelopes. I yells, 'Delivery,' and when Carlyle don't answer, I looks around the door, and geez, there he is on the floor, the top of his head blown away." He swaggered a bit for the crowd's benefit, proud of his part in the drama. "Man, I never seen nothin' like it, blood and pieces of—"

"Thank you, Mr. Buckholtz," Sally cut him off. His story hadn't changed significantly from the first telling, and she didn't need a repeat of the gore he seemed to relish. "You can see if Detective Claborne wants you for anything else."

The delivery boy glanced around, not wanting to lose his starring role. His eyes lit on the small end office and Vonnie Meechum's window. "Hey," he said, glomming onto the thought, "there's some nosy dame always staring out that window. She mighta seen somthin'. Naw," he added reluctantly, "never mind. This is Saturday. They're closed."

"Thanks. I'll check anyway," Sally said, and headed for the south alley entrance, thinking her partner, Stan, had probably already interviewed everyone available. The door opened onto a short passage that connected with the front sidewalk. Stan Holcumb stood at the corner pushing coins into a pop machine.

"Hi, Stan," Sally said, "find out anything?" The doleful strains of a Randy Travis tune wafted through the air.

"Naw, nobody in the restaurant saw or heard anything. Took forever. They don't speak English very well."

The music seemed to be coming from the end office, and it looked as if there was a light on. Maybe they weren't closed after all. Sally nodded toward the frosted glass door. "You do this one yet?"

"Nope, just headed there." He pulled a can of Mountain Dew from the machine as Sally opened the door. The rank, over-heated air of the closed office hit her like a cudgel.

"Stan!" she yelped, then pressed the button on her radio and spoke into the transmitter. "Another body, south end of the building." She heard Stan's swiftly caught breath as he stood in the doorway.

Her eyes swept the room. She stepped quickly to the body and placed her fingers on the woman's neck where the pulse of the carotid should have beaten, knowing she would feel nothing. The skin was cold.

She stepped back and began the note-taking process. She saw the half-eaten Twinkie, the open Pepsi, heard the soft hum of the still-running IBM. She had worked in hundreds of tiny offices like this, been one of the hundreds of women beating their fingers off, trying to make a buck. At least it seemed like hundreds. Thousands. God, how she had fought to get out of that cheap labor pool. And yeah, Sally thought, the seats by the window were the best.

She sighed and bent over the woman's body to look at her work in progress. Blood splotched the paper; the crisp black type dwindled off into a string of symbols like the comics use to indicate swearing. Appropriate.

"Anything on that?" Stan asked hopefully.

Sally shook her head. Life should be so easy. She felt her throat tighten, and fought an urge to smooth back the woman's stringy hair.

***

Detective Jay Claborne leaned back in his chair, and gave Sally a slow, appreciative smile. "Hi, McIntosh. What can I do for you?"

"Just wondering if you got anything new on the Carlyle and Meechum case?"

"Still bucking for my job, huh?"

"You bet," she answered with a grin. He was good-looking in a tough, wiry kind of way, and never missed an opportunity to give her a hard time about her driving ambition. On the other hand, he seemed pleased by her eagerness to learn and never brushed off her questions.

"There's nothing new on that mess," he said. "We're at a standstill. It's gone to the bottom of the pile." He gestured to the jumbled stacks of papers and manila envelopes piled on one end of his desk. He ran his hands over his face and through his hair. His smile disintegrated into lines of weariness.

"All we've got is the bodies and the bullets that killed them. No witness, no weapon, no evidence and no suspects. That's not quite right," he added. "I've got a long list of suspects who had it in for Pierson, anyway. Fourteen of them. They all lost a pot of money because of him, and my gut tells me one of them did the shooting."

"What about the woman, Vonnie Meechum? There weren't any connections between Pierson and the typing service?"

"Nothing that linked the two together, nor any reason to believe that someone had it in for the My Gal Monday operation. And the female victim's ex-husband is Army, remarried and stationed overseas."

"So the original supposition still seems the most likely?" Sally asked. "Somebody who had it in for Pierson uses the back entrance thinking the alley is deserted, and shoots him. Somewhere along the line, he sees Vonnie Meechum watching him out the window and kills her, too, so she can't ID him."

"There's no real way to know who was killed first. But that seems the logical scenario. Actually, we think the killer shot Pierson, then went out the front door of the office and down the covered sidewalk to My Gal Monday. The prints on the inside front doorknob of Pierson's office were smeared."

"Intentionally?"

He nodded and made a twisting motion with his hand. "Probably wore gloves. Same thing on the other pertinent knobs. The only clear prints were those we expected to find—yours, the delivery boy's, and a couple from some of the other officers."

"Do you mind if I look at the file?"

He rooted around in the stack of papers and pulled out a fat file folder. "Help yourself."

She thumbed through the reports. "And you checked out all fourteen of Pierson's customers?"

He gave her a hard look. "I know my job, McIntosh," he said, but his tone was light.

"Sorry, I didn't mean it that way." Her tentative smile brought an answering one.

"They were checked and re-checked. Some promising prospects, too. A couple had records, one had a history of violence, but nothing panned out. Everything's a dead end. Look, I've got to get busy on some of this active stuff."

Sally jumped up and looked at her watch. "Wow, me too," she lied. Actually, she was off duty. She hoped she hadn't worn out her welcome. Hurriedly, she shuffled the papers back into the folder, but stopped when a familiar blood-stained sheet of paper caught her eye. Now it was encased in a clear plastic envelope. The type was still crisp, and the streak of blood still slashed through the last line Vonnie Meechum had ever typed. XII. TASK CONFIGGURRRRNX#@$%. Feelings of sadness, depression, and anger engulfed Sally. She tucked the envelope back in the file and set it on Claborne's desk.

"You can't win them all," he said quietly. "That's one of the most important things you have to learn."

"I know," she said, but she couldn't get the picture of the

dead woman, slumped over her typewriter, out of her mind. "And ... thanks. Sorry I kept you so long."

"Hey, it's okay, McIntosh." He grinned and added, "But if you really want to help, find me a witness."

Sally went back to the duty room; she had one more report she wanted to fill out before she left for the day. Her partner, Stan, was at the old typewriter, doing his usual hunt and peck. He looked up.

"Hi, Sal. Thought you left."

"No. I wanted to see if there were any new developments on the Vonnie Meechum murder."

"Ha! Don't kid me, you just got the hots for Claborne, I know—shit!" He threw his hands up in the air. "You know you shouldn't make me talk while I'm trying to type. Now I gotta do it all over again."

Sally laughed. "No, don't take it out; I'll fix it for you. Get me some whiteout. What did you do this time?"

"Oh, I hit the Caps Lock and I got a bunch of crap instead of numbers."

Sally began dabbing the correction liquid on an asterisk, then stopped, the little brush paused above the paper. She stared at the line of symbols that should have been numbers, then down at the keyboard. "Oh my god." She shoved back the chair and raced for the door.

Detective Claborne was still at his desk. "I need to see the file again," Sally said breathlessly.

"Look, McIntosh ..." he began, a bit wearily, but reached for the file.

"No, please, I won't bother you, but I've got an idea." She snatched the plastic envelope from the file and peered at the paper. Yes, she had remembered it correctly. Two letters and four symbols.

"Look, this is kind of crazy, but ..." She put the envelope on the desk in front of him and pointed to the last line of type on the paper. "The woman was typing a heading, so she had the Caps Lock on. It was probably going to be TASK CONFIGURATION. Her finger paused on the R, so she got some repeats. Maybe that's when she saw the killer, or when she was shot. Then she made six more strokes. That R is on the top row of alphabet keys, and the N X are on the bottom. The symbols are back up on the very top row. That's a pretty far stretch for random, or reflexive strokes, don't you think? And if she meant numbers instead of—"

He caught her meaning quickly. "A license plate!" He glanced down at his own keyboard to see which numbers were on the keys with the symbols. 3245. NX3245.

He pulled a thick, stapled report from the file and flipped through the pages until he found what he was looking for. "You might just get my job after all, McIntosh. Here it is: Roman Wycoff, tan Honda Civic, license plate NX three two four five."

"At least it's a starting place," Sally said, but the detective seemed lost in the files.

"Said he was out ice fishing that day," he mumbled. "Mmmm, might have to do a bit of dredging."

He looked up at Sally, his eyes bright with the gleam of the hunt. "A starting place is all you ever need, McIntosh. Thanks."

Hugh Holton

HUGH HOLTON is the 1995-1997 regional vice president of Mystery Writers of America and president of the Midwest Chapter. After attending meetings and serving in various offices and publishing numerous short stories, Holton's first novel, *Presumed Dead* was published by Tor/Forge in 1994. Not really science fiction nor totally police procedural, *Sun Times* book columnist Edward S. Gilbreth calls it "an updated Chicago-ized version of 'The Phantom of the Opera'—part fantasy, part action/suspense and part whodunit—with a stunner of an ending that will leave you bone-chilled." Holton's second book, *Windy City,* also published by Tor/Forge, July, 1995, made the *Chicago Tribune's* Best Seller List. His third novel, *Chicago Blues,* was released in March of 1996.

A twenty-seven-year veteran of the Chicago Police Force, Holton is well known in the mystery field as an unstinting resource on police work and columnist of *Mystery Scene Magazine.* He holds both bachelor's and master's degrees in Journalism and History from Roosevelt University. In addition, he is a graduate of the nine-month Police Traffic course at Northwestern University—the West Point of police academies. A second-generation cop, Holton lives in Chicago, of course: it's the law.

NICK CASTLE—PRIVATE EYE
BY
Hugh Holton

"The warehouse the Nazis were operating out of was on a side street not far from the docks," author Hutchinson T. Holiday wrote as he began the final chapter of *Nick Castle Vs. the Nazi Spy-Master*. "I could smell dead fish, rusted iron from the old tubs lying at anchor, and something else. It took me a minute to recognize it: the smell of fear—and it was coming off me.

"I flattened myself against the wall of the building across the narrow alley from the lair Hitler's boys were using as their home base for the Fifth Column war against the United States. It was nineteen thirty-nine and the world teetered on the brink of a global annihilation that would make the last war look like a Sunday school picnic. Some say that war is inevitable, so what the hell, why not start it now? Nick Castle's own private war against Der Fuhrer and his boys. I liked the sound of that.

"I snatched my Army-issue Colt semi-automatic pistol from its shoulder rig and checked the load. They called these Nazis supermen, but they didn't wear costumes with an 'S' emblazoned on their chests, so bullets did damage them. As I inched along the wall I reminded myself that bullets from their Lugers could kill me as well.

"A drizzle was falling and a dense fog drifted in from the harbor. That made my job easier, as I could move toward their lair without being seen, and harder, as I couldn't see what kind of opposition I was up against.

"I leaped through the dark to the other side of the alley. I almost ran head on into a wall, but brought myself up short just in time. My left foot kicked something wet and furry. An alley cat let out a howl louder than an air raid siren and ran off into the dark. A flashlight snapped on at the other end of the alley. Its beam swung toward me.

"'*Was is das dort?!*' [What is that?!]

"'*Ich weiss nicht!*' [I don't know!]

"It didn't sound like the two guys passing the time of day on the other side of that beam were from Brooklyn. I had two options at this point: to take it on the lam like a yellow belly, or stand and fight. Despite being Nick Castle, private eye, it took me a moment to make a decision.

"'Halt!'

"The beam framed me through the fog. I probably looked more like a drowned soul, who had just climbed out of the bay, than what was about to become these guys' worst nightmare. But I must have made an impression on them because the light trembled. I held the automatic down at my side ready to do my talking for me in a language they'd understand.

"'*Kennen sie ihn?*' [Do you know him?]

"'*Nein, Herr Major.*' [No, Major.]

"They had lowered the torch enough for me to get a look at them. They wore fedoras, black leather coats and wire-rim glasses. Your average Gestapo undercover uniform. They also carried a couple of mean-looking machine guns, which were pointed right at me. Well, as my Uncle Luke Castle always used to say, 'Every war begins with the first bullet.' So I raised the Army Colt and opened fire.

"I caught the boys from the Master Race by surprise. It took them a full second to react. They unleashed a hive of steel-jacketed death bees that thought I was a mayflower. Three seconds later it was all over.

"I was the only one left standing, but I had problems of my own, though not as serious as the two krauts stretched across the floor of the filthy waterfront alley. The gunfight had taken place within a space of fifteen feet. For my trouble I'd gotten a hole in the crown of my black pork-pie hat, a crease through my right trench coat sleeve, which had dug a hunk of flesh out of my arm, and a ringing in my ears which was making hearing difficult. The Fuhrer's boys had come out of it much the worse for wear and tear.

"One, the blond with the blue eyes and square cranium, who had 'Major' stamped all over him, had a bullet hole in the center of his forehead. The other one, who looked like Willie Martinelli, who played shortstop on my high school baseball team in Jersey, had one through his throat and another in his chest.

"'Nice shooting, Castle.' I complimented myself, but I knew it wasn't over yet.

"I stored the forty-five back in my shoulder holster and picked up the major's machine gun. I had to admit it was a nice piece, lightweight and easy to handle. Of course, the Germans always made the best weapons. I was glad they hadn't learned to exchange gunfire with New York private eyes in dark alleys. I couldn't expect that our brief exchange of gunfire had gone unnoticed inside the warehouse, despite the neighborhood and the time of night, so I moved out fast. I found the entrance just beyond the place where the major and the Martinelli look-alike had first turned the flashlight on me. It was just a door with a couple of mean-looking locks the Master Race goons had left unlocked. I hesitated before going inside.

"This was the lair of the most dangerous beast on Earth. I'd tracked his kind, but never this particular species of vermin, who hid behind the front of political fanaticism. But then it didn't really matter. A killer in Queens, a stick-up man in Manhattan, or a rapist in Brooklyn. Nick Castle, private eye, dispensed justice the same to all, quickly and efficiently. Saved the taxpayers money and allowed overpaid cops more time to take coffee breaks in mob-owned taverns.

"So I went through that door on a March night in nineteen thirty-nine not knowing what or who I'd meet on the other side. It was dark as a confessional in Hell. Dark and cold, as if a freezer door had been left open or Death had laughed in my face. I made my way along, carefully keeping the machine gun up and ready to answer any questions like the ones I'd been asked in the alley.

"Suddenly a blinding light hit me at the same time my head exploded with pain. The damp cement floor rushed up to meet me as I dropped the machine gun and fell face first. The world blurred, refocused and blurred again. A hard boot slammed into my ribs and the breath rushed out of me. I turned over in a weak attempt to protect myself and the boot crashed into my chest. I generally had a high tolerance for pain, but not this much. There was steel over those toes and in another couple of kicks I'd have some things broken I'd need working if I was going to get out of this mess. I was trying to cover up before the next punt when a terribly familiar voice said, 'Stop!'

"There were no more kicks.

"I took the respite to try to pull myself together. I lay on the floor with my eyes closed feeling the throbs from around my body that gave me the bad news: I was hurting; and the good news: I wasn't dead yet.

"Then I heard that voice I'd first heard in Hank's Bar and Grill in midtown Manhattan. A voice that belonged to a songbird with red hair and green eyes you wanted to die for. A voice that sang 'Stormy Weather' and 'Lover Man' and made them sound like they were meant just for me. A voice that now said '*Herr Oberst Vogler, darf ich ihn vorstellen. Das ist Herr Nick Castle.*' [Colonel Vogler, allow me to introduce him. This is Mr. Nick Castle.]

"I looked up into the face of the woman I thought I loved. She was standing beside a man with the face of a living cadaver topped with a monocle like a cherry on a cake. The fact that this was Colonel Erik Vogler of the Gestapo, head of the Nazi spy ring in New York and the man I'd been hunting since Christmas, hardly mattered now. What did matter was that the woman I loved and planned to marry had betrayed me. Vera Ryan was a Nazi!"

***

The phone ringing in his Chicago study interrupted Hutch Holiday's narrative train. He waited for his answering machine to pick it up. On his last birthday, Holiday had turned sixty-six years old. He decided at that point that it was time to slow down a bit, as his doctor had ordered. So he stopped smoking filterless Pall Malls, which were Nick Castle's brand, and switched to filter-tipped Carltons. He also began putting ice and water in his bourbon. He was a widower and had been married to the same woman for thirty years before her death two years before. Unlike Nick Castle, he was not a ladies' man and had not remarried.

The phone rang a third time and the answering machine kicked on.

Hutchinson T. Holiday was a former high school English teacher turned author. He wrote his first Nick Castle mystery at the age of forty-two.

Nick Castle Vs. the Nazi Spy-Master would be his twenty-seventh and last. At the end of the book the private detective was going to die and set the stage for a new character who would not live in the pre-World War II past, but in the 1990s.

The machine hummed, playing the recorded message for the caller: *"This is Hutchinson T. Holiday. I am not available to take your call, but ..."*

His new character would be named Becky Snow. A female who would probably outlive Holiday. But that had always been his desire. To leave something on this Earth after he'd gone. His conscience nagged him. Nick Castle would live on as well; Hutch hushed this inner voice with the admonition "But only in reprints."

The caller's voice came over the machine speaker: "Hutch, this is the Mayor! It is urgent that I speak with you!"

Responding to the urgency in the mayor's tone, Holiday bounded across the study with amazing spryness for a man of his age and snatched up the receiver while the mayor was still talking.

"What's up, Your Honor?"

The mayor's voice was taut with strain. "Hutch, you're the only one I can turn to. You've got to help me. Can you come and pick me up right away?"

"Sure. Where are you?"

"I'll be at the LaSalle Street entrance to City Hall in exactly fifteen minutes. Drive your fastest car."

"That's the Ferrari, but it only seats two."

"There will only be the two of us."

"No bodyguards?"

"I can't explain now, but I can't trust anyone else."

"I'm on the way."

But after hanging up the phone Holiday didn't move. For years he had written about Nick Castle's ability to overcome the "snakes of fear knotting his guts," but he'd never had to personally overcome any fears of his own except being a little anxious when riding in scenic elevators. Now the mayor was asking for his help. Asking him to do something he had only experienced in fiction.

He walked over to the liquor cabinet on wobbly legs and poured himself a straight shot of bourbon. Tossing it down caused his insides to burn from throat to stomach. Nick Castle did this ten times a day and didn't even grimace. But Nick Castle wasn't real. However, Holiday was and had an old, dear friend in trouble. He put the glass down and headed for the door.

* * *

The black Ferrari shot west on Randolph and screamed into a right turn on LaSalle. Hutch Holiday was a senior citizen, but he could still drive. Maybe not as good as Nick Castle, but what the hell.

It was a hot, humid August night a few minutes before midnight. Initially, Holiday thought the west entrance to City Hall was deserted. Then he saw the mayor.

He came out of the west doors and waved his hands in the air. Holiday thought he was dressed in a gaudily colored red and white shirt. With dawning horror the author realized the mayor's white shirt was stained with blood.

Holiday cranked a hard U-turn that brought him to the curb inches away from where the mayor was staggering across the sidewalk. He jumped out of the car and raced around to help his friend. The mayor collapsed in his arms and his weight forced Holiday to lower him to the pavement.

The mayor gasped, "Anton Constanzo ..."

"The banker?" Holiday said. "He did this?"

The mayor nodded weakly and clutched at Holiday's arm. He was weakening fast. The author knew he'd have to get the injured man to a hospital. He tried to lift him. Then he became aware of two men standing a few feet away.

Holiday turned, but he could only see one of their faces. In a Nick Castle novel he would have described it as angular, pockmarked and mean. However, it wasn't the face which drew the writer's attention; it was the gun he carried.

If Holiday was Nick Castle he would dive out of the line of fire, roll over the hood of the Ferrari and come out blasting from the other side with his .45. But he wasn't Nick Castle, who had only aged three chronological years in the last quarter of a century.

The bullet hit Holiday in the chest and knocked him to the ground. The author had no words to describe the pain other than "It hurts like hell." Then he passed out.

* * *

Nurse Zelda Perry stood over Hutch Holiday's hospital bed and checked the tubes and monitors that were keeping the author alive. She felt a particular kinship with this patient. Her mother had named her after a heroine in Holiday's *Nick Castle and the Pharaoh's Curse* and she'd been a fan of Nick Castle not only in print, but also in the movies, all her life.

As she looked down at the unconscious, aging writer she imagined that in his youth he'd probably looked a lot like the dark-haired, lantern-jawed private eye. In the seventeen movies which had been adapted from Nick Castle books, six actors had played the part of the legendary private eye. A couple of them, Zelda thought, had been adequate; the majority were miscast. She had her own idea of what the tough, cynical detective with the heart of gold had not only looked like, but also how he acted. In her estimation, Nick Castle was a real man with fists of iron and deadly accuracy with any firearm, but also possessed the soul of a poet. He could charm a duchess out of her jewels, as he'd done in *Nick Castle and the Manor House Affair* or blow a bad chick out of her high heels as he'd done in *Nick Castle and the Deadly Secret*.

A lightning bolt split the sky and Zelda crossed to the window to close the drapes. She didn't want her prized patient's recovery period disturbed. Rain was falling on the city in torrents, as if the sky itself was crying in protest over what had happened to Mr. Holiday and the mayor, who was in critical condition in another wing of the hospital.

Before shutting the drapes, she looked down at the phalanx of police cars encircling the hospital grounds. She questioned whether the entire police force could keep Mr. Holiday and the mayor safe. Of course, if Nick Castle were here ... She silently scolded herself. This wasn't the time for fantasy.

She returned to the bed and again studied the unconscious writer. He was almost like a member of her family, although they'd never met. She reached down and took one of his hands.

"Who did this to you, Mr. Holiday?" she said into the cold antiseptic silence.

A deep voice replied from the shadows on the other side of the room. "A slime bag named Anton Constanzo and a couple of his boys tried to take out the wordsmith and the mayor. Constanzo's making a move to take over this town, but he botched the job. He's not the type to give up easy. That's why I've got to stop him."

Shocked and more than a little outraged at this violation of Mr. Holiday's privacy, Zelda stomped across the room to confront the shadowy figure. But as she got closer a strange unease took hold of her. The intruder's silhouette looked oddly familiar, from the dark hat that was tilted down over the right eye to the broad shoulders with the suit jacket tailored to conceal the shoulder-holstered Army-issue semi-automatic .45 Colt.

"You're not supposed to be in here, sir," she said in her most outraged medical professional's voice. "This is a restricted area."

"I'm part of his family, doll."

That voice, along with an accompanying bolt of lightning, sent a shiver down Zelda's spine.

"Mr. Holiday doesn't have any family," she declared.

"Sure he does, doll," the man said. "Allow me to introduce myself." As a Zippo lighter snapped on to illuminate the lantern-jawed face with the crooked grin, he said, "Nick Castle, private eye, at your service." Then he lit a filterless Pall Mall.

Zelda was too stunned to speak. She watched him inhale and then expel a thick cloud of smoke. He extinguished the flame and his features were once more cast in shadow. She finally found her voice.

"There's no smoking allowed in the hospital, sir."

With the cigarette dangling from the corner of his mouth he stepped around her and walked over to the bed. Slowly, she followed him. She noticed the way he carried his shoulders, and his walk; every movement was exactly like Nick Castle's. However, her reference for the image of Nick Castle was not one she'd read about or seen in a movie. It was the image of the fictional private eye she'd developed in her own imagination.

He stood looking down at the wounded man for a long

time. Then he looked at her. The watery glint of tears reflected from his eyes as he said a choked, "Take care of him, doll. He's all I got."

She became so frustrated she snapped, "Look, I don't know who you are or how you got in here, but there's a policeman right outside this door, so if you don't leave I'm going to have you arrested."

His face twisted into a half smile she could only characterize as a smirk. The cigarette in the corner of his mouth bobbed up and down as he said, "If you want to help the wordsmith you'll keep the cops out of this. They didn't do such a good job protecting him and the mayor in the first place. Constanzo's put a lot of people, both in and out of city government, on his payroll."

Zelda started for the door, but something stopped her before she reached it. She found that she was beginning to trust this man. She turned to face him. "Anton Constanzo's one of the richest men in town."

He sneered. "He's also a lowlife who is going to come after the wordsmith and the mayor again, cops or no cops." He gave her a long, cold stare. "And I don't think a nurse will stop him either."

Zelda's blood ran cold. "What are you going to do?"

He opened the drawer of the night table beside Holiday's bed and removed the writer's wristwatch and key ring. Strapping on the watch, he said, "I'll need to borrow this because Holiday broke mine in a Brooklyn warehouse a few hours ago."

Zelda's head was reeling, so this made as much sense as everything else that had happened since he showed up.

He gave the writer a final look before turning away. "I'll see you later, doll."

She watched him vanish into the darkness. She heard herself say, "Be careful, Nick."

* * *

Zelda paced the floor of Hutch Holiday's hospital room until the sky began brightening. During the night she'd checked the author's vital signs every few minutes. Finally, she sat down in the chair beside his bed. She dozed. When she woke up the curtains were open and bright sunshine streamed in through the windows. Also, Nick Castle had returned.

In the light of day the image she'd had in her mind and the man in this room with her meshed. They were exactly the same. However, since she'd first set eyes on him last night, he had changed. His right cheek was bruised and a trickle of blood dripped from one corner of his mouth. His clothing was disheveled and he looked exhausted. Yet there was a satisfied glint in his eye, which Hutch Holiday always wrote was Nick Castle's End of the Case look.

"So, doll," he said, "how's the wordsmith?"

"Resting peacefully," she responded. "How are you?" she added with concern.

With a tired smirk he pulled up a chair and straddled it backwards. As he sat down, his trench coat fell to the floor and his suit coat flopped open. Zelda saw blood on his shirt. A great deal of blood.

"You're hurt!"

Again the smirk. "I've been worse, doll."

He pulled out a pack of Pall Malls and lit one. From his inside coat pocket he removed a half-pint bottle in a paper sack. He unscrewed the cap and took a pull which made him grimace.

Zelda watched all this with fascination, as she had experienced it many times before in one form or another. Nick Castle, with a drink in one hand and a cigarette in the other, was wrapping up the case. She'd read about or seen movies in which he'd done this in Hank's Bar in Manhattan, in the Oval Office of the White House, and even in the main chamber of the Taj Mahal.

"I managed to slip into the police pound and reclaim the wordsmith's Ferrari without too much trouble. It wasn't a Caddie or a Buick, but it got me where I wanted to go.

"A peek in the phone book got me the skinny on where this Constanzo hung his hat. A penthouse apartment on Lake Shore Drive, no less, with a doorman who had the face of an ex-pug and a thirty-eight in his back pocket. I stashed the Ferrari on a side street and strolled to the back of the building. The doorman eyed me as I walked past, but he took me for just another guy out for a walk. He never saw the overhand left I dropped him with.

"The elevator deposited me right in Constanzo's penthouse apartment living room. The decor was contemporary American gangster: expensive and tasteless. There was a glass and chrome bar running along one wall so I decided on a shot of Wild Turkey to clear the Ferrari's exhaust fumes from my throat. I had just tossed down a shooter and was thinking about doing an encore when I heard a sultry voice say 'You must be looking for trouble, handsome.'

"There was a blonde stretched out on the couch in the middle of the room. I must've been blind to miss her when I came in because she was wearing a negligee, which left little to the imagination. I gave her my best Nick Castle ready-willing-and-able leer and shot back 'I'm ready for all the trouble you can dish out, doll.'

"She gave me a smoldering look that could melt sunspots and said 'Oh, I'm not going to be the one giving you the trouble. They are.'

"With that these two goons jumped me." Nick Castle slumped a little lower, let out a sigh and took a pull from his bottle before continuing. "It happens every time I close a case. The wordsmith puts a couple of bruisers into the story who want to play tag with my face. They started bouncing me from one end of the room to the other until I managed to catch one with a lucky punch that dispatched him to the land of nod. I snatched a lamp from an end table and planted it across the other one's skull. I was reaching for the forty-five to back my fist play when a familiar voice yelled 'Freeze, Castle!'

"I went into my mannequin impersonation, as somebody came up behind me and gave me a quick frisk. Whoever it was removed my piece, stepped back and said 'Turn around.'

"That's when I looked into that cadaver's face with the monocle on top like a cherry on a cake. Then I began to figure this thing out. The guy facing me with the Luger was Colonel Erik Vogler, formerly of the Gestapo. I'd last seen Herr Oberst Vogler, as Vera Ryan had called him, in a Brooklyn warehouse in nineteen thirty-nine. Somehow he'd gotten from the fictional world into the real one.

"'Well, hello, Colonel Vogler,' I said. 'Long time no see. Whatever happened to Vera Ryan?'

"Vogler smiled, revealing a couple of rows of teeth which would have done a Great White Shark proud. 'I no longer need your Manhattan songbird, Herr Castle. Now I have a much more powerful ally.'

"On cue, Anton Constanzo walked out of the next room and joined Vogler. I studied the banker-turned-criminal. The suit was tailor-made, the hair perfectly barbered and the skin deeply tanned, but dressing up a rat in expensive duds doesn't make it anything else than a rat.

"Constanzo read the look I was giving him and said a sarcastic 'Don't take it so hard, Castle. After all, it was because of you that I met my most valuable assistant here.'

"It was only a flicker, but I noticed. When Constanzo called Vogler an 'assistant' the Nazi flinched. I filed this away for future reference.

"Maintaining my cool, but slowly tensing my muscles so I could make a move when the opportunity arrived, I said to Constanzo 'You want to explain how you figure I'm responsible for any of this?'

"The gangster's smile dripped venom. 'I have no problem with that, Castle. It will be the last thing you hear, anyway. You see, when I made my move on the mayor and your pal Holiday got involved, some type of fissure opened between the real world and the fictional one. This allowed you, at least what appeared to be you, to slip through.'

"'And him?' I asked, pointing at Vogler.

"Constanzo laughed. 'He's why I'm grateful to you. There is a balance in the cosmos. A yin and a yang, so to speak. So whoever's pulling the strings couldn't just let you through without sending Herr Vogler to balance the scales.'

"'That's Herr *Oberst* Vogler,' the Nazi snapped.

"Constanzo looked at him with mild annoyance before saying 'Okay, Herr Oberst Vogler, earn your keep and get rid of him.'

"'I am not kept!' Vogler shouted. 'I am an officer in the Gestapo. A confidant of the Fuhrer himself.'

"'Save the Nazi crap,' Constanzo said. 'You guys were a bunch of losers. Now do what I told you.'

"And Vogler did open fire, but not at me. He shot Constanzo three times. The gangster seemed surprised before he died. I wasn't. Then the Nazi turned the gun on me. That's when I made my move.

"I leaped across the six feet separating me and the Nazi and grabbed his gun hand. We struggled. Two shots rang out."

Finally, in Hutch Holiday's hospital room, Nick Castle ran out of gas. He slumped forward with his chin coming to rest against the back of the chair he was straddling. His hat toppled off to join his trench coat on the floor. Zelda jumped up and reached him just as the whiskey bottle in the paper sack began to slip from his grasp. She caught it and also removed the still-burning cigarette from the corner of his mouth.

She checked his wound. There was a bullet hole on the left side of his abdomen just below the rib cage. It was oozing blood, accompanied by a soft sucking noise. Nick Castle had a punctured lung.

"I've got to get a doctor in here to look at you," Zelda said.

Nick's head came up and he said, "Your sawbones won't help me. Only the wordsmith can save me."

"But Nick Castle's not real," came the raspy voice from the bed.

Zelda spun around to find that Hutch Holiday was awake. "He was real enough to save your life!" she cried. "You've got to save his."

As the writer and nurse looked on, Nick Castle toppled out of his chair onto the floor.

* * *

"Although I'd left him for dead, Colonel Erik Vogler had survived. It took me awhile to recuperate from the hole in my gut, but when I did I went looking for the ex-Nazi. The trail led to, of all places, Las Vegas."

Thus began the first chapter of *The New Adventures of Nick Castle–The Lady Luck Case* by Hutchinson T. Holiday.

ANN BLAINE

ANN BLAINE is a member of Mystery Writers of America. She just recently completed her second suspense novel and is in the process of marketing it. Although her novels are yet unpublished she has been active in the field of writing for years and is an award-winning poet and short story writer.

In 1993, Blaine received the Literary Arts Award of Distinction presented by the Livingston Arts Council of Michigan for her support and development of the literary arts in her community. She is currently serving as a board member of the council.

She has organized and co-chaired the annual writers conference held in Brighton, Michigan, each spring for the past seven years and has served as a mentor in the literary program for gifted students. She regularly gives poetry and writing workshops for high schools and elementary schools in her area. She is the editor and founder of Livingston County's only literary magazine, *Willow Walk*, which is published twice a year.

In addition to suspense stories, Blaine has written several songs and two musicals, which were produced locally.

Mrs. Blaine lives in Michigan with her husband Bill, and her two children, Nick and Heather.

ONE SHOT—HE'S DEAD

by
Ann Marie Blaine

Police Chief Nick Murdock hated his job on nights like this. He parked across the street from John Freedmont's house and stared at the glimmer of silver light that showed between the half-drawn drapes of the living room window. Twice he thought he saw Betty Freedmont walk past the window. She was restless. Nick looked at the luminous dial of his watch. Just past midnight. He pictured his own wife and thought about the many times she had been waiting at the door when he'd come off the night shift. He knew Betty Freedmont was worried about John. She was right to worry. John was late and Nick's job was to tell Betty that John wouldn't be coming home tonight. He wouldn't be coming home ever: John was dead.

Inside the house Betty went into the kitchen and poured herself a cup of coffee. Her dark hair, usually pulled back in a barrette, hung loose to her shoulders. Betty was thirty-seven years old. She had a trim figure and an attractive face, but because she was a quiet woman people rarely noticed these things. She normally didn't drink hard liquor, but tonight she was nervous so she opened the small cupboard over the refrigerator where they kept a half-empty bottle of brandy. She poured a small amount into her coffee, set the bottle down, shrugged her shoulders, picked it back up, and added another shot to her cup.

The silence of the empty house was getting on her nerves. She took a sip of her brandied coffee and carried it into the living room. She looked out the window and saw a plain gray sedan parked across the street. A man had been sitting there for the last ten minutes, but it was too dark to see who he was. She flipped on the TV and watched Jay Leno making wise cracks at some rock singer she'd never heard of.

Outside, Nick Murdock looked in his rearview mirror and saw what he was waiting for. A red sedan rounded the corner and pulled up behind him. That would be Julie Sloane. Julie was the only female officer on the Lowell police force. A petite blond, she had a university degree in criminology. She was young for the job, but she tried hard and the men respected her for that. Nick thought there ought to be a woman with him when he told Betty. That's why he called in Julie on her night off. It was a small town and both Murdock and Sloane knew the Freedmonts. Even if John hadn't been a personal friend of Nick's, he would have known of him: John Freedmont had been the city mayor for the past twelve years.

Nick climbed out of the car and zipped his jacket. He was out of uniform and his baggy slacks and sweater hid the well-toned body of a man who believed in being both mentally and physically fit.

He wore his dark blond hair in a crewcut and his slate blue eyes were permanently crinkled at the corners from being in the sun so often.

"Chief," Julie said, addressing her superior.

"Thanks for coming over, Julie. I appreciate it."

"This is a tough one," Julie said. "I'm glad to help out. I just wish it hadn't been for something like this."

"Yeah," Nick answered.

They crossed the street and walked up the short sidewalk to the Freedmont's front porch. It was a small house. The

Freedmonts could have afforded better, but they never had kids and so they never felt the need to move to a bigger place. Nick pushed the lighted doorbell and stepped back. Betty answered immediately.

"Julie," she said. "Nick, what are you doing here?"

She looked pale, as if she already knew. Her hand went to her throat in a nervous flutter.

Nick got it over with quickly. "Betty, I'm sorry. It's John. He was shot in his car about an hour ago. He's dead."

Betty never said a word. She looked at Julie and saw the confirmation on her face, then she fainted.

Five hours later Nick was back at his desk downtown. He had showered and shaved, but he was badly in need of a cup of coffee. His spiky hair and pale countenance testified to the sleepless night he'd just spent. The small station consisted of three rooms and what was euphemistically called the waiting area. The waiting area was about six feet wide and eight feet deep, between the front door and the glassed-in front desk. Only officers or those accompanied by an officer were allowed behind the bulletproof glass. Even small towns took precautions these days. You never knew when some crazy would pass through on his way out of, or into, the big city.

Detroit was less than sixty miles away geographically, but it was a different world than the one Murdock lived in. His town was rural suburbia—a cross between small farms, whose owners had held onto their land in spite of rising taxes, and bedroom suburbs where commuters lived on evenings and weekends. It was a quiet town. The last murder was committed in 1976 and that had been a family dispute. The police force did more traffic surveillance than anything else. An occasional larceny, or somebody beating up on the wife or kids broke the monotony, but all and all it was a pretty safe town. Until last night.

The senseless killing of the town's leading citizen was bound to raise a furor in the local weekly paper and the terrible thing was that Nick didn't have a clue as to who did it and even worse than that, he probably never would. It was that kind of crime.

The information in the report on his desk was sketchy. Sergeant Troy Higgins was on duty and cruising the district when he saw the car parked at the intersection of Grand and Sibley. The light was green and the car didn't move. Higgins pulled up beside it and saw the mayor slumped in the seat, blood trickling from the wound in the side of his head. The window on the passenger side of the car was blown out.

Higgins automatically looked at his watch, 11:09 PM, and then radioed for backup. Nick was listening to the scanner and headed out as soon as the call came through. It was less than a mile from his house. By the time he got there another squad car and two more off-duty policemen were at the scene.

During the day it was a fairly busy intersection with businesses on the four corners, but at night only the gas station and party store were open. The guy at the gas station and the woman at the all-night party store on opposite sides of the street hadn't seen or heard anything. The gas station attendant had dozed off behind the counter until the flasher on the police car woke him up. The woman in the party store was watching TV.

There were houses on both sides of the street farther from the intersection. All the windows were dark; the police nevertheless went from door to door, looking for a witness. There weren't any. Murdock put the report down. A man gets shot at an intersection practically in the middle of town and no one knows anything. His frustration level was heading for seizure level by the time the office clerk came in and handed him his morning cup of coffee.

"Bad thing about last night," Lois said. She was middle-aged and dumpy, with short, straggly brown hair, but she was a whiz at her job. She'd been with the department longer than anyone, including Murdock. "This is a double whammy for Betty."

"Yeah, why?"

"Her mother passed away three weeks ago," Lois said.

"I didn't know that," Nick answered. He passed his hand over his face in a tired gesture.

"Trouble comes to some people in bunches, doesn't it?"

"Yeah, I guess so. I don't think Betty has any other family. It's a tragedy she never had kids."

Lois left his small office and went out to the front desk. Nick sipped his coffee and contemplated how unfair life was.

At eight o'clock he walked across the street to the county courthouse. Office space in the building was rented to the city for the mayor's use. The courthouse doors didn't officially open until nine, but Murdock knew the office workers came in at eight. He figured by now everybody knew of the shooting. He figured wrong. The minute he entered the room he knew he was the bearer of the bad news. The three women that worked in the mayor's office were following their usual early morning routine. It was obvious to Murdock that nobody knew what had happened.

"What can I do for you, Chief?" Gladys Smith, the office manager, asked.

It was the second time he had to tell the grim story and he didn't like it any better than the first. Two of the women started to cry, and the third, Susan Bronson, turned white and left the room. She didn't return. Chief Murdock asked the usual questions and got the expected responses. The mayor didn't have any enemies. The whole town loved him. He'd been re-elected six times.

"I suppose that leaves me to supervise the downtown renovation project," Gladys said. "At least now it'll be done right." Then she covered her mouth as she looked at the others. "I'm sorry. I don't know what I'm saying. Who cares at a time like this? The man's just been murdered. I'd be glad to take over, but I didn't mean ... I mean, I'm sorry he's dead." She was babbling, but Murdock understood. There was a lot of unfinished business that would have to be taken care of and it would probably fall on Gladys' shoulders, at least temporarily. Murdock wasn't getting anywhere here, so he excused himself and left. The ladies had a lot of people to contact and they'd best be getting on with it. He passed Susan Bronson in the hall on his way out. She was putting on her coat. She looked like she'd just been sick. Murdock offered his assistance, but she said she was going home; she seemed deeply affected by the tragic news.

His next stop was Betty Freedmont's. It was a distasteful job, but he had to ask the questions she'd been too distraught to answer last night. He didn't figure on getting any better answers than the office staff had given him, but it was part of the routine. He'd already made up his mind that it was a random drive-by shooting, one of those senseless acts of violence you read about in the Detroit paper every day. Now that violence had come to his back yard and he didn't like it.

Betty was dressed in brown slacks and a cream-colored blouse. Her dark hair was pulled back from her face. She was pale, but calm. Murdock didn't think she'd slept any more than he had.

"I don't understand any of this," she said. "John was a

good man. He worked hard for the city. He went to church on Sunday. How could this happen to us?"

Nick didn't have the answers. He left a half hour later feeling worse than when he'd come.

The funeral was held two days later and half the town turned out. Chief Murdock and the rest of the department wore their uniforms in honor of the dead mayor and stood respectfully at attention as the coffin was lowered into the ground. Two things stood out in Murdock's mind after the service was over: Betty Freedmont didn't shed a tear as they lowered her husband's body into the ground, and Susan Bronson was the only member of the mayor's staff who didn't attend the funeral. Strange, he thought, she seemed more upset than anyone when he'd broken the news the other day.

The first break in the case came as he was about to get into his car to leave the cemetery. Abbie Greenspan stopped him with a hand on his arm. Abbie was an old friend.

"Nick, I don't know if it has anything to do with the mayor's death, but there's something we need to tell you."

The "we" was her teenage daughter standing off to one side.

Nick nodded at the girl. "Hi, Marsha," he said, then turned his attention to Abbie. "What is it, Abbie?

Abbie pushed her daughter forward. "Tell the sheriff what you just told me."

Marsha looked frightened, but she did as she was told. "I was babysitting at Harper's Wednesday night. It's their bowling night and they usually have a few drinks after so it was about eleven or so when they got home. I was walking home and I took the shortcut down the alley behind the gas station. When I crossed Sibley I heard a car backfire."

"Go on," the chief said.

"Well, like I said. I thought it was a car backfiring, but now I don't know."

"Did you see the car?"

"That's the part I wanted her to tell you," Abbie said.

"I saw two cars at the light," Marsha answered. "The one in the passing lane was just sitting there. The other one was pulling away."

"Could you identify the make?" Nick asked.

"Better than that," Abbie said. "Marsha's a nut about license numbers; she likes to play that game."

The Chief tried to keep his face calm. "What did you see Marsha?"

Marsha looked at her mother for encouragement and then plunged ahead. "I don't know anything about cars, but it was like medium-sized and a dark color and there were flames or something painted on the trunk. I saw them reflected in the light. It was so quick and I just glanced at it. I mean I didn't even know about the mayor until the next day."

"What about the numbers?" Nick asked.

"I caught a glimpse of the plate as it was pulling away. I didn't catch it all, but the first three letters were DBH, you know, like dark blue horses, DBH, and then the number eight."

"You're sure about this?"

"Positive," Marsha said. "Like Mom said, I'm a nut about license plates. They stick in my head. I automatically read them. It's a thing I have."

"Yeah," Murdock said. "A thing. Look, you two, I want you to follow me downtown. I'll have to take an official statement."

Murdock drove to the station trying not to feel excited. It wasn't much, but it was something. Cases had been solved with less.

When they arrived at the station Murdock entered the three letters and one digit of the plate number, along with the general description of the vehicle, into the computer, which directly interfaced into the Secretary of State's files. In less than two minutes he had a listing of possible match-ups. There were twenty-three names and addresses on the list; they were scattered across the state. He decided to enlist the aid of the state police to investigate the leads. Even with their help it might be days before they tracked down everyone on the list.

The next evening the city council held an emergency meeting to appoint a mayor *pro tempore* until a regular election could be held. Murdock attended the open meeting along with Julie Sloane. Murdock reflected on his decision to hire the young woman the previous fall and was glad that he had. She took a real interest in the community and often volunteered to come in on her off time.

The council unanimously voted to appoint Gladys Smith as the temporary mayor. Gladys deserved the honor and the position; she had been the mayor's assistant ever since he came to office and was intimate with all aspects of city government.

When the meeting broke up, Nick and Julie went up to congratulate her on her new position.

"I never anticipated this," Gladys said, a worried frown creasing her forehead. "Now I'm going to have to replace two people in the office."

"Two?" Julie asked. "What other job is open?"

"Besides my own, there's Susan Bronson's position," Gladys answered. "She just up and left the day we found out about Mayor Freedmont. Then yesterday she called and said she wouldn't be returning. She's decided to move up north to her sister's."

"That was sudden," Nick said.

"You're telling me," Gladys said. "I never understood why John hired her in the first place. If you ask me we were doing just fine without her and now when we really could use extra help she up and runs. But that's life: when it rains it pours."

"Yeah," Nick agreed.

Gladys excused herself and hurried off to catch a departing councilman.

"How long has Gladys worked in the mayor's office?" Julie asked.

"She's been there a while. She worked for the last mayor before Freedmont was elected."

"Really?" Julie asked. "That's unusual, isn't it?"

"A bit, but Gladys knows the ropes. A lot of people thought she should have run when the last mayor died."

"Why didn't she?"

"Couldn't get the backing, I guess. It's still a small town in some ways. A lot of men didn't want a woman running things."

"Oh." The one word spoke volumes coming from Julie's lips.

"Don't go *oh* like that. Gladys was never a women's libber. She understood why it wasn't feasible for her to take over. She never resented it."

"Right," Julie said.

He said goodbye to her on the courthouse steps and then drove home. Murdock thought about Julie's reaction. It was no secret that Gladys wanted to be mayor, but she wouldn't kill for it. It took a real stretch of the imagination to think that.

He thought about the last time he'd seen Susan Bronson outside the mayor's office. She was pale as a ghost. The mayor's death had deeply affected her. Susan had moved to Lowell just a little over a year ago. Why would John Freedmont's death be such a personal tragedy to a low-level city employee? Unless there was something else going on.

The next morning Nick drove by Betty Freedmont's house again. This time it was a personal visit. His wife had made a casserole and asked him to drop it off on his way to work. The automatic garage door began to open just as he parked his car in the drive. Betty was about to get into her car. Nick tooted his horn and got out.

"Nick, I wasn't expecting any company this morning," Betty said. She was immaculately but plainly dressed, as always.

"I probably should have called. Myra asked me to drop this off." He handed Betty the still-warm casserole.

"That's so thoughtful," Betty said. "I still have food left over from the funeral, but I'll put this in the freezer for next week. Tell Myra thanks. It was a thoughtful thing to do."

"I will," Nick said. He felt awkward. Betty wasn't an easy person to talk to. She never looked you in the eye. She was the exact opposite of John. He had been the most gregarious man in town, one of the reasons he'd been such a good mayor. He could out-talk anyone. Nick looked past Betty into the garage.

Several empty boxes were piled by the back door, otherwise the place was immaculate. John's tools hung neatly above a bench in one corner. Two or three old license plates decorated one wall and the other wall held shelves filled with the usual leftover paint and gardening supplies.

Betty followed his gaze to the boxes.

"I'm packing up John's things and taking them over to the church," she said.

Nick nodded. "It must be tough."

"Yes," she answered.

"Well, I have to be going," Nick said. He said goodbye

and climbed into the cruiser. He was halfway down the block when he realized that Betty hadn't asked him about the investigation. It was just as well. He didn't have anything new to tell her anyway. His mind went back to his conversation with Gladys Smith the evening before. Susan Bronson's abrupt departure bothered him. Call it a hunch or instinct, he knew he had to look her up and talk to her. Something wasn't right there and he intended to find out what it was.

It took less than ten minutes to get Susan's northern Michigan address and phone number. Nick studied the card for a minute and then decided not to phone. He would conduct this interview in person and he didn't want Susan to know he was coming.

"Lois," he called. "Is there anything important on my calendar tomorrow?"

Lois leaned on the doorjamb as she checked the daily planner.

"Looks like your luncheon with Princess Di was cancelled so you're free. Why? You thinking of taking me to lunch?"

Nick grinned. "It's a hard offer to refuse, but I'm going to be out of town for a few hours. Think you can hold down the office?"

"Chief, I was handling things here when you were still borrowing your daddy's razor. I think I can keep it going for a few hours tomorrow."

Nick continued grinning. "Lois, I don't know why they just didn't make you sheriff when Riley retired."

"They did offer me the position, but I turned them down. These hips wouldn't fit into one of them uniforms," Lois said as she flounced back to her desk. Murdock grinned. At least somebody still had a sense of humor.

The drive north took two hours, but Murdock had an early start and by ten o'clock he had arrived at his destination. The town of Doveslow wasn't much to look at: three streets and a crossroad with the usual local restaurant/tavern and church. He checked the card on the dash for the correct address and in three minutes he was parked outside Susan Bronson's house. It was an old pseudo-Victorian two-story house with clapboard siding and a wide veranda across the front. Nick got out of the car and climbed the steps. The bell was the old-fashioned kind that turned like a key. Through the lace curtains on the door Nick could see Susan Bronson descending the stairs. He also saw her hesitate as she saw who was at the door.

"Chief Murdock, isn't it?" Susan said as she opened the door. "What on earth brings you here?"

Nick took off his hat and brushed his hand over his crewcut. "I'm sorry to intrude without calling first, but it's important that I speak to you."

"About what?"

"About the death of Mayor Freedmont and your sudden disappearance from Lowell."

Susan's face blanched. "I don't know anything about John's death and as for my sudden disappearance, I simply decided to take some time off. I needed a rest."

Nick had another one of those hunches. "You were very close to John, weren't you, Susan?"

"I don't know what you mean," she stuttered.

"I don't know exactly, but Gladys thought ..."

"Gladys is an old busybody." Susan's lip was trembling. "She had no idea what a fine man John was."

"John was a very fine man, that's why I'm trying to find out who killed him. I think you might be able to help me. May I come in?"

A tear slid down Susan's cheek and Nick couldn't help but notice how young and vulnerable she looked. She opened the door wider and he followed her into the living room, where they sat down.

"How long were you and Mayor Freedmont having an affair?" Nick asked.

Susan crumbled completely. "Is that what she told you? Gladys always thought she knew everything, but she doesn't know anything. It wasn't like that; it was never like that. John was an honorable man. That night he drove me home we had been working late. He was so tired and Betty was out of town. I offered to make us a late supper. We talked and had a little wine. It wasn't his idea. He had no idea that I was in love with him."

"So you slept with him that one time?"

"Afterward he was miserable. He really loved Betty. I knew that, but it didn't seem to matter that night."

"Did Betty know about the affair?"

"Yes, she did. John was a fool. He couldn't stand the guilt, so he confessed that he'd slept with me. She was angry and hurt at first, but then she realized it wasn't his fault and she forgave him."

"So you were in love with him, that's why his death affected you so hard. That's why you quit."

Susan looked him in the eye. "I would have been leaving soon anyway. I'm pregnant."

It was Nick's turn to be taken aback. "Did John know? Is it his baby?"

"Of course it's his baby. I've never been with another man, not that it's anybody's business but my own." She was silent for a moment as she wiped away a tear and composed herself. "Yes, John knew. I called him at home a week ago Tuesday as soon as I was sure." Susan looked down. "I know what you're thinking, but I'm not that kind of girl, Chief. I've never been with any other man. I didn't want anything from John, but I thought he should know."

"How did he react?"

"It was extraordinary. He didn't say anything. Just hung up the phone. The next day he told me he was taking me to the mayor's conference in Detroit on Wednesday."

She saw the reaction on Murdock's face. The mayor was killed at eleven o'clock on Wednesday night.

"Yes, he must have just dropped me off when he was shot at the intersection."

Nick thought hard. "What happened between the two of you the day of the conference?"

"We argued all the way to Detroit and back. He told me how he and Betty had never had children. How she'd had three miscarriages and the doctors said it was dangerous for her to try again. Children weren't important to John, but they were to Betty. He wanted me to go away to have the baby and give it up to them for adoption."

"He was going to tell Betty about the baby?"

"I don't think so. Betty wanted to adopt years ago. It was John who hesitated. He didn't want to raise somebody else's child, but this child would be his. He actually thought it was God's gift to him and Betty."

"You must have been devastated."

"That doesn't even half cover it."

"What did you tell him?"

"I told him I'd consider it. The next day I found out he was dead."

They talked for a few more minutes and Susan offered to make them a light lunch before he left. Murdock declined. He had a lot to think about as he cruised south, but none of it brought him any closer to solving the case.

Two days later he was back at Betty Freedmont's house. She was in the garage sorting through John's tools.

"I'm giving these away," she said. "I wouldn't have any idea how to use them anyway."

There were more boxes stacked in the corner.

"Looks like you've been doing more packing."

"Yes, you probably heard that my mother died a few weeks ago," Betty said. "I've decided to move into her house. It has fewer memories than this place. I'm going to sell this house."

A stack of old license plates sitting on the workbench caught Nick's attention. He examined them absently as he spoke.

"I'm sorry we haven't made more progress on the case, Betty. We followed up on that list of plate numbers we had, but nothing panned out. It just doesn't make sense." He looked up and saw that Betty was suddenly tense.

"I'm sorry, I didn't mean to upset you."

"It's all right," she said as she grabbed the license plate in his hand. Flustered, she dropped it into the trash barrel. "I've been meaning to get rid of these, too." She dropped the rest of the stack into the trash. "You'll have to leave now, Nick, I'm terribly busy."

Nick looked at the number on the license plate she had grabbed from him. DPH 6703. He reached into the bin and picked it up. Betty's face turned white. He ran his finger over the letters. There was something sticky on the metal.

Thinking out loud, he said "It would be relatively easy to doctor a license plate number. A little adhesive tape or paint and a P looks like a B."

Betty stiffened and when she spoke her voice was overly

loud and shrill. "Are you insinuating that somebody doctored that license plate number? That would be illegal. We would never do anything like that." She grabbed the plate and threw it back into the garbage bin.

"I wasn't insinuating anything," Murdock said, surprised at Betty's reaction. "I was just thinking out loud."

Betty's face took on a dark, angry look. "They always suspect the wife first, don't they? Well, I was at church the night John was killed. Wednesday night is choir practice. There are a dozen people who will verify it. I can't believe you're standing in my garage looking for clues to convict me when the real murderer is on the loose somewhere out there."

Nick was totally embarrassed.

"I'm sorry, Betty. I wasn't implying anything. I know how close you and John were. I guess I've just been working too hard. I'm getting on everybody's nerves, including my own."

Betty seemed mollified as Nick left, but before he reached the station the thought *What if Betty* did *do it?* tumbled around in his mind. He called the secretary of the Presbyterian church as soon as he sat down at his desk and verified that Betty had been at choir practice that night. Practice broke up around ten-thirty. It always did. Plenty of time for Betty to pull up next to John at a dark intersection. It was a ridiculous thought, but it nagged at him. He decided to let it go for now.

There was a message on his desk. Susan Bronson needed to speak to him, urgently. He called immediately, but it was Susan's sister who answered the phone.

"Susan's not here right now, Sheriff Murdock, but I know she wants to talk to you as soon as possible."

Murdock glanced at his watch. It was after two, but this was worth another drive north.

"I'll be there around four."

On the way out of town he passed the Presbyterian church. The minister was in the parking lot with Betty, helping her unload boxes.

Nick spent the time driving north going over in his mind what he already knew. John was shot just after eleven o'clock. Gladys Smith had disapproved of the way John ran the mayor's office. She hadn't liked Susan Bronson. Would Gladys kill for a job?

John had gotten his office clerk pregnant. What if Betty knew about the baby? Would she have wanted John dead? Women had killed their husbands for less.

Or maybe Susan Bronson, angry at being cast aside, killed him in a fit of jealousy or despair?

More likely than any of those scenarios was the one he had come up with first—an anonymous drive-by shooting.

Once again Nick Murdock found himself seated in the fussy Victorian living room of Susan Bronson's sister's house.

Susan fidgeted with a fold in her skirt.

"There was something I didn't tell you the other day. I figured it wasn't any of your business and you didn't ask."

Murdock waited.

"Mrs. Freedmont came to see me the day after John's funeral."

Murdock tried not to register surprise.

"She said that Gladys was at her house after the funeral and stayed to help tidy up after the other guests left. Gladys is such a mean old busybody. She told Mrs. Freedmont that she thought I was in *trouble*—meaning pregnant. Mrs. Freedmont put two and two together and figured out it was John's."

"Why did she come to see you?"

"That's the weird part. She said she wanted to do the right thing. She asked if it was John's baby. I told her the same thing I told you. She offered to pay for my expenses until the baby was born, and she wants the baby. She said it's all she'll have left of John. She wants to adopt it after it's born just like John wanted to."

"What did you tell her?"

Susan looked down and began fiddling with the fold in her skirt again.

"You've got to understand, Sheriff Murdock. I don't have much money. Mrs. Freedmont is rich. She could do a lot for the baby and I could start all over again someplace else."

"It's all right, Susan. I understand. It makes sense." He stood to leave. "Thank you for calling me. You were right to do so."

She showed him to the door. It was beginning to get dark; nightfall came early this time of year. Murdock was tired and it was a long drive home.

Thoughts swirled in his head. He didn't know if Susan's confession had any bearing on the case. Betty had always wanted children. It made sense that she'd want to raise John's baby. She didn't have any other family. Betty had forgiven John for the one-night stand before he was killed and she didn't know about the baby until after the funeral. That pretty much left her without a motive. He could scratch one suspect off the list.

As far as Susan was concerned it would have been in her best interest if John had lived. That let her off the hook, too.

He had dug up a lot of dirt, but none of it pointed to murder. It was just like he thought from the start: a senseless drive-by murder that no one would ever solve. Murdock glanced at his watch. He figured if he drove hard he might still make it home in time to take Myra to a movie.

A few miles out of town he pulled up to a flashing red blinker on a deserted section of the two-lane highway. In the corner of his eye he saw a car pulling up next to him. Funny, he hadn't seen any headlights.

He looked to his left and saw the barrel of a gun. Instinct took over. He dove to the floor of the car just a fraction of a second too late. He felt the searing heat of the blow before the pain hit. Heard the roar of squealing tires before he passed out.

***

Officers Sloane and Higgins approached the front door of the Freedmont house. Betty answered the bell dressed in a robe and slippers. Her dishevelled hair and slightly swollen face suggested she'd been sleeping heavily. Her face froze when she opened the door.

"Elizabeth Freedmont," Julie Sloane said formally, "You're under arrest for attempted murder." Sloan began reading Freedmont her rights.

Betty didn't react. "How did you know it was me?" she asked as Julie finished.

"You should have checked the car," Julie answered. "It was only a shoulder wound."

The next day Sheriff Murdock came into work on time as usual. His shoulder was taped under his freshly pressed uniform shirt and his left arm was in a sling. He sat at his desk shuffling papers. Lois came in and set a cup of coffee on the desk. She started to make conversation, but recognized he wasn't in the mood and left. After a few minutes Murdock passed Lois' desk.

"Are you all right, Chief?" she asked. He didn't hear her. Several men who had arrived for the day shift were buzzing about the arrest. They quieted down as he walked through. He stood in front of the jail cell where Betty sat on the edge of the bed, staring at the wall. She was dressed in prison grays, her hair pulled neatly back in a barrette.

"I don't get it, Betty. Why'd you do it?"

"You found out about the baby. It was just a matter of time until you confronted me. Then the whole town would know."

"But John. Why'd you kill John?"

Betty turned her gaze from the wall and stared at Sheriff Murdock.

"We were married for eighteen years. I thought that meant something. I could forgive a one-night stand. It was hard, but anyone can make a mistake. I left choir practice early because I had a headache. Then I passed her house on the way home. I saw John's car parked out front. He told me he'd be at a conference all day. Instead he'd spent the day with her. I couldn't forgive that. I figured it out on the way home. It only took a minute to change the license plate and doctor the numbers with adhesive tape. There were some flame decals in the garage and I pasted them on the car for good measure. I thought even if somebody saw the car they'd never identify it. When I drove back to Susan's he was just leaving. I followed him to the intersection."

"You must have really hated him."

Betty looked surprised. "Hated him? How could I hate John? He was my whole life. I just couldn't let him leave me for another woman." Betty's face turned to stone. "He was my husband. He will always be my husband. Nobody else could ever love him as much as I do."

Murdock shook his head. He thought about John and how much he'd loved his wife in spite of his one indiscretion.

He thought about Susan all alone in that house up north. Then he thought about the baby and how much John had wanted to raise it with Betty. Now John was dead, Betty was in prison, and the baby would probably be given up for adoption anyway.

Some days he hated this job.

Mark Richard Zubro

Mark Richard Zubro is interested in chocolate, history and politics, in the works of J.R.R.Tolkien and of Walter Brooks, and in folk music. He is an 8th grade English teacher and union president for the Summit Hill District #161 in Frankfort, Illinois.

He is the author of two series: a police procedural featuring a Chicago Detective, and an amateur sleuth series featuring English teacher. His latest work is *Another Dead Teenager* published in August 1995. His newest novel, *Rust on the Razor*, has just been published.

Tea For Two
by
Mark Richard Zubro

"But I don't want to go to a tea party. I can't imagine how I ever let you talk me into this."

He is not attractive when he whines.

"Put your party smile on and ring the bell. It's a good cause. You like good causes."

"I love good causes. I hate tea parties."

"You've never been to a tea party."

"There's good reasons I've never been to a tea party. I don't drink tea. I've never had tea. I hate tea."

"How can you hate it, if you've never had it?"

"You sound like my mother."

"Obviously a wise woman. Ring the bell."

"Our hostess will probably have sixteen cats. I'm allergic to cat hair."

I thought of telling him people were allergic to cat dander not cat hair, but he was grumpy enough already, so all I said was, "You never mentioned any cat allergies before today."

He sniffed. "I think I'm going to sneeze."

"The Friends of the Podunk, Illinois, Library Literary Society and Horseshoe Tossing Guild need help. I promised Meg. You promised Meg. You won't be swamped by obnoxious fans. These will be charming, sweet people who read books and talk about Chaucer."

"I'd rather toss horseshoes." He paused. "Is that the real name of the group?"

"No." I reached in front of him and rang the bell.

Moments later Mildred Finistermine, a woman in her sixties, opened the door of the Victorian mansion. I'd met her at one of the planning meetings for the party. She beamed at me and then at Scott. She'd done a lot of beaming at the meeting where I met her; I suspect she beamed at everyone. She'd also offered her home as a place for the party. For that we all beamed at her.

She wore a flower print dress. She extended a white-gloved hand to me. She let her fingertips touch my palm. I introduced Scott. He got a dose of the fingertips.

The foyer she led us into was wallpapered in a French café motif. Poodles and wine bottles chased each other around delicate black chairs at a street-side eatery against a background of numerous Eiffel Towers.

Next to the door was a mahogany hat rack with a matching umbrella stand. A flight of stairs carpeted in dusky rose led up to the right. A set of wrought-iron chairs and a table nestled under a painting of a man in a high collar and black robe. She nodded at the portrait, "Judge Wiley, my grandfather. He was one of the first settlers of Syskeston. The first judge in Syskeston County."

A long-haired, gray cat crept down the hallway that led farther into the house. Scott nudged me and nodded his head in the direction of the animal. The cat stopped and turned yellow eyes on us. Scott sneezed.

We were at a fund-raiser set up by a joint committee of the Library Board, Friends of the Library, and the Literary Society of Syskeston, Illinois. My lover, Scott Carpenter, was the main attraction. As a star baseball player, he would bring people and their checkbooks out to the fund-raiser. You win a few World Series games and everyone takes notice, and at fund-raisers, the money often flows. They would get to meet, shake hands with, and talk to him, as well as get a free autographed baseball. At the moment, I was dragging Scott to a special pre-fund-raiser reception/high tea to be attended only by those who had already contributed more than one hundred dollars to the library. Also invited were the staff of the library, the officers of both organizations, selected best friends, and significant others of each member of each such group, and probably their idiot cousins from the outback. The not-quite-elite who'd paid less than one hundred would attend the big reception two hours from now in the local high school gymnasium.

Syskeston was in deepest downstate Illinois, somewhere north of Cairo, fifty miles from the nearest interstate highway. We'd driven most of the afternoon through a part of the state unrecognized in the Chicago area where we came from, except by politicians needing votes every four years.

Meg Swarthmore, who had roped us into this, had grown up here, and still had strong connections to the area. She ran the library at the high school where I taught, River's Edge, a suburb of Chicago. We were close friends. She had asked for

our help for the nearly bankrupt library, and with some pushing from me, we had acquiesced.

I heard the tinkle of spoons in tea cups, voices murmur-
ing softly, and discreetly played chamber music.

Mildred rolled back a pair of sliding doors on our left to
reveal a sunroom/parlor which stretched the entire length of
the east side of the building. All eyes turned on us, or rather
on Scott. People look at him. He's handsome. He's famous.
He's rich. He was what had drawn them here.

Once inside, I noted that the people present stood in two
separate groups. Nearby, twenty-five or so hunkered down around
the buffet table. At the far end of the room, another crowd with
slightly fewer people surrounded a table with two gigantic urns,
one silver-plated, the other gold. Everyone I could see clutched
nearly translucent tea cups and/or tiny dishes with small mounds
of delicately prepared foods.

On one side of the grand piano near the center of the
room was a four-member chamber group playing softly. I saw
Meg chatting with an elderly, white-haired gentleman on the
other side of the piano. She spotted me, waved, and hurried
over with her companion. She introduced him as Dr. Brewster.
He clasped hands with Scott enthusiastically. He was rotund
and cheerful. With a beard, and red, tasseled hat, he could
play Santa in a pageant.

While Dr. Brewster blathered, Mildred looked uncertainly
from group to group.

Meg saw Mildred's hesitation and said, "Millie, why don't
I get everyone's attention, and you can introduce the guests to
all of them, and then they can chat with them individually?"

Mildred nodded.

Meg walked over and spoke to the musicians. They stopped
playing. The people in the room quieted down. The groups did

not move toward Scott eagerly as had so many over the years. Each shifted a few feet in our direction and stared at us. No one in either aggregation looked toward anyone in the other.

Mildred eyed both groups, sighed, cleared her throat, and began a simple but elegant introduction and thank you to Scott. Finished, she hesitated for an instant when neither cluster of people moved. Her beam looked forced. Dr. Brewster stepped forward, placed one hand gently on Scott's elbow, and led him toward the group near the tea table. Murmurs of conversation began from each group.

I leaned over to Meg and muttered, "Is this Librarian Wars?"

"Don't say that word."

"Wars?"

"The L word." She pulled me toward the door through which we had entered and the farthest point from either group. When she was sure no one was in earshot, Meg whispered, "This is awful."

"What's going on?"

"They hate each other."

"Who hates who?"

"Them." She inclined her head, first toward one group and then the other.

I watched Scott being gently engulfed by the faction on our right, the garrison around the tea table. Two slender men who looked to be in their mid-forties led the slow eddying towards him. The men wore dark gray suits, starched white shirts, and red ties.

"Milly never told me all this, or I never would have asked you and Scott to attend. She and I grew up here in Syskeston and even went off to and graduated from Vassar together. We've been friends for years. She would have told me. I don't think the controversy started until about six months ago. Long after you agreed to attend. So it's not really her fault."

The parts of Scott's schedule that he allows for appearances and speaking engagements are filled for over a year in advance. He'd barely been able to squeeze in this visit.

"A big fight about censorship? Isn't that the usual?"

"No censorship problems here. Not yet anyway."

"Did somebody not return a book? A librarian lose her stamp pad? And why am I not supposed to say librarian?"

"The people at the tea table want to be called information specialists."

I glanced surreptitiously at the generally younger crowd. Some of the women wore pant suits, although gray and conservative. A few wore flower print dresses. The few men not in dark gray suits tended to wear khaki pants, blue shirts, patterned yellow silk ties, and Bass Weejuns.

"The ones at the buffet table insist they are librarians."

This faction tended heavily to the wool skirt and cardigan over-the-shoulders end of the scale. Several wore white blouses with Peter Pan collars buttoned to the top. Two wore white gloves and a few a daring strand of pearls. Sensible oxfords were the shoes of choice. The men in the group all wore black or gray suits with black shoes and dark ties. No khaki here.

"Is there a big deal difference between librarian and information whatsis?" I asked.

"Specialist. Yes, to them there is."

"You aren't making this up?"

"No. The whole situation's been aggravated by a dispute that has split both the Library Board and the Friends of the Library into almost equal factions."

"Major altercation over a new card catalogue?"

"Hush," Meg said. "That battle is just starting."

"Oh."

"The big fight started when they landed a medium-sized grant from the government. The two who wrote the proposal had a falling out about how the money was supposed to be used."

"I thought those government things were pretty strict."

"Usually they are, but this one had some flexibility. The man who worked on it, Joe Conestoga, assumed it was for his pet project, expanding the book collection. The woman who worked on it, Jennifer Jones, assumed it was for her pet project, overhauling and improving the facilities."

"I thought you told us they were broke."

"Nearly. They haven't been able to spend the government money because of disagreements. That money isn't enough to solve anywhere near the problems they have. Their misunderstanding exacerbated problems the system has had for years. Unless this fund-raiser is a huge success, they could be forced to close permanently."

"Why don't they just cut back, retrench, exist on what they've got?"

Meg clutched my arm. "Say that any louder and both sides might lynch you."

"Why not just take a vote?"

"They did. The board voted in September to do it Jennifer's way. Then in November they elected a new board, which decided to do it Joe's way, but Jennifer's faction had enough clout in the community to get everything delayed. Now both sides have gone to court. They've even got spies in each other's camp. They're to the point of having people casually lingering around corners to try to overhear conversations. Strange behavior for adults, I'd say."

"This is nuts."

"The whole thing is more complicated because, according to cheap, tawdry gossip—"

"The best kind."

"Jennifer and Joe were having this secret, torrid affair."

"Are they married?"

"Not to each other."

"Oh. I'm supposed to take this seriously? I mean, even an affair among these people can't be all that big a deal. Can it?"

"It would be among the two involved and their spouses."

"Well, yeah. Were the spouses aware of what was going on?"

"I don't know. Neither is divorced yet."

"So the library is going downhill because the people involved are human? They'd let this place go to hell? I thought you told me this was one of the oldest libraries in the state."

"It is. This part of the state was settled long before the Chicago area was. The library has been around since before the Civil War. Lots of fierce pride in the community about everything connected to it. They still work partly in the Carnegie Library that was built seventy years ago. The other section is in the basement of one of the churches in town." She sighed. "Being human isn't the problem." She smiled at me. "It's just the people involved." She patted my arm and began easing away from me. "I've got to try to smooth things as best I can. Will you be all right if I leave you on your own?"

"I didn't bring my machine gun."

She grinned briefly, squared her shoulders, and marched away.

I eased my way to the corner near the end of the buffet table that held the dish with the squares of cheese impaled by toothpicks. On the lavish spread I recognized spinach dip surrounded by fresh sourdough bread, mounds of small sandwiches with squiggles of paté on them, dishes of fresh shrimp and sauce, and numerous items I could not name, but which looked inviting. But then I know gourmet canapés as well as most fish know nuclear physics.

I caught snatches of conversation as people eddied and swirled around me. I wished they wore signs so I could have known which faction was which. Might have made it more fun. I heard:

"I can't wait. I hope we get enough money for all the computers."

"That old card catalogue has got to go."

"She's got to change her mind. We can't have people drinking coffee at their desks."

"Didn't drink coffee at their desks in my day."

"She's so old, she farts dust."

"Una, dear, you made my favorite dish."

"I tried a new twist on my usual."

"It's delicious. You must give me the recipe."

"I wish we didn't all have to bring something to eat."

"A potluck for such a famous person, really!"

"It isn't dignified."

"Blame them!"

"And he walked right up to her and called her a librarian. I have more degrees than anyone here, and she just lets him! Doesn't correct him. I put a stop to that. I stepped right in and said *I* was the librarian. I could answer his questions. These clerks! Honestly!"

"We can't ever get rid of the old card catalogue. I remember as a kid hunting through the old system. It was such a comfort to look and touch and hold all those different little cards."

"They'll try to get those computers in here any way they can."

"It's all their fault."

A woman in her mid-thirties with soft, blond hair reached for a canapé from a plate of stuffed mushrooms wrapped in bacon. She added it to several other items on her plate. On her saucer, sodden white tea bags nestled next to her cup.

Meg appeared next to me and said, "Tom Mason, this is Jennifer Jones."

One of the major combatants Meg had mentioned. I couldn't tell if she was on the pro or con side of the Great Computer/ Catalogue Controversy. Her gold-rimmed glasses hung on a chain around her neck that let them dangle over her white blouse. She wore a gray skirt and jacket. She smiled at me.

"You came in with Mr. Carpenter?" Jennifer asked.

"Yes, we're lovers."

"Oh," she said.

Jennifer sipped her tea. Meg left us and for the moment Jennifer and I were alone at a corner of the buffet table. She stood next to me and together we observed the crowd. Next to Scott was a man in his early thirties, handsome, but with the look of someone who should have started going to the gym and begun cutting back on the calories last Christmas. He would be heavily into middle-age spread within weeks.

"Look at him," Jennifer said.

"Who?" I asked.

"Joe Conestoga. The man is practically drooling over the big deal sports player."

"I thought that was the idea," I pointed out reasonably.

"I'm sorry. Don't take me wrong, but Joe will brag about meeting Scott Carpenter for the rest of his life. He'll twist it all out of proportion just like he does everything else."

I made sympathetic murmurs. I may not have wanted to hear more, or take this all that seriously, but I was moderately bored and sufficiently curious to hear what she had to say. It took very little prompting. The bitterness and anger were obviously near to the surface.

"I want to make sure," she said, "that everyone who comes into contact with that vile man knows exactly what a rat he is. He's a liar, a cheat, a two-timer, a backstabber ..." The list became quite lengthy. "I wish I could make him disappear from the face of the planet."

"He must have done something pretty awful."

"I'll say." She gave me the outline of the same story I got from Meg, but with far more numerous negative adjectives added to Joe Conestoga's name.

"And yes, someone will tell you we had an affair. You've probably heard already. No one in this town can keep their mouth shut. The truth is he was a lousy lover. He began to brag about it to all his friends in the bar at the Interstate Twin Motel. It wouldn't have been long before the news was on CNN."

I decided not to mention that the Interstate Twin was the motel we were staying at. Who knew it was the hotbed of male gossip? It was also the only place remotely close with rooms available.

Jennifer drained her tea cup daintily, turned to the buffet table, and picked up a piece of celery stuffed with cream cheese. She took one bite, gasped, and pitched over onto the table. Her teacup flew into the air. The liquid sloshed onto the front of a blue-rinsed matron's silk blouse while the cup continued on its journey to the floor. Jennifer's face landed in the guacamole dip and her left elbow in the pickled herring. Meg and I reached for her. She flailed with her arms for a moment, then slipped to the floor.

Several people nearby stifled laughs and giggles. A few gasped. For a moment I thought she was choking on something. Meg tried the Heimlich maneuver, but it quickly became apparent that choking was not her problem.

Dr. Brewster, two men I didn't know, and I, carried Jennifer to a room across the hall. Within moments she began to vomit and go into convulsions. The nearest hospital was at least half an hour away. Dr. Brewster did what little he could for the few minutes it took the paramedics to arrive from the volunteer fire department. Jennifer stopped gasping for breath a few moments after they walked in the door. They did their best, but she died without regaining consciousness.

A short time later Dr. Brewster and I walked back across the hall. The people in the room became silent when they saw us. Meg, Millie, and Joe Conestoga stood near the door. Dr. Brewster gave everyone the bad news.

An elderly woman in a Peter Pan collar with tears streaming down her face said to Joe Conestoga, "I hope you're satisfied."

Several people gasped. Mildred stepped forward and led the woman away.

The sheriff arrived to find the factions divided and placed as I had when we arrived. He was Mildred and Meg's age with a mostly bald top of his head, but with a few lank strands pulled from front to back. On the sides, his hair touched the tops of his ears. He wore dark brown pants, a tan shirt, a badge, and a gun. In his left hand he carried the kind of hat I thought only Texas Rangers wore.

Meg, Mildred, Scott, and I stood in the center of the room. He strode over to us. He was introduced as Arnie Church.

"Wanted to get here earlier, Millie, sorry. Was out in the country at Sam Patch's place. Wife busted him up pretty bad again."

Meg explained what we knew about what happened to Jennifer. She finished, "It didn't look like choking. I thought it was so sudden, maybe poison of some kind."

"Come on, Meg, murder?" Arnie said. "You've been up in Chicago too long. Haven't had a murder here in a decade."

"I think you've got one now, Arnie," Meg said.

Dr. Brewster added, "Her convulsions and vomiting are typical symptoms of poisoning."

***

After two hours the police had managed to get statements from only half of those present. The organizers of the event, led by Millie, urged Arnie to let Scott move on to the big reception.

They hadn't gotten around to me yet. Scott, Millie, Meg, and the others who'd been questioned were allowed to leave ten minutes later.

Jennifer's death hadn't prevented the living from devouring most of what was on the buffet table by this time. I was standing next to the tea table. Joe Conestoga, whom I had not been introduced to yet, wandered up to a newly arrived electric coffee maker, which sat next to the gold urn.

"Finally, coffee!" Joe said. He filled his cup and glanced around the table, then pulled a packet of diet sugar out of his blazer pocket. He poured two into his cup, stirred, took a sip, made a face, put the cup down, pulled out another packet, and dumped it into his cup. He took a hefty gulp.

"Stuff is awful," he said.

He staggered slightly and reached out to steady himself against the table. I put out my hand and grabbed his elbow.

"Are you all right?" I asked.

"Fine, thanks." He took deep breaths, as if he were repeating a relaxation technique. "I've been under too much tension and stress lately. Doctor says I'm supposed to cut down on caffeine." He quaffed more coffee.

I thought of reiterating the caffeine warning, but then I wasn't his mother or his physician.

"I heard you've had problems," I said.

"That doesn't surprise me. Nobody around here can keep their mouth shut." He gestured with his coffee cup toward the crowd. "Half of them think I murdered Jennifer. I wouldn't kill the silly twit. We had an affair. We were both adults; no one was at fault. You'd think these people had never heard of people having an affair. Good thing you're a stranger."

I moved closer. "Why's that?" I asked.

"You haven't heard all the lies and rumors. Look at them." He nodded toward the crowd everywhere in the room, except near us. "Two hours ago, half of them believed my side of the story. My side of the controversy. Took my side in all my battles with Jennifer. Look at them. Friends! Ha!"

"What were the fights about?"

"She took my ideas. She tried to take my money. When she couldn't do that, she tried to smear me with everyone in the community. She told lie after lie. Distortion after distortion. She was a vomitous pig. I'm not sorry she's dead."

"But you must have been close at one time. If you had an affair ..." It wasn't my business and normally I'm not that bold, but by now I was intrigued with all these fighting people. And it was true, he did make the best suspect. And truer still, cheap tawdry gossip is cheap tawdry gossip no matter where you are or how well you know the people.

He raised an eyebrow at me. "I saw her talking to you just before she died. With her dying breath she was probably spreading her lies. This used to be a quiet place to work. A good town. She ruined it."

He downed the rest of the cup of coffee, turned back to the machine, and poured himself another cup. He took out more packets of diet sugar and dumped them into his coffee. "You'd think they'd keep diet sugar as well as real sugar when they have these get-togethers."

"Did the breaking off of the affair start the rift, or the internal politics of the library begin the fight?" I figured I might as well ask. You don't ask, it's tough to get answers.

"You know a lot for a first-time visitor."

"Like you said, it's hard to miss. Stand in one spot around here long enough and you can hear most of it."

"Truth is, she was a rotten lover. Plus, she began to blab to everyone about us. Told the women at the beauty parlor, no doubt. It wouldn't have been long before the news would've been on CNN. She had such a big mouth."

He poured another cup of coffee and started dumping in diet sugar. He saw my strange look. "All Arnie drinks is coffee. They surely wouldn't have gotten it for me. Old Jennifer would make sure of that. Her war against me continued to the most minuscule thing. No coffee. No diet sugar. Getting control of the party entertainment and fund-raising committee was one of her latest coups."

He clanked the spoon against the side of the cup, placed it carefully on a napkin on a clean plate. This time he sipped instead of gulped his coffee.

"You always carry so much diet sugar?"

"Around here. When Jennifer started her war against me, she tried to keep me from drinking coffee at my desk. She had to have special tea, specially made, for her special needs. She and her cronies would meet in the basement of the library, brew tea, and hatch paranoid plots."

He sipped the coffee, smiled, swallowed another mouthful, and with a dull thump pitched face first into the sugar bowl. The electric coffee-maker tipped over, the glass container flipped over, and brown liquid sloshed onto the lace tablecloth. Joe gasped once and flailed his arms. The gold and silver urns toppled to the floor. Their lids flew off and their contents spilled onto the carpet.

For a while he seemed to be breathing normally. Dr. Brewster, the paramedics, and the police tried reviving him. Then Joe began vomiting and having convulsions. After his body became still, they tried CPR. Nothing they did helped. Joe Conestoga was dead.

You kind of stand around aimlessly at times like that. The cops were bustling themselves and the rest of us hither and yon. Meg and Mildred returned from the big reception. The turnout was great, but the death of one of the library staff cast a vast pall over the entire event, and now this second demise made the day that much more of a calamity.

More to have something to do and to save Millie some work, Meg and I began to help clear debris from the carpet. Sopping up all the liquid and laundering the carpet thoroughly would probably take professional cleaners.

After we'd been at it all of two minutes, a young police officer barked at us and told us to stop. I flipped the wad of napkins I'd been using into a trash basket.

I said, "At least we didn't have to pick up gobs of mushed-up food or sodden tea bags."

"We didn't use tea bags," Meg said. "It was all brewed in the big urns just before the party."

"I saw Jennifer with tea bags on her saucer."

"Must have brought her own tea bags and gotten hot water from the kitchen."

"She the only one who used tea bags?"

"I don't know. Why?"

"If she was poisoned ... Where'd she get the tea bags?"

"We'll ask Millie."

Millie was sitting on a gold damask couch. Dr. Brewster

was holding her hand and comforting her. He rose at our approach. Meg sat next to Millie.

"Are you all right?" Meg asked.

"I don't know," she said. "I honestly don't know."

Meg patted her shoulder and murmured soothing words to her for several minutes. Finally Meg said, "Tom and I wanted to ask you several things. Are you up to it?"

Millie nodded.

"Did Jennifer brew her own tea today?" I asked.

"Oh, yes. She always did. She'd make up special concoctions every Sunday night from teas she ordered from a catalogue. She'd put each of them in little bags and use them all week."

"So that's why she was the only one I saw with the tea bags."

"I'm sure she was. Jennifer always insisted on her little ways. Before you got here, I gave her a kettle to heat water in the kitchen."

"You think somebody doctored her tea bag?" Meg asked.

"Maybe," I said.

"We better talk to Arnie," Meg said.

We told him our suspicions. He called over a young cop. "Somebody got those tea bags from the floor near Jennifer's body?"

The cop returned in a minute with two tea bags in a clear plastic container.

"These all the tea bags?" Arnie asked.

"We found three more in her purse and two more in the dead guy's pockets."

"Where?" Meg, Arnie, and I asked.

He repeated his statement.

"Bring them all," Arnie commanded.

"What could they have put in the tea bags?" Millie asked.

"Would poison have worked that fast?"

"If it was powerful enough to kill her, wouldn't she have detected an odd taste?" Meg asked.

"Depends on the type of poison," Arnie said.

Dr. Brewster's face looked ashen.

"What's wrong, Ben?" Meg asked.

"If it was poison ... or narcotics ... oh, my god." Abruptly he sat down next to Millie and Meg.

We all turned to him.

"They were both on prescription medications. Jennifer started several months ago with a tranquilizer. She said the stress was incredible. Joe began two weeks ago. I had to be careful with his dosage because he was on high blood pressure medicine as well."

"He's young to have high blood pressure," Millie said.

"He was in his late thirties and he'd begun to put on weight. He hadn't exercised in years. His blood pressure was way up."

"He was guzzling coffee just before he died," I said.

"If even half my patients did as I told them ..." Brewster shook his head. "Although I don't know if the caffeine would have killed him." He shrugged.

I asked, "You can give knock-out drops to somebody and it would kill them?"

"Not usually, but some narcotics don't mix well with certain prescriptions, but who knows? We'll have to wait for the autopsies. This is awful."

"Who knew what prescriptions they were on?" I asked.

"This is a small town, as I'm sure you've noticed," Dr. Brewster said. "There aren't many secrets. I told no one. I have no idea who they told. The nearest pharmacy is in Bridgeton, ten miles away. That's where most everybody fills their prescriptions. I'm sure they'll question the staff there."

"Could it have been placed in the tea bags?" I asked.

"Depends on what narcotic it was, but yes."

"And in the diet sugar packets," I said.

They all looked at me. I explained. Arnie ordered the diet sugar packets impounded.

***

Four hours later Scott and I sat together in the bar of the Interstate Twin Motel. We expected Meg to join us shortly. We'd extricated ourselves from the uncomfortable clutches of the police and the local townspeople and driven to our motel in depressed silence. So far I'd noted that the bar seemed to be a haven to absolutely nobody. We were the only customers. If this was a hotbed of cheap, tawdry gossip, they weren't doing it while we were around.

After our waitress stopped gawking long enough to deliver our diet sodas and get autographs from Scott for her kids, Scott said, "That was the most depressing fiasco I've ever been involved in."

"I prefer my fiascoes to be the cheerful kind. I make it a policy to attend only bright, happy fiascoes."

"How can you make a joke?"

"I remember a few wild disasters and mad panic situations you've gotten us into."

"Name one."

I didn't have to think a second. "How about the time in Tashkent, with the train conductor, the camel seller with the patch over one eye, and the missing heroin dealer?"

"That wasn't my fault."

"Precisely."

"You said they'd talk about Chaucer and be civilized. Nobody talked about Chaucer. Nobody even mentioned books.

They just kept killing each other."

"A situation Chaucer probably would have appreciated and understood. Just think, for the rest of your life you can say you've been to a tea party."

He was silent for a minute, then took a drink of soda. Finally he said, "I know it wasn't your fault."

"I appreciate your willingness to help out."

Meg walked into the bar, spotted us, and came over. She placed an order for more diet soda. She took off her glasses, rubbed her hands vigorously over her face, and sighed deeply. She said, "If I ever try to drag you two down here again, shoot me first and if that doesn't work, tattoo the words 'you can't go home again' on my forehead."

"What happened after we left?" I asked.

"The deaths were bad enough. Talking to the survivors was ghastly. I have never seen so many people so upset. Even worse, Ben Brewster proposed again at the police station."

"The doctor?"

"Yeah. He proposed to me when he took me to the senior prom several centuries ago, as I remember it. Managed to bring it up several times since, never on quite as inauspicious an occasion as this. Old Ben is sweet and nice and was quite a looker as a kid, not that bad now either for that matter, but he has no sense of timing. Plus, I just don't want to marry him. Didn't then, either. I need this on a day with bodies flopping into the dip?" She suppressed a smile and then looked around guiltily. "I don't mean to be making a joke."

I said, "Macabre gallows humor sometimes helps people get through horrible tragedies."

We all sipped soda.

"What happened?" Scott asked.

"They were trying to kill each other," Meg said.

"Jennifer and Joe?"

"Came loaded. Some of the lab reports started to come in before I left. Ben told me all the details. Old boyfriends are good for something after all. The diet sugar packets Joe had and the tea bags Jennifer had were both laced with narcotics. They found diet sugar packets that had been tampered with at her house. She may have tried to kill him before. Joe had to dole out her tea bags only a couple at a time. Both had to be careful they wouldn't be seen."

"A surreptitious reach into a purse or pocket and the poisoned packet would be delivered," I said.

Meg nodded.

"Maybe they were just trying to make each other very ill," Scott suggested. "Maybe neither one intended murder."

"We'll never know," Meg said. "The point is each knew the other was on a prescription drug. Spies from each camp had reported to the other about what effect the tensions had on their opponent."

"None of the spies were in on it?" Scott asked.

"At the moment they don't think so. They were just people indulging in salacious gossip that turned fatal. Noting down which pills the other was taking, how many and how often. Didn't take much for Joe or Jennifer to do some library research and come up with successful combinations of drugs that would kill when mixed with what they were taking."

"And one would be alive to enjoy it, if they hadn't planned it on the same day," Scott said.

I said, "Lots of people, lots of suspects around. More people than usual because Scott was there, made it as good a time as any for an attempt. These people were nuts."

"Very angry, very human, very flawed," Meg said and sighed. "I'm afraid I'll never forget the first moments after

Jennifer's face landed in the guacamole."

John Lutz

JOHN LUTZ's first short story was published in 1966, and he has been writing ever since. The author of over twenty-five novels and approximately 200 short stories and articles, Lutz is a past president of both Mystery Writers of America and Private Eye Writers of America. He won the Mystery Writers of America Edgar Award in 1986, and the Private Eye Writers of America Shamus Award in 1982 and 1988. In 1989, he won the Trophee 813 Award for best mystery short story collection translated to the French language. He is the author of two long-running private eye series, the Carver series, set in Florida; and the Nudger series, set in his home town of St. Louis, Missouri. Also the author of many non-series suspense novels, his *SWF Seeks Same* was made into the hit movie *Single White Female*, starring Bridget Fonda and Jennifer Jason Leigh.

His novel, *The Ex*, was made into the film of the same title, for which he co-authored the screen play.

The latest book in the Nudger series is *Thicker Than Blood*, published by St. Martin's Press. His next Nudger novel, as yet untitled, is due to be published in September, again by St. Martin's Press. Latest in the Carver series is *Lightning*, Henry Holt. He is currently at work on a new Nudger novel titled *Oops!*

YOU BELONG TO ME
By
John Lutz

Someone was banging on something metal down in the street, and one of the homeless began chanting in time with the steely rhythm, an inane paean to the breaking day. It was someone else—a man's voice, in the street but close by and snarling with anger—who demanded quiet and actually drew Joel up from sleep.

His first thought of the new day took form like an opaque cloud in his mind, a clinging remnant of yesterday. Or last night. He was relieved that he wouldn't have to shave his legs. His particular reluctance to do that surprised him. Maybe he didn't know himself as well as he'd thought.

Sleep still fogged his mind. He was lying on his stomach, his right arm numb and wedged beneath him, his cheek mushed into the pillow. Slowly, he opened his exposed and gritty eye.

Meredith was already awake, glowing golden in the bright morning haze from the skylight as she stood bent forward like a graceful bird, bony elbows extended behind her as she fastened the clasps on her brassiere.

Without moving, Joel asked where she was going.

"Got an appointment," she said, straightening. He could tell she was slightly irritated that he was awake; she'd been planning to leave their loft apartment without his knowledge.

He didn't ask her what kind of appointment or with whom. Joel Green and Meredith Clark had been living together for six months, and they allowed for each other's independence. Knowing of Joel's possessiveness and occasional outbursts of jealous invective, Meredith had made unquestioned individual activity one of the prerequisites for their shared lives.

"I microwaved yesterday's coffee," she said, slipping into a pearl-colored cotton blouse. She buttoned the cuffs, striking a peculiarly masculine pose, as if next she would straighten her tie and caress her chin to make sure she'd shaved close enough. "There's some left, and a couple of glazed doughnuts from last night."

"Sounds fine," Joel said, not able to think about breakfast. He wasn't yet fully awake and there was a horrific taste in his mouth. He moved his tongue experimentally. Were his teeth really the size and texture of mossy tombstones?

"You going in to Bailey's this morning?" Meredith asked.

Bailey's was the restaurant where Joel waited tables. "Uh-huh. 'Bout eleven. Gotta be there for the lunch crowd."

"What about rehearsal?"

She was certainly nosy about him, considering her own penchant for privacy. "Why do you ask?"

"I thought we might go out tonight and see Nora at the Low Note."

Nora Doan was a good friend and a bad stand-up comic, a longtime acquaintance of Joel's whom Meredith had taken to immediately. He did want to go with Meredith to the Low Note, where Nora was opening to do another perilous week of stand-up in front of a crowd that only occasionally seemed to notice she wasn't funny. But it was impossible.

"Rehearsal tonight," he said. "How about if I join you there afterward?"

She cocked her head to the side and looked upward at a

slight angle, the way she often did when she was considering, as if she were glancing at a cartoon balloon where she might read the information she was seeking.

"No," she said after a while, "I think I'll do something else."

She walked toward him, slender, graceful, body like a flame, a glamorous girl with straight brown hair almost to her waist. He'd threaded handfuls of that hair through his fingers, buried his face in its perfumed tangle.

She smiled as if knowing his thoughts and bent over him, kissing him on the forehead. Her lips were soft and cool, her breath a warm promise at their center.

"Have yourself a good day," she said.

He didn't move. "You too."

He listened to the *tap, tap* of her high heels as she crossed the wooden floor, the rattle of the chain lock, then the door closing and latching as she left the apartment.

Joel was a slender, muscular man, not very tall, with a curly-haired, boyish handsomeness despite his thirty-six years. His even features lent him a youthfully compelling presence on the stage. He knew he was watchable. He had a compact way of moving from his years as a dancer. An actor now, despite his days spent as a waiter at Bailey's, he was finally meeting with success. He'd recently been cast as one of the two male leads in *Chris Cross* at the Grayson Theater on West 29th Street. It was off-off Broadway, but it was a play that would garner *Times* and *New York* capsule reviews, and, if everything went well, would represent a solid acting credit. He often told himself he was an actor first and a waiter second, but at times it was difficult to believe it with his heart. There were a thousand actors waiting tables in Manhattan, and most of them were destined for other careers in distant cities.

He warmed a cup of coffee in the microwave, sat down at the table, then sipped the steaming black brew while he munched a stale, glazed doughnut. Mentally checking his confidence level as he often did, he found it high. He'd once been told he had a Napoleonic complex because of his small stature. But he wasn't *that* small, so he didn't believe it. He knew he was confident because he was good. It certainly wasn't insecurity that made him possessive and occasionally temperamental.

That was how Joel saw himself, anyway.

He wondered if Napoleon had ever seen himself the same way.

***

Joel's character in the comedy *Chris Cross*, Chris Evans, was one of two young law school graduates with androgynous names who masquerade as women so they'll be accepted by a prestigious law firm committed to hiring female associates. The other male lead's character, Lou Garvey, convinces Chris that after they are hired, the law firm will be unable to fire them when they reveal they are men, fearing a reverse sexual discrimination suit. The two naive young lawyers plan on becoming media celebrities, if not successful attorneys.

As the play progresses, none of this turns out as planned, as in life.

Chris Cross was scheduled to open at the Grayson in a month and was in the early phase of character read-throughs rather than more extensive rehearsals. Usually these occurred in mornings or afternoons, as *Leave Her to Purgatory* was running at the Grayson during the evenings. But a matinee was scheduled for today, so the read-through was in the evening. Joel's hours at Bailey's were flexible, and he'd easily been able to trade shifts with Todd Marks, a waiter who normally worked the lunch crowd.

Because *Chris Cross* required cross-dressing, the director, Barry Edwards, thought it would be a good idea if Joel and his co-star Vic Nurville, who played Lou, did the read-throughs in costume so they could get comfortable as soon as possible in female clothing.

At first Joel hadn't thought that was necessary, but he soon learned it wasn't easy to handle small objects wearing long false fingernails, or to walk with a seemingly natural gait in high heels. It took several rehearsals before he *was* comfortable enough in costume to forget from time to time that he was wearing a blouse, skirt, panty hose and high heels. Not to mention artificial breasts.

In the brick-walled, musty dressing room in the Grayson, makeup artist Beth Smallwood grinned at him as he sat before the mirror and smoothed back his hair. Beth was a tall woman with dark eyes, arched brows, and a prognathous jaw. Joel saw her long-faced, toothy smile and grinned back.

"You apply your makeup yourself tonight," she said. "You've gotta learn to put your lipstick on straight sometime, baby. I'll be right here to supervise."

"I'll go along with that until it's time to get into my unmentionables," Joel said.

"Go easy with the shading on your cheeks," Beth advised. "We don't want you looking fashion-model gaunt."

"Or like a corpse."

"Same thing. I like 'em with blood."

Joel smiled at her reflection in the mirror and began applying foundation makeup. He'd shaved closely with a new blade less than an hour before leaving for the theater, and his complexion soon took on an uncharacteristically flawless pale cast. Years disappeared from his face. He found himself wondering why older men didn't wear makeup. Cosmetic companies could market it under the name Brute Power Powder or somesuch and it would probably sell.

Not so the false eyelashes. They made for a drastic change in appearance and they were trouble. After applying blue eyeshadow, he lightly coated the false lashes with glue, then fit them over his own eyelashes with a recently acquired skill. Then he used dark eyeliner to lengthen his eyes and blend the lashes at the corners. Beth looked on and nodded approvingly. More makeup of a different shade then, to soften the size and line of his nose and emphasize his cheekbones. He cocked his head, peering at himself from one angle, then another, checking blend and shading. Fine. It was time for lipstick.

"Looking like a county fair queen," Beth told him.

"Is that what we want?"

"Sure. What we don't want is for you to look like a drag queen. One of the reasons you got the Chris role is because you have the facial structure and the slight build to pass as a genuine female."

He applied lip liner, then filled in with lipstick to thicken and shape his upper lip, then to make his lower lip appear fuller. County fair queen indeed! He was beginning to admire the woman in the mirror.

Beth did step outside while he slipped into the special codpiece that would minimize the bulge of his genitals, then the undergarment with the built-up hips and buttocks. But she was back to watch him work into his pantyhose. The nylon was just dark enough so that the hair on his legs wouldn't be visible. He put on the tailored skirt, then his false breasts and his blouse, fumbling with the buttons running down the left side instead of the right. Was there a reason why the buttons on men's and women's garments were reversed?

"It's easier if you put on the blouse first," Beth told him, "so it'll be tucked in when you zip your skirt."

It occurred to Joel that the women he'd seen get dressed had often put on their blouses before skirts or slacks, while he and most men customarily put on their pants before their shirts. That was probably because, unlike pants, many skirts zipped up the back and required effort. He nodded to Beth in the mirror and sat back down at the dressing table. She helped him with his blond wig, then touched up his makeup, her long fingers moving with an easy dexterity.

"You're catching on to this," she said. "You're almost ready for the *Village Voice* personal ads."

When they were finished with the wig, Joel worked his feet into his size-nine high heels. Men's feet were larger than women's, even in proportion to their height, and the shoes were designed to minimize this discrepancy. Joel was surprised by the attractive turn of his ankles. Had the casting director checked out his legs before hiring him? He felt a vague annoyance as well as amusement at the thought, and he gained a glimmer of insight as to why women resented assessment of their skills resting so heavily on physical attributes.

He stood up, a bit unsteady on the high heels, and Beth helped him shrug into the blazer tailored to minimize his waist. It also had special shoulder pads that made it appear they were responsible for what was actually the natural width of his shoulders.

He studied himself in the full-length mirrors, front and back. He might have been looking at one of the smartly dressed young career women he'd seen strolling down Second Avenue on their lunch hour.

"Trust me," Beth said approvingly, "you're a babe."

And since she was among the best in her business, he did trust her.

***

The read-through went smoothly, and Joel and Vic followed stage directions at one point to get used to moving in female clothing. They had to remember how to sit down with their thighs pressed together, how to cross their legs at the knees and sometimes twine one almost around the other, how to feign absentmindedly pumping one calf, letting a shoe dangle from their toes. Joel had trouble walking with his elbows tucked in close to his waist, but other than that he was learning female body language with an ease that amazed him. "Getting in touch with your feminine side," Barry had told him with the seriousness of a man who had been in deep therapy for a long time.

"Rent a video of *Tootsie*," suggested Reginald Ames, an impossibly distinguished actor who would portray a senior law partner.

Joel thought Ames might be joking, but he decided that studying Dustin Hoffman's cross-dress performance could only help.

Barry thanked everyone and told them goodbye until tomorrow, and most of the cast drifted away. Vic had a date, so Joel stayed out of his way while he got out of costume, removed his makeup, then dressed.

By the time Vic, his old masculine self again in Levi's and red chambray shirt, told him goodnight and left, the main theater was dark and Joel was alone.

He loved the feel of an empty theater almost as much as that of a sold-out house. The ghost of every performance was present; the emotion of countless audiences seemed to float out there in the dark auditorium like a low-voltage electrical force. In the faint musty smell and the shadows and thick silence crackled the potential of recharging that force.

"I said 'tort,' not 'tart'!" Joel proclaimed in Chris' husky female voice, listening to the line from Act One play out over the empty seats all the way to the back of the theater.

He smiled slightly, knowing he was in the right business.

He walked into the dressing room carrying his high heels in his hand, still wondering how women managed to spend an entire day in footwear that concentrated all their weight on their scrunched-up toes.

He'd had time to speculate about what Meredith was doing that evening. Probably she'd gone to the Low Note to see Nora as originally planned, but Joel doubted that she'd return home directly afterward.

Where would she go? Who would she see?

And why?

He sat at the dressing table and studied his reflection in the mirror. The woman who might have been his attractive sister gazed back at him. "Women!" Joel said softly.

The woman in the mirror shook her pretty blond head in sympathy.

What would it be like, Joel wondered, if his attractive sister went out in public? Would she pass as female without drawing a second glance from other women? Would men stare at her admiringly?

Learning those answers might be constructive in building the persona of Chris.

But he knew what he was really considering.

As Chris, Joel could easily check up on Meredith. He could go into the Low Note, for instance, and sit at the bar, watch her at her table, see if she was with anyone, perhaps even eavesdrop. Meredith would never suspect from across the dimly lit room that he was the attractive blond woman perched on a bar stool.

Joel debated with himself. He raised a hand to remove his blond wig, then lowered the hand.

He was an actor, he told himself. He could easily bring it off. That was what this part was about, and he knew he could play it. And he could leave the latch on the Grayson's back door off, return later tonight, and remove his makeup and costume.

No one would know the difference, and even if they did, he could tell them he'd decided to try his Chris persona on the street to help him gain confidence for his role. They'd believe him; actors did crazy things all the time.

Like the one I'm considering.

He gazed into his eyes in the mirror and gave a smile that surprised him with its loveliness. Then he worked his feet back into his high-heeled shoes.

Your eyes should be green instead of blue, he told himself.

Half a block away from the Low Note, Joel paced back and forth on the sidewalk, trying to get up his nerve to enter, to actually try passing as a woman in a room crowded with both sexes. If he was to be convincing on stage at the Grayson, it should be easy for him to play his role in a dimly lit Village bar.

But "should" was a long way from reality.

Only when a light drizzle began to fall and he automatically became concerned that it might muss his hairdo, did he smile and stride confidently on his high heels toward the entrance to the Low Note.

He kept his thighs close together, his elbows tucked in, easing more into character with each step. A cab slowed and swerved to the curb near him as the driver peered inquisitively at him through the windshield. The lady might need to get out of the rain. Joel shook his head and the cab sped away. He didn't recall a cabby ever showing such concern when he was dressed as a male.

It was almost eleven-thirty and he knew Nora would be most of the way through her second act. Joel had seen her a week ago when she was rehearsing. Nora was a small, pretty brunette with devilish blue eyes above a gentle and disarming smile, and a delivery that tried to be subtle but unfortunately lacked timing, as well as funny material. She worked hard, and her problem was that the audience saw her labor. It was half-drunk and amiable crowds like those at the Low Note that fed her delusion that she'd someday be what she ironically called a "serious comedian." Joel had once tried to talk her into concentrating on her singing, which was actually very good when she sang blues standards. But he remembered the hurt in her eyes, the glow fading from them, and he'd never again tried to dissuade her. People should be allowed their dreams. He knew.

He didn't glance at anyone as he entered, so he didn't know if anyone looked at him. He was immediately aware of laughter falling from a crescendo. Good. Nora seemed to be going over tonight.

Then he heard her soft voice and saw her on stage as he made it to the bar on his high heels and perched on one of only two vacant stools.

"...and for seventy-five dollars I'll do it while drinking a glass of water," Nora was saying. The audience roared.

Joel looked toward the stage and there she was, petite and shapely and blending her broadsword brand of comedy with a gentle sex appeal. He thought it was her innate gentleness that kept her from being shredded by more discerning audiences.

She nodded her thanks to this audience, smiling almost while her eyes sparked challenge. She was game, all right. "I read the label on this cough medicine," she was saying, "and it said 'Caution: might cause a rash in sensitive people.' So I figured hell, I was safe. [Moderate laughter.] But I was up scratching like crazy all night. How'd I know it'd cause sensitivity in rash people?"

Joel watched with fascination, admiring her courage. It was like seeing a one-armed trapeze artist work without a net.

Joel heard a voice say, "Miss? Miss?"

The bartender, a mustached, redheaded man named Willy whom Joel had seen before, was talking to him. But there was no recognition in Willy's eyes as Joel used his stage alto voice—Chris' voice—to order a scotch and water on the rocks.

He felt better when his drink had arrived and he'd paid for it. Careful about how he sat on the bar stool—knees pressed together, ankles crossed, elbows still tight to his sides—he looked around for Meredith.

It took him a few seconds to locate her. She was seated alone at a table near a post, about ten feet from the stage and twenty feet from where Joel sat. She looked beautiful, smiling slightly as she watched and listened to Nora.

He felt guilty right now, ashamed of the jealousy and suspicion that had driven him to the Low Note. But at the same time he experienced a delicious sense of secrecy, sitting here as someone else entirely, watching her. It was like being invisible.

Nora finished her act with the story about the midget who

went to the masquerade party dressed as a hot dog. Everyone liked it and she told them what a great crowd they were. They were drunk enough to believe it, and maybe they were right. Meredith stopped clapping, lowered her hands to her lap, then looked around for one of the servers to bring her another drink. Her gaze slid over Joel without pausing, and he let out a long breath. Why *would* she take a second look, he asked himself, at the pretty blond woman at the bar?

A man three stools down caught Joel's eye in the mirror and smiled at him. Big guy wearing a tropical-pattern shirt with a pair of wire-rimmed glasses protruding from the pocket. He looked hopeful. Joel broke off eye contact. It was working almost too well, he thought. Chris was passing the test with what might be a record score—if there were a record to shoot for.

Though Joel felt perfectly comfortable now in the female Chris' clothing, he decided he'd finish his drink and then leave. It was almost midnight, and he had to get the clothes and wig back to costume at the Grayson before returning to the apartment. Meredith might well be home before he was tonight.

He watched as Nora approached her table, and the two women spoke briefly. Then Nora walked away, accepting congratulations and signing a few autographs before leaving the Low Note.

She'd walked past Joel on her way to the door, not three feet away from him, so close he could smell her perfume, and she hadn't recognized him.

Meredith was looking at her watch now. She never had caught a server's attention, so she drained what was left of her wine, then stood up.

She was moving toward the bar. Toward Joel!

He sat tense with fear. He momentarily considered bowing his head and placing his hand over his face, but he knew that would only draw her attention.

Barely glancing at him, she went to the pay phone in the alcove near the door.

Joel felt his heartbeat quicken. This was why he'd come here, to view her life close up when she wasn't in his presence. To see how she moved, spoke, laughed, when he wasn't around. It was a sad compulsion, he knew, yet he was glad now that he'd come here as Chris.

After speaking for a few minutes on the phone, Meredith angrily hung up, then stomped to the door and pushed outside.

Joel slid down off his stool and followed.

"If you're gonna be here tomorrow night, so will I," a man seated nearby said. "Or should we go to your place right now?"

What a total jerk, Joel thought. How much success could the guy have with a line like that?

It was illuminating in a lot of ways, this being a woman.

***

As soon as he stepped outside into the cool night air, he saw Meredith half a block away, striding past a row of glowing windows that had a strobe-light effect on her and seemed to speed her movements. She was walking at a fast pace, her purse slung by its strap over her left shoulder and diagonally across her upper body, her arms swinging freely.

Where was she going?

She walked to Christopher Street, then toward the river. It was drizzling again, not hard, but enough to keep people off the streets, so keeping her in sight was no problem.

Listening to the tap of his high heels on the sidewalk, Joel slowed his pace and fell farther back. He had to stay well behind her or she might turn around and notice him; she might remember the attractive and faintly familiar blond woman from the Low Note.

She walked for a while parallel to the river, then she stopped near a low, stone wall that followed its bank. Joel could see buildings and several parked trucks about a block beyond where Meredith was standing motionless and staring out at the black water.

He sat on a bench near a tree and watched her from the darkness. It was still drizzling, almost a mist, but she didn't seem to notice. She was obviously there to meet someone.

Joel felt the old anger welling up in him, roaring through his veins. *She* could trust *him*. And he'd kept the faith and trusted her, but apparently he'd been wrong. He'd played the fool.

The hell with this! Joel thought. Why torture myself?

He stood up to leave, then realized his sudden motion had made him visible, drawn attention to him.

Meredith was looking directly at him.

Joel hesitated, shifting his weight from one leg to the other. The feet in the high heels wanted to carry him swiftly away from Meredith's curious gaze. And there was still time. He could make a hurried exit as Chris, and tonight wouldn't have happened.

But why should *he* feel guilty? Meredith was the one secretly meeting someone. The one who owed the explanation.

She continued to stand motionless, staring in his direction.

All right, Joel thought, his hands trembling with anger. Let's see what this is all about.

He began striding toward Meredith, walking fast. She continued watching him, her right hand unconsciously moving to rest on her purse. Fearing robbery? Assault by a strange woman?

She'd recognize him soon, he was sure, and he waited for

her reaction as he approached her in the dark.

When he was ten feet from her, she backed away a step, squinting at him. Then her lower jaw dropped. He could see her eyes widen with surprise and realization.

"Joel?" She extended both hands toward him with a strange awkwardness, as if trying to fend something off and reach for it at the same time "Joel! What is this?"

"We need to talk," he said.

"Do we ever! But not here. Not now."

"Come over here," he told her, and began walking toward the bench and tree.

"What is this?" she repeated in a stunned voice, following him. "What's going on?"

"Let's sit down on that bench and I'll explain. Then you'll explain."

But when they reached the bench, Meredith didn't sit down.

"What is this?" she asked for the third time. "I mean, why are you made up like that?"

"I'm the one with the more important questions."

"Listen, Joel, whatever's going on, this isn't smart, you being here. I—"

He was leaning with one hand on the tree, watching her, when she suddenly stopped talking and toppled over the bench.

His first confused thought was that she'd had a sudden heart attack or suffered some kind of stroke. She was lying very still on her back with one leg twisted oddly beneath her, precisely as she'd fallen.

"Meredith?" He moved toward her.

And instantly he was aware of a man approaching about a hundred feet away, holding what looked like a small rifle with a telescopic sight. He was close enough for Joel to see him clearly, a glimpse of short blond hair above a square-featured face with a dark slash of eyebrow.

The man's step faltered, and Joel realized he hadn't been seen in the shadows, leaning against the tree by the bench, until he'd moved toward Meredith.

Joel looked down at Meredith, at the hole perfectly centered between her eyes, and at how almost all of one side of her head was missing

"God!" he heard himself say softly. "God, God, God!"

Then there was a loud *Chunk!* that sounded like a hatchet striking the tree he'd been leaning against, and bits of wood and bark flew. A tiny piece of something–probably bark–struck his right cheek just below the eye, stinging for a moment.

Joel realized a bullet had ricocheted off the tree, exactly like in the movies.

People died in the movies!

He saw the man go down on one knee, taking aim again.

Joel started to run, stumbled for half a dozen steps, but somehow kept his balance. He removed his high heels and sprinted like mad toward Christopher Street. He thought he heard a bullet snap past his right ear, but he wasn't sure. The gun was obviously equipped with a silencer.

He ran harder, stretching out his stride, feeling his thighs ache, a sharp pain pressing like a weight against his ribs.

Finally he reached the street and buildings.

But not people. The light rain was still keeping everyone inside.

Everyone other than Meredith, Joel, and Meredith's killer.

Joel kept running hard down Christopher, feeling the cold wetness beneath his nyloned soles. At a cross street a cab skidded with a gravelly rushing sound on the soaked pavement, almost hitting him. Still clutching his shoes, Joel climbed in through its back door.

"Away!" he said to the cabby.

"Away where?"

"Just away, damn it!"

Joel realized he'd used his masculine voice, but the cabbie didn't seem to have noticed. He was accustomed to such fares in the Village.

"Whatever," he sighed, and hit the accelerator.

Joel fell back against the seat as the cab pulled away.

He probed at the pain in his ribs, making sure he merely had a stitch in his side and was winded and not shot. Then he craned his neck and stared behind him out the rain-streaked rear window.

He saw only shadows, angles, stillness.

The dark and empty street.

***

He lay curled on his side in bed, listening for police sirens.

And of course there were almost always sirens in New York, wailing, desperate loops of sound that screamed the urgency of life and death in a city that strained the limits.

Meredith dead! His mind couldn't contain the thought.

Joel had instructed the taxi driver to let him out a block away from the Grayson, then he'd returned the female clothing and gone home to the apartment in a daze. He'd found himself in bed without remembering how he got there, and he thought about Meredith being dead and he wept for almost an hour.

His jealousy and possessiveness dissipated in his pain as he recalled their shared moments, the brief tangential passage when their lives had touched and struck warmth and love. Ended now, already receding into the past to be altered and lost in memory. There was so much poor Meredith would miss, even as he missed her. A suffocating sorrow enveloped him and held him paralyzed and inert with its weight.

Then reason, and fear, infiltrated his grief. He wanted to phone the police, to tell them what had happened and describe the blond man. The Nazi, as Joel thought of him, with his machined handsomeness and sophisticated, silent weapon of death. Meredith's dispassionate murderer. Once he'd even reached for the phone, then withdrawn his hand as if he'd felt heat.

Think about this! he'd told himself. *Think about it before you use the phone and say something you have to live with forever!*

What would he tell the police? That dressed in women's clothing and wearing high heels and makeup he'd spied on Meredith, then followed her and seen her killed? No one would be able to corroborate that. No one at the Low Note would be able to identify with certainty the blond woman who'd been there only briefly. Joel read mysteries. He watched TV and went to movies. It was no secret who'd be the prime suspect, at least initially. It was usually the spouse, the police said. Joel and Meredith weren't married, but he was the next best thing to the classic spouse suspect. And since the police wouldn't believe his wild story of cross-dressing and following Meredith as his character in the play, he had no alibi. If he couldn't prove he'd been Chris, then where had Joel been at the time of Meredith's murder?

The Chris story simply wouldn't fly. Even he was beginning to think of last night as Chris as a horrible dream, one that, in the light of reason, was already melting away like soft wax. Only the fact of Meredith's murder remained like rock.

Terrible, undeniable reality.

Her death would not go away.

Joel knew then how it had to be. He'd tell them he'd returned from the read-through at the Grayson and spent the rest of the night alone in the apartment. Even if he couldn't prove he had, they couldn't prove he hadn't. That would be his invented reality, and he would cling to it so hard that he'd be convincing. Forging make-believe into plausibility was his profession, his calling; he could do it.

Another chilling thought removed all doubt about what should be his story.

There was always the possibility—no, the probability—that if the police discovered he'd left the Grayson as Chris, they'd assume it had been his cover so he could kill Meredith without fearing later identification by witnesses. As for motive, his history of sometimes violent jealousy was well known. He could imagine ex-wife Gail testifying to that in court, along with friends of Meredith who'd witnessed his often irrational jealous furies over the past year.

Sirens sounded louder, nearer. He drew his knees up tight to his chest and for a horrible instant actually thought he was going to faint from the waves of terror and nausea that swept over him. Then the sirens, directly outside in the street below, or certainly no farther away than the next block, drifted away and faded to silence.

Joel made himself straighten his legs and lie flat on his back so he was staring straight up at the shadowed ceiling. At that moment he wasn't sure of anything. Not even how to feel about Meredith. He loved her, he missed her, and she was gone, and in an illogical but persistent way he felt guilty as well as great sorrow, as if her death had been his fault.

But there was nothing he could have changed. He knew that. He might as well not have been near her when she died. The gunman hadn't even known he was there when the bullet had—

Trying to block out the image of Meredith's ruined head, the improbable spreading layer of blood emanating from it, he swallowed the bitter taste at the base of his tongue and stared hard at a rectangle of black shadow on the ceiling. He wished he could merge with the shadow, disappear into it forever.

He sucked in a deep breath as if trying to drown quickly and mercifully in deep water, then let it out slowly.

He felt somewhat better, steadier. Meredith had spoken of a mother in New Jersey. Maybe she'd be the one the police would contact, would ask to identify Meredith's body when it was found.

My God, when would it be found? Was Meredith still lying on the hard, wet concrete, her blood congealing, her head—

Joel rolled onto his side again. Then he pushed himself up and sat slumped on the edge of the mattress.

The rain had stopped and he could hear voices in the street below. A TV was playing faintly somewhere in the building despite the hour, an infomercial about non-stick cookware that was also self-cleaning. Everything seemed so normal. Meredith might walk in at any moment, moving slowly and quietly so she wouldn't wake him.

More than once, he'd pretended to be asleep when she'd come in, watching her place her purse on the chair near the door, then remove her shoes and noiselessly move in stockinged feet to the bathroom, where she'd silently undress. Minutes later she'd tiptoe across the floor and ease her body into bed alongside Joel's, while he lay with his eyes closed, wondering where she'd been earlier that night, how she'd used the freedom they accorded one another. He would listen to her breathing, even try to smell the scent of recent sex on her. How ashamed he was of that now, of the jealousy that was his addiction.

Meredith wouldn't slide quietly into bed beside him tonight. Or ever again. And now Joel had to choose between a desperate lie or an almost certain murder charge. Already it was too late to call the police. That should have been done immediately after his escape from the killer. He should have taken the cab directly to the nearest precinct house, or had the cabby use his radio to bring the police.

Too late now. Too late for Meredith and for Joel.

He cried for a long time, then he pressed his face into a pillow wet and warm from tears he knew had changed nothing. How futile to weep in the face of death. How futile it all was.

Trapped by his actions of the night before, he lay awake until morning, frightened, resigned, cursed, and listening.

Waiting for the police.

***

Meredith's mother phoned Joel at nine o'clock the next morning and tearfully told him Meredith was dead. She'd been notified two hours earlier and had been driven to the morgue to identify the body.

There was at that moment a loud knock on the door. Joel, feigning shock at the news of Meredith's death, told her mother he thought the police were at the door and hung up.

He opened the door and was face to face with a large, shambling NYPD detective who said his name was Frank Hennigan as he casually showed identification. He was disheveled and had a dead, curved-stem pipe clamped in his jaw. His manner was amiable, his patter disarming, but after a few minutes of questions and answers, Joel knew that his mind-set was obsessive.

By the time Hennigan left, Joel was sure that he was the prime suspect in the case. Hennigan obviously wanted to arrest him, but couldn't. Yet. Joel's story about rehearsal, then studying his lines alone in his apartment, was apparently good enough—but only for so long.

If the police scared Joel, something happened that afternoon that scared him even more. The man with the short blond hair, dark eyebrows and square features passed Joel on the street outside the apartment. He was wearing black slacks and a black shirt with a black leather vest. His manner of dress and stern demeanor, his cold blue eyes and oddly military bearing, made Joel think again that he'd be perfectly cast as a Nazi zealot.

That night Joel was shocked to see him sitting at a table in Bailey's, waiting to be served. He merely stared at Joel as his order was taken. More staring as Joel placed his food before him. He left no tip.

Joel knew what the Nazi was doing. He'd found out Joel and Meredith had been lovers and was watching him, hoping he'd lead him to the female acquaintance of Meredith who'd witnessed her murder. To Chris. And when he found Chris, he planned to kill her so she couldn't identify him. He *had* to kill her. And if he happened to follow Joel to the Grayson, if he happened to witness a dress rehearsal ... Joel shuddered and veered his mind away from the thought.

It was when Nora was driving him back from Meredith's funeral in New Jersey that Joel knew what he had to do. Only two blocks from the cemetery, they passed the Nazi seated in a parked car. The killer was determined, Joel knew, and *Chris Cross* was soon going to be advertised. Show posters were going to be mounted outside the Grayson. Handbills would be given out in Times Square. Joel would surely be found out. He was Chris; Chris was the witness to murder. The Nazi thought his time was limited; Joel knew it was his own.

He had to take a chance. Another.

Back in Manhattan, he asked Nora to pull her car to the curb a block from his apartment, and he told her everything, then pleaded for her help. After her initial astonishment, she seemed to believe him and sympathize with him.

Then, as soon as she'd dropped him off, she phoned Detective Hennigan.

***

Unseen, Joel left the Grayson early the next evening with his Chris clothing and makeup, then changed in his apartment. Scheduled to work that night at Bailey's, he'd called in sick.

He didn't dare go into Bailey's as Chris, but he browsed through the shops across the street until they closed. Then he sat at an outdoor table at the coffee shop two doors down from Bailey's.

Though he'd been around Bailey's every night since Meredith's death, this night the Nazi didn't show.

Despondent, Joel finally gave up. He smoothed his pantyhose, stood up from the table, and walked toward his apartment. He planned on changing clothes and identities before going to the Grayson to replace Chris' clothing while the dressing room was empty during tonight's performance of *Leave Her to Purgatory*. The odds against him seemed insurmountable now. If the Nazi didn't discover his female persona and kill him, Hennigan would finally arrest him and he might as well be dead.

It wasn't until he was out of breath after climbing the first two flights of stairs to his apartment, and had removed his burdensome high-heeled shoes, that he knew something was wrong. There was the slightest of sounds from the shadows on the landing, where the stairwell turned. He stood there barefoot, terrified, feeling vulnerable, feeling female, feeling doomed. He got an inkling then of what it must be like to be a woman alone and marked and stalked.

"Bitch!" a hoarse voice whispered. And suddenly the Nazi, snarling like an enraged animal, had him around the waist.

Joel surprised him with his strength and flung him against the wall. The Nazi staggered and half fell down three or four steps, then was coming at Joel again. This time Joel saw the knife in his hand.

The Nazi slashed out at Joel, and Joel, standing dazed in a deadly dream, suddenly remembered the shoes in his hands. He struck at the Nazi over and over with the stiletto heels.

His face battered and bloody, the Nazi kept advancing and plunging the knife into Joel's chest. Sensing the kill, he clutched Joel's hair with his free hand, trying to make him a steadier target for the knife.

Then he stumbled backward, holding Joel's blond wig and staring at him in disbelief.

That was when there was a loud clatter on the stairs. Shouts. Screams.

Nora was there. With Hennigan and several uniformed officers.

It took them less than a minute to disarm and handcuff the Nazi.

Joel slumped on the steps, as Nora held him close and tight and Hennigan assured him an ambulance was on the way.

Ambulance?

As if in response to his thought, a siren began its distant, urgent wail.

Joel suddenly remembered he'd been stabbed, but the blood on his blouse seemed to be from the Nazi's injuries and not his own. He explored fearfully with his fingers and discovered that his foam-rubber breasts had absorbed the brunt of the knife attack. He'd suffered only shallow stab wounds that required six stitches at the hospital emergency room.

The next morning, Hennigan told Joel and Nora about Meredith's former romantic involvement with the Nazi, who turned out to be a major European cocaine dealer. Meredith had known too much, and the people the Nazi did business with had demanded she be killed, and that he do the deed to prove and guarantee his loyalty.

"The things people do for money," Nora said.

"And for love," Joel said.

"For survival," Hennigan added.

***

The publicity from the Nazi's arrest resulted in *Chris Cross* playing to sold-out performances. Nora was able to obtain several lucrative bookings by working what had happened into a black comedy routine.

At the end of the play's run, Nora moved into the loft apartment with Joel. He realized she was a performer and attractive to men, and he promised never to be jealous.

She refused to make the same promise.

Edward D. Hoch

EDWARD D. HOCH, past president of the Mystery Writers of America and winner of its 1967 Edgar Award for best short story, was born in 1930 in Rochester, New York. Following two years in the army and a year at Pocket Books in New York City, he returned to Rochester and published his first short story in 1955. Since then he has published nearly 750 stories and forty books, including novels, collections and anthologies, and his stories have been published in more than twenty countries and several of them have been adapted for television.

Hoch worked in public relations for fourteen years, but has been a full-time writer since 1968. His stories have appeared in every issue of *Ellery Queen's Mystery Magazine* since 1973, and for the past twenty years he has edited *The Year's Best Mystery and Suspense Stories*. He married Patricia A. McMahon in 1957; they reside in Rochester, where he is a trustee of the Rochester Public Library.

THE NARROW HOUSE
by
Ed Hoch

It was Andrew who taught Emily Rhodes the fundamentals of growing marijuana, but it was from the gang at the Shades of Purple Lounge that she first learned the advantages of growing it indoors. The narrow three-story brownstone that she leased in Greenwich Village provided a back yard only a bit larger than a postage stamp, and the one time she'd tried growing a few plants among the wild ferns there, they'd been dug up and stolen before she could harvest the leaves.

Andrew was gone by then, off to San Francisco with a gay lover who'd stolen him from innocent and trusting Emily. The gang at the Shades of Purple sympathized. "Make sure the next one is straight, honey," the bartender told her, pouring a drink on the house. When she came in a few weeks later to grumble about the stolen pot plants, he didn't pour her a free drink. Instead he sent her over to Lou and Toni Nelson.

The Nelsons were a Village couple who turned up at the Shades of Purple once or twice a week. Emily didn't know them well, but they seemed friendly enough. Lou was a bearded man in his late thirties who'd crashed in New York after a decade of dullness as a suburban breadwinner. Emily knew he was into drugs because once at a Village party he'd brought enough pot for everyone. Toni, who was probably his wife, had the drawn look of an addict. Emily liked her and felt vaguely sorry for her, though Toni never complained.

She told Lou about her latest misfortune with the stolen plants but she found him surprisingly unsympathetic. "You're still living back in the sixties, kid," he told her. "First of all, no one grows pot for the leaves any more. You smoke sinsemilla, the bud of the female plant. Whoever stole your plants just didn't know any better."

Emily reminded him of the party a few months back when he'd brought a plastic bag full of marijuana leaves. "What about that?"

"I like you, kid. You've got a good memory. I was going to

throw them out when Toni said I should bring them along. She figured the crowd at that party wouldn't know the difference and she was right."

Toni nodded, exhaling a bluish cloud of tobacco smoke. She was rarely without a cigarette or a joint. "You got your own house, Emily. You should be growing indoors. Then you don't have to stay up half the night with a shotgun stuck out your back window."

"I wouldn't know the first thing about that." She laughed at the idea, shaking her head. "I'm not in the business. I was just growing a little for my own use."

"If you grow it, you're in the business," Lou Nelson assured her. "If you want, Toni and I could drop over and look at your place, see how much room you got."

"Do you grow indoors?" Emily asked.

"Sometimes," he answered vaguely.

So it came about that the Nelsons called on Emily at home two nights later. Her living and dining rooms were on the main floor, along with the kitchen. The bedrooms and bath occupied the second level with the top story being unused. "Storage!" Lou Nelson exclaimed upon seeing it. "You use this lovely third floor merely for storage?"

"It's a bit large for a single room and I'd have to get the owner's permission to make any substantial changes." She sighed, staring at the walls. "It's such a narrow house."

"Poe called a coffin a narrow house," Toni Nelson interjected. "And I suppose it is."

"You could grow a thousand plants up here," Lou decided while pacing off the room, "and no one would ever be the wiser."

"Wouldn't I need special equipment, lights, all sorts of things?"

He smiled benignly. "We could advise you on what you'd need. We could even supply some of the manpower—or womanpower—if you wish."

"I think a thousand plants would be a bit much. Wouldn't I be breaking the law?"

Toni coughed lightly and took out another cigarette. "A hundred plants means a mandatory five-to-forty. Years, that is. No parole."

Emily felt a shiver run through her. "My God, you can kill somebody and get less time than that."

"They have to catch you first," Lou Nelson assured her. "With me and Toni helping you, that's not a worry."

"What sort of equipment would I need to do it fast?"

"With six hundred-watt sodium lights you can harvest buds in sixty days. That fast enough for you?"

"Just right," she decided. Two months and she could turn a good profit and be out of business before the law caught on. "Where do I get the seeds?"

"I have a little stash. How many would you want?"

"Less than a hundred. Why tempt fate?"

"Any special variety?"

"I don't know. The ones that were stolen were a Northern Lights hybrid."

Lou nodded. "That's good pot."

But Toni interrupted. "Hell, Lou, you get a hundred of those in a room and they smell like sulphur. Sell her some Bubble Gum seeds."

He was quick to agree. "The Bubble Gum hybrid is best for indoors. It's got a nice sweet smell like candy or chewing gum. You still better keep the door closed, but at least the odor isn't offensive."

So it was decided. Lou and Toni would come over the following week with the necessary supplies, and because Toni was hopeless with her fingers he'd bring along Carol Knox to help with the installation. Emily had met Carol at a couple of Village parties. She was tall and slender like Emily, not particularly pretty, but with shoulder-length red hair that attracted attention. Like the Nelsons, she was into marijuana-growing in a big way.

Emily was employed by a temporary agency that sent her out to various office jobs in lower Manhattan. She barely earned rent money working as a temp, but she had a few hundred dollars saved up. It was enough to pay Lou for the plastic tubing, ceramic heater, carbon dioxide tank, four sodium lamps with timer, and other equipment she'd need.

"How many seeds?" she asked him when he handed her the packet.

"Ninety-five. You said to keep it under a hundred."

"Fine. How much space will they need?"

"These hybrids don't need much space; they get very tall before they start producing buds. We could grow them all on a large tabletop."

"What about that folding table in the dining room?" Carol suggested. She had an odd throaty voice that commanded attention.

"Good idea," Emily agreed. "I won't be throwing any dinner parties while that stuff's growing up here."

The table was six feet long when unfolded, and three feet wide. The seeds, each in its own peat pot, easily fit on top. "You'll have a sea of green in sixty days," Lou promised. Then, while Emily and Toni watched, he and Carol Knox went to work running the tubing that would supply water to the plants.

The heater was for the roots and the sodium lamps provided the closest thing to sunlight twelve hours a day.

"Remember," Carol instructed Emily, "drapes closed, door closed at all times. You can check on them if you want, but don't leave the door open. This tank will supply carbon dioxide to sweeten the air, and they'll have heat, light and water. So long as the system's working you don't have to lift a finger until it's time to harvest the buds. Then I hope you'll remember your friends."

"You'll all get some," she promised. "But I'll be selling the rest. I need the money now that Andrew's gone."

The weeks after that passed uneventfully. Emily saw the Nelsons occasionally at the Shades of Purple, and once she saw Carol Knox there too. "How's it coming?" Carol asked.

Emily gave her a thumbs-up sign. "Perfect. Only a few more weeks."

When the time came they helped her with the harvest. There were multiple buds on most of the plants and when she smoked them she achieved a glowing high. Lou sold the rest at two hundred and eighty dollars an ounce.

It was time to dismantle the equipment and return the table to the dining room, but Emily decided it had been so easy she'd try it again.

***

When the second planting was halfway through its two-month cycle, Emily dropped in at the Shades of Purple Lounge for their monthly drag queen night. She was watching the entertainment with half an eye when Carol Knox came in and headed straight for her. "Bad news, Emily. Your old beau Andrew's back in town. He was here earlier and told the Nelsons he was heading over to your place."

"Damn!" Emily was on her feet. "Thanks for the warning, Carol."

"He doesn't have a key, does he?"

"I hope not." She went out the door fast.

She'd been too casual about keys while Andrew was living there, she realized now. Once she'd let him borrow hers to have a duplicate made, and he'd returned it when he moved out. But there was nothing to have stopped him from making a second duplicate. The room on her third floor wasn't even locked. If he got in and happened to wander up there ...

She ran the last two blocks to the narrow house. There was no sign of entry and the place seemed empty as she turned her key in the lock. Then she heard it—the sound of her stereo playing up in the bedroom. Andrew was back.

Her heart was thudding as she climbed the stairs to face him. "Hello, Andrew. What are you doing back here?"

Seeing him now, his lanky body spread across her sofa while he flipped through her pile of CDs, she wondered how she could ever have loved him. "Don't you buy the new stuff any more?" he asked, tossing the CDs aside.

She held out her hand. "I want my other key. Then I want you to get out."

"Hey, just a minute! I thought we had something going."

"What happened to your friend?"

"I'm sorry about that, Emily. I must have been drunk or crazy to go off with him."

"Give me the key, Andrew."

"Can't we—"

"No, we can't."

He stood up and reached into the pocket of his jeans. For an instant she feared he was going for a weapon, but when his hand came out it was only holding the key. "Sorry about that. I thought you'd be pleased to see me."

"I'm not. Goodbye, Andrew."

He went down the stairs and out of her life once more. For the final time, she hoped.

***

Emily usually checked the third floor in the morning, and it wasn't until after breakfast that she went up and found the door to the plant room slightly ajar. She was certain she'd closed it tightly the previous morning. Didn't she always close it?

Andrew.

Had he been up there snooping around?

The room seemed undisturbed and nothing had been taken. The sodium lights still bathed the plants in a healthy sunny glow, and a small electric fan circulated the air. Water and fertilizer were delivered automatically by the plastic tubes. The tank of carbon dioxide helped freshen the air. Everything was as it should be.

Except that the door hadn't quite been closed.

Was Andrew planning to return in a month when the pot was ready for harvesting? She had two pounds of buds last time. At $280 an ounce that meant nearly nine thousand dollars.

He'd surrendered the key, but maybe he had another one. Maybe he had a whole box full of keys.

She decided it was time to get the lock changed. She phoned the landlord and told him she would pay for it herself. He offered no objection, but insisted a duplicate key must be sent to his office. Later, at the Shades of Purple, she told Carol and the Nelsons about it. They agreed she'd done the right thing.

"He might have found a new companion," Carol speculated. "I haven't seen him around the last few nights."

Emily went to jobs for the temp agency most mornings, and finally landed a month-long position at a travel agency. It was easy work, mainly simple computer things, and she liked the people. It did involve a certain amount of overtime with the vacation season approaching, and most weeknights she'd head straight home instead of stopping at the Shades of Purple. She hadn't seen the Nelsons in several days when Toni phoned her one evening just as she walked in the door. "There's a bit of a problem, Emily. I don't want to discuss it on the phone. Could I come over?"

"Come ahead. If you haven't eaten yet you can join me in some macaroni and cheese."

Toni Nelson arrived within thirty minutes, looking serious. She sat down in the living room and said, "We've got problems. Lou's been arrested."

"What for?"

"Dealing. He went down to Wall Street this morning with a plastic bag of freshly harvested buds. He'd never had any trouble before, but this time his customer turned out to be an undercover cop. Would you come with me to see him?"

"Of course. Let me get my coat."

Lou was being held at Centre Street overnight, awaiting arraignment the following morning. Toni was allowed to see him while Emily waited outside in a cramped visitors' area. She'd been there about five minutes when a large black man wearing a photo ID pinned to his shirt came over to talk with her.

"I'm Sergeant Wendt," he said, settling down on the bench next to her. "You came to see Louis Nelson?"

She nodded. "But they'd only let his wife in. I'm just a friend."

"This is my case. I'm anxious to wrap it up."

"Then let Lou go. He didn't do anything."

Sergeant Wendt smiled at her, revealing a gold tooth. "He says he grew the pot himself and I tend to believe him, but that doesn't change the charge that he was selling it. Possession of a small amount of marijuana has been decriminalized in New York State, but it's still a crime to sell it. And growing it can be a federal offense. Would you be knowin' anyone in your neighborhood growing pot?"

"Nope."

"Wouldn't be likely to tell me if you did know." His smile had faded. "What about Nelson and his wife?"

"I've never been to their place. I see them at the neighborhood bars."

"Let me give you some advice, Miss. Stay clear of Nelson and his wife. This investigation is just starting, and folks that get caught up in it are goin' to be facing big troubles."

"Thank you for the advice, Sergeant," she said primly.

***

Toni didn't speak until they were back in the car. Then, as she took a firm grip on the steering wheel she said grimly, "He thinks they're going to throw the book at him. He couldn't say much with them listening, but he wants me to post bail for him as soon as it's set. He doesn't think it'll be too high. It's not as if he was selling cocaine or heroin."

"Do you have the money?"

"I have it. But I'll need your help on something else tonight, Emily."

"Sure. Any way I can help—"

"I have to get rid of all the indoor gardening equipment tonight. That detective, Wendt, could have a search warrant by tomorrow morning." She thought some more and added, "I'm sorry now that I took you along, Emily. Maybe you need to get rid of your garden, too."

"I'm only ten days from harvest, Toni. I need the money. I can't quit now. You and Lou just brought in your crop. It's different with you."

Toni shrugged. "You're taking a chance. The heat's going to be on."

"They need probable cause to get a search warrant, don't they? They've got no reason to suspect me of anything."

Toni parked in her usual spot a block from the place they were renting. Emily had been mostly truthful when she told the detective she'd never been there. She'd never seen the basement room where the pot was grown, and seeing it now for the first time was almost more than she could grasp. There were twice, no, *three* times as many plants as she had—certainly way over the safe limit of one hundred—and most of them were just starting to bud. Tubes carried water and fertilizer back and forth across the basement floor.

"Everything goes," she said. "This basement has to be bare in an hour's time."

"But there's a small fortune here!" Emily objected.

"There's also life sentences for Lou and me if it's found like this. Are you helping me or not?"

"Of course I'm helping."

There was a Dumpster next door behind some stores, and they filled it with everything that would burn, including the plants. Then Toni threw in a lighted match and they watched the fire from a block away. Carol came by to watch with them, holding her nose at one point. "That's high-grade stuff for a bonfire."

"Lou's locked up," Toni explained. "They'll be here with a

search warrant."

"God, Toni! What are you going to do?"

"If he gets bail we'll probably skip."

A fire engine came roaring out of the night, finally dousing the blaze with a high-pressure hose. The three of them moved on quickly.

**

Lou made bail the following morning, and they celebrated at the Shades of Purple that night. As the word got around, all of their friends showed up. No one put it into words, but everyone seemed to know it was really a farewell party. By the weekend, when Emily dropped in the place again, Carol Knox told her they were gone.

"Doesn't that make him a fugitive?" she asked.

"I think they were heading west. There's lots of space out that way. Maybe they'll find a wheat field big enough for ten thousand plants. Hell, it's the biggest cash crop in America, now."

Emily went home that night and climbed the stairs to the third floor. The buds were almost ready. Just a few more days and they'd be money in the bank. Then she could dismantle the system and lay low for a while. Lou wasn't around to sell the stuff for her, but she wasn't worried—there were plenty of buyers at the Shades of Purple on any given night.

It was just at harvest time that the travel agency got especially busy. She was supposed to have dinner with Carol, but had to call up and cancel. As it turned out, she finished the computer work sooner than expected, and, by eight-thirty, was headed home.

As she fit the key into the shiny new lock on her brownstone's door, she noticed scratches she was certain hadn't been there before. She entered cautiously, hardly breathing, and stood in the downstairs hall. After a few moments she heard a sound from far above. Someone was in the plant room.

She tiptoed to the kitchen and took a hammer from one of the drawers. Andrew had come back, just as she'd feared, and picked the lock when his old key wouldn't open it.

Emily moved cautiously up the stairs, the sounds growing just a bit louder as she reached the second floor in the dark. The door to the plant room, at the top of the next flight, was slightly ajar as she'd found it that other time after Andrew's visit. She could see the beam of a tiny flashlight moving back and forth among the plants.

This last flight was the most dangerous because of the squeaky steps. She avoided the worst of them, keeping her eyes on Andrew's flashlight. Then she heard the snip of clippers and the rustle of a plastic bag. He was cutting them off, cutting the buds.

In a fury she burst into the room as the flashlight went off. "Damn you, Andrew! I'll kill you for this!"

His strong hands grabbed at her wrist, went for her throat. They tussled for a moment in the dark and then she swung the hammer in a high, deadly arc. There was a crunch of bone as it connected and her assailant went down without a sound, scattering some plants as he fell.

She snapped on the sodium lamps and gasped.

The figure on the floor of her plant room, in a widening circle of blood, wasn't Andrew. It was Carol.

She'd killed Carol Knox.

***

Emily slumped to the floor, half-fainting, and sat for a long time staring at the body. She was finally forced to move by the thin trail of blood inching across the floor toward her. She stood up then and realized for the first time that she was no longer holding the hammer. It lay there among the plants, blood red at its tip. She went out in the hall and turned on the lights.

Trying to collect her thoughts, trying to realize what she had done, Emily looked back into the plant room and reached down to pick up the plastic bag full of clipped-off buds. Carol had indeed been stealing them, and chances were it had been she who'd sneaked up once before and left the door ajar. Andrew had nothing to do with it. Carol, her good friend Carol, had been trying to rip her off. She still felt bad about what had happened, but maybe Carol had deserved it.

Now the problem was what to do about it. All she'd done was kill a burglar, really, although the papers would immediately brand it a drug-related killing and that never sounded good. Perhaps she—

Her thoughts were interrupted by the ringing of her doorbell. God, who could that be? Lou and Toni were gone. Could it possibly be Andrew, after all?

At first she didn't answer it, but the ringing continued. It was only nine o'clock and whoever it was could see that the upstairs lights were on. Finally, she crept down and tried to see out through the curtains. There was a large shape silhouetted against the glare from the streetlight. She turned on the hall light, checked quickly to be certain there were no spots of blood on her, and opened the door.

It was the black detective, Sergeant Wendt.

"Oh! Hello."

"Sorry to bother you this late, Miss Rhodes, but I need to ask you a few questions about the Nelsons. May I come in?"

"Of course." She led him into the living room, turning on

lights as she went. "How can I help you?"

"Lou Nelson has dropped out of sight. He missed a sched-uled court appearance today and that probably means he's skipped bail. It would go a lot easier on him if he came back and surrendered."

"I have no idea where he is," she answered truthfully.

"When's the last time you saw him?" he asked, his eyes shifting from her face to study the room.

"Last week. I think it was the night he got out on bail. They had a little party at the Shades of Purple Lounge."

"Nothing was said about Lou and his wife leaving town?"

"Nothing. I was a friend. I'm sure they would have told me. Maybe he just forgot about the court date."

"The place they were renting is empty of all their personal stuff. They're not coming back."

She shrugged. "I couldn't tell you."

"I understand there was a fire in a Dumpster near their place the night he was arrested."

Fire!

Suddenly, all in a flash, she saw the way out. "I heard the fire engine and went down to see what was going on."

"Any idea who started it? Was Toni Nelson involved?"

"I doubt it. More likely it would be a girl named Carol Knox. She hangs around the Shades of Purple and she's been acting strange lately, especially about fires. She was here one night and set a couple of paper napkins ablaze, just to see them burn."

He made a note of that. "Carol Knox, you say?"

Emily nodded. "Tall, slender, long red hair. You can't miss her."

"Where does she live?"

"They could tell you at the bar. I try to stay away from her when I can. She's been acting spooky lately."

"A friend of the Nelsons?"

"She knew them. We all did."

That seemed to satisfy him and he closed his notebook. "Thanks for your help, Miss Rhodes. I'll call you if I need anything else."

As she closed the front door behind him, Emily felt her body relax for the first time since he'd entered.

***

She worked quickly after that. There was no way she could get Carol's body out of the house by herself, and she had no friends to ask for help. Now that Lou and Toni had left town she was alone. She could hardly walk into the Shades of Purple and tell them she'd just killed Carol Knox.

No, Carol would have to stay there along with the plants, and that meant Emily's only chance was to destroy everything. The detective's mention of the fire had given her the idea. The narrow house was going to burn tonight, and Carol's body along with it. She'd already noticed that they were about the same size, and now that she forced herself to carefully study the body of her victim she saw that even the bone structures of their faces were similar. The main difference in their appearance was the hair. Emily's was short and black, but Carol's long red hair would be destroyed by the fire. Her fingerprints would be gone too, if they were ever on file.

What else? Dental records, of course! The police were always checking dental records for identification. Emily had gotten this far in her young life without any cavities, although her wisdom teeth had been removed. She forced herself to pry open Carol's mouth and discovered that she was in luck. No wisdom teeth there either, and only one cavity that she could see, along the upper left side. In a bad fire, with falling debris, that could easily be knocked out and lost. She picked up the hammer and aimed one more blow.

When it was over she was breathing hard. Somehow she realized for the first time that she'd become a criminal. The blow that killed Carol had been something of an accident. This blow, knocking out the tooth, had been deliberate.

She had a quart bottle of kerosene for an old lamp in the living room that she'd never lit. Now she sprinkled the kerosene around, especially onto Carol's face and hands. She put crumpled newspapers in the plant room to feed the fire once it got started. It didn't really matter if some of the pot-growing equipment survived the blaze. The body would be identified as Emily's and the police would be searching for the missing Carol Knox.

Next, she rigged up a crude fuse made from a length of clothesline dipped in the remains of the kerosene. She gathered up a few clothes and some money, and even took twenty-four dollars in loose bills she found in Carol's pocket. There was no identification. Emily lit the fuse on her way out.

She watched from down the block until she saw the bright glow in the third-floor windows. Then she hurried away. She was disappearing into a subway entrance when she heard the first distant siren.

***

Emily dyed her hair blond and took an apartment on the upper west side of Manhattan, many miles from her previous home. The newspaper accounts of the fire mentioned suspected marijuana-growing and stated that the dead woman had been tentatively identified as Emily Rhodes. Police were investigating.

She'd determined that New York was a big enough city to hide in, especially if everyone thought she was dead. Staying clear of the Village was no problem and the upper west side had always appealed to her, anyway. What she needed was a new identity and a job. Lou Nelson had shown her once how to doctor social security cards. "Don't change the first three numbers," he said, "because those are the code for the state that issued the card. But do change the first letters of your last name. Computers do everything by the alphabet. If Rhodes becomes Jodes they'll never find you."

Emily knew the number would be quickly revealed as a fake if anyone checked it, but she also knew the employment agency wouldn't bother to check unless they had a reason. She chose a small agency near her new apartment, and they sent her out the first day. Her resume said she was from Ohio and listed a couple of stores she knew were out of business.

She worked in the office of a catering service for a few days and felt like she'd been there for months. The apartment was a good one for the price, with a partial view of the Hudson River. There was a tiny spare room and she even found herself pacing off the square footage and thinking of a new plant room.

But no, not yet.

Oddly, on the weekend she thought of her mother back in Ohio. How had she taken the news of Emily's death? It was better not to speculate about that.

On the following Monday morning she was back at work at the catering service. Shortly before eleven the manager summoned her to his office. She walked in and faced two big men standing there. One of them was Sergeant Wendt. He sighed and said, "That's her." Then, in a formal voice, he added, "Miss Emily Rhodes, I am placing you under arrest. You have the right to a lawyer. Anything you say may be used against you—"

"What's the charge?" she asked.

"You are suspected of murdering Carol Knox and setting fire to your residence in Greenwich Village. There may be additional charges involving drugs."

They had to handcuff her when they took her out. That was the rule. "How did you find me so soon?" she asked in the car.

Wendt was silent at first. Then he said, "I figured if you were still in New York you'd try for more temporary employment. We've been checking agencies for the last several days."

"I was supposed to be dead. How did you know Carol's body wasn't mine?"

"That was the easy part," he said. "Carol Knox was a man."

Loren D. Estleman

LOREN D. ESTLEMAN was born in Ann Arbor, Michigan, in 1952, and graduated from Eastern Michigan University in 1974 with a BA in English Literature and Journalism. Since the appearance of his first novel in 1976, he has published thirty-seven books, including the Amos Walker detective series, for which he is best known, and the Detroit historical crime series: *Whiskey River, Motown, King of the Corner,* and the latest, *Edsel.* Another, *Stress,* was published by Warner Books in March 1996. A winner of seven national writing awards, Estleman has also been nominated for the National Book Award and the Pulitzer. Estleman lives in Michigan with his wife, Deborah, who writes under the name Deborah Morgan.

PICKUPS AND SHOTGUNS
by
Loren D. Estleman

Fifty minutes after I arrived for my appointment five minutes early, Lawrence Otell's secretary, a tawny-haired angel whose placard read **Ms. ROLAND,** hung up her telephone and told me I could go in. I left off studying an actuarial chart on the wall that informed me I'd been dead for two years, passed through the door marked PRIVATE, and shook the hand of the big, square, middle-aged type seated behind a desk shaped like a lima bean. He managed my name and indicated the chair on the customer's side, helping himself to a lump of hard candy from the jar on the desk without offering me one or apologizing for making me wait. I didn't give it much thought. I'd been working off and on for Midwest Confidential Life, Automobile, & Casualty for fifteen years and had yet to receive so much as a Christmas card from its headquarters in downtown Detroit.

"I see you've handled a number of assignments for us, Mr. Walker." Otell peered through a pair of black-rimmed readers at a file with my name lettered on the tab.

"You gave me the last six personally."

That upset him quite a bit. He glanced at me over the tops of his glasses, then closed the folder. "Have you ever investigated arson?"

"I went along on a couple of torch jobs. Is that the beef?"

"My usual man is out sick this week. He seems to be taken ill every year during the first week of deer hunting season. You don't hunt?"

"I used to, with my father. It isn't so much fun now that I do it for a living."

"I don't go in for blood sports myself. This case shouldn't be too complicated. The only reason I'm suspicious at all is the policyholder refused permission to the local fire department to investigate the premises. By law the investigators are required to ask permission. Otherwise they must seek a warrant. They're in the process of doing that now, but the circuit judge is away on a hunting trip and can't be reached."

"Can't they get another judge?"

"It's a small town, and it's Friday afternoon. They might not be able to locate another before Monday, by which time the integrity of the scene may be violated. Of course, this could be simply a case of a disgruntled homeowner sticking his finger in the spokes just to cause trouble. Do you know the term 'pickups and shotguns'?"

I shook my head, which pleased him. Otell was a frustrated pedant.

"It's a phrase advertisers use when they divide the population into consumer groups. Huron's a small town in a farm community yielding slowly to suburban development. Pickups and shotguns outsell sports cars and cuff links five to one."

"I was there once. You're overestimating sports cars and cuff links."

He slid another folder out from under the one with my name on it and held it out. "This contains all the information you'll need to start. The commander of the sheriff's substation is Sergeant Early. You'll want to let him know what you're up to."

I didn't ask him why. It was hunting season, and there were bound to be a lot more shotguns circulating around the neighborhood than pickups.

***

Huron had changed since my last visit. The local newspaper office was closed, probably having been wolfed down by a larger competitor and relocated. The restaurant was boarded up, real estate offices had taken over several of the retail stores in the business district, and the town had sprouted a tail along the main highway made up of chain department stores, fast-food franchises, and an antiques mall with all the old-world charm of a sperm bank. The twenty-first century was bearing down on Huron like an iron heel in an Air Jordan.

Sergeant Early was a solid-looking number with a military brush mustache in a cocoa-brown uniform with a sheriff's star embroidered on each sleeve. He looked at my credentials, then got up from behind his desk and rescued his cap off a peg. "Supreme Court ought to have its head examined. Why a private cop can go into a place where sworn authority is barred is the first question the shrink should ask."

"It's a waiver the policyholder signs when he applies for insurance," I said.

"He must've been drunk when he signed it. Mike Hopper won't even sign a traffic citation. But he's no insurance fraud."

Early accompanied me in my car to a plot just outside the village limits containing a small barn, a couple of other outbuildings, and a pile of charred timbers that had once been a house. He leaned against a fender while I pulled an old rubber raincoat and a pair of galoshes out of the trunk and put them on. "What do you look for, exactly?" he asked.

"Suspicious burn patterns, combustible materials where they don't belong, obvious evidence of arson. If they're not present I leave the actual cause of the fire to the experts. I'm just a troubleshooter."

"Well, you won't find any trouble here. Hopper's a pain in the butt. He's also one of the most honest men I know."

According to the file Lawrence Otell had given me, the Hopper family had sold its acreage short to developers years before, then watched the developers make back ten times the investment by subdividing, building houses, and selling the plots for a hundred thousand apiece. Meanwhile Mike, the last of the family, had become an independent trucker to survive. He had been alone at home, sleeping on the second story, when the fire broke out, and had escaped with only the pajamas he was wearing. The house was totally engulfed by the time the fire department arrived.

Sergeant Early remained outside while I waded through a muck of sodden ashes, turning over lumps of melted and half-burned furniture and shining my flashlight into corners made inaccessible by the piles of debris. The stench was one I could never get used to, which was why I didn't specialize in arson investigation. I'd only taken the job to remind Midwest Confidential I was still in business. The company had saved me from a negative balance more times than I could count.

I fished out a couple of bowling trophies, smeared with soot but undamaged, and a thick spiral-bound book charred around the edges that upon opening I found to contain what looked like family snapshots going back to the 'thirties, judging by the cars and clothing that appeared in them. These items I wrapped in one of the kitchen trash bags I'd carried along to store evidence and laid it atop what used to be a cabinet television. The sky looked like rain or snow, and such mementoes are irreplaceable. That was it for the ground floor, as well as the second story, which had collapsed along with the rest of the house.

Finding the stairs to the basement I switched on my flashlight and descended, testing each step before I trusted my full weight to it. The half-cellar was dank and airless, and the stagnant water from the firemen's hoses came up almost to my boot-tops on the concrete floor. Something nudged one of my calves. My light found a red plastic can, half-burned, that

I might have thought was a watering can floating on the surface if it weren't just the kind of thing I was looking for. I picked it up by what was left of its handle and smelled the inside. Gasoline never smells like anything but what it is.

Advertised warnings to the contrary, a lot of people store gasoline in their cellars. I did some more looking. In a corner relatively untouched by the flames, I found two more cans just like it. Training the flashlight beam around the room, I spotted another floating object and waded over to it. It was a wooden dowel about two feet long, partially-burned, with a husk of what might have been charred oilcloth wrapped around the end. On this end I smelled more gasoline. I carried the cans and the makeshift torch upstairs and showed them to Sergeant Early.

"It's not conclusive," I said. "Experts may be able to tell if the fire started in the basement, or maybe not. Right now it looks like someone doused the place with gas, then lit a torch and threw it in from the top of the stairs where he could get out before it got going."

Early took off his cap, ran his fingers back through his short thinning hair, and put it back on. "Mike's got enemies. One of 'em might have been sore enough to burn him out."

"If that's true, he did him a favor, at least financially. The place was insured for a lot more than he would have gotten for it on the market."

"Let's go talk to him."

***

Mike Hooper's tractor-trailer, bearing his name on the cab, was parked behind a motel on an as-yet undeveloped section of state highway, one of the old-fashioned kind with bungalows lined up on either side of the office. We were greeted at the door of #11 by a big man with narrow eyes, a reddish-brown beard and mustache that concealed his mouth completely, and a strip of untanned flesh at the top of his forehead where a cap would rest normally. He was shoeless and had on an undershirt and stained workpants. One of his big hands was wrapped around a beer can.

"Mike, this is Amos Walker. He's with your insurance company. We need to talk."

"I said I didn't want nobody snooping around my place. I was born there. Nobody goes in without an invite but family, and I'm all the family that's left."

"It's gone past that." I held up one of the gasoline cans. "Is this yours?"

"I sold my pickup for a down payment on my rig. It's diesel. I got no use for gas."

"What do you owe on your rig?" Early asked.

"I'm three payments behind, not that it's your damn business. What the hell goes on here?"

I read it like a primer. "You get much behind, the company repossesses your tractor-trailer. Without a rig you starve. That's what goes on here. Did you put a match to your place for the insurance?"

He almost caught me square on the jaw, but only because I thought he'd need more reaction time. As it was, his fist clipped my left ear when I moved my head. The sergeant caught his wrist and twisted it behind his back, using Hopper's own momentum against him. "Hold on, Mike. Walker doesn't know you. Can you think of anybody you've had a run-in with who might want to set fire to your house?"

When the answer didn't come right away, Early twisted harder. "No. Crap, Tom, who do you think I hang out with? I tee somebody off, he takes a swing at me. He don't come around in the middle of the night and try to fry me in my bed."

"Mike's right. His crowd isn't that original."

"In that case, Sergeant, I'm informing you that Midwest Confidential intends to press charges against Mr. Hopper for attempted fraud."

"You heard him, Mike. I'm going to have to put you in custody."

As he said it, Early gave me a black look that told me all I needed to know about which man he'd rather put handcuffs on.

***

He was still wearing the look an hour later, when he returned to his desk in the substation after seeing Hopper off to the county lock-up in the back of a squad car. "I never had to arrest a friend before," he said. "I like it a lot? Hell no, I don't."

I said, "I don't much like being the bad cop, but he knows you."

"I still don't think he did it."

"Neither do I."

He touched his mustache, watching me. I liked that way he had of waiting for answers to the questions he didn't ask. He had a lot of city cop in him for a glorified security officer.

I offered him a cigarette, and lit one for myself when he shook his head. "I wanted to get a look at him, just to see if he was the type who would throw away family treasures in return for the fast buck," I said, depositing the match in a clay ashtray that looked as if Early had a kid who went to summer camp. "He isn't. He was telling the truth when he said he didn't want anyone but family poking through the ashes of his birthplace. If he burned his own house, he might sacrifice his bowling trophies to make it look good, but he'd find some way to save family pictures. He almost lost an album full of memories in the flames. He didn't set that fire."

"Who do you think did?"

"I don't know. Maybe nobody. Maybe somebody sneaked in after the fire and planted the gasoline cans and the torch to make it look like arson."

"Somebody'd have to hate Mike a lot to try to frame him. He's got some enemies, but he's got a lot of friends, too. I'd hate to think what they'd do to someone who'd sink that low. If you didn't buy it, why'd you have me arrest Mike?"

"If whoever it was thinks it worked, he may not be looking over his shoulder when we come up on him from behind. It would help if someone saw somebody hanging around the scene after the fire was out."

"That's a tough one. There are always gawkers. Pesky kids. Wait." He touched his mustache again. "Al Ludendorf—that's the fire chief—told me he caught Lloyd Golson skulking around the night after the fire. Golson's a petty thief. Al thought he might've been there to loot the place, but he searched him and didn't find anything on him. He ran him off."

"Where would I find Golson?"

Sergeant Early smiled for the first time since we'd met. "Hell, that's easy. I caught him shoplifting a circular saw out of the Huron Hardware yesterday. He's locked up in the same wing with Mike Hopper."

***

I drove straight from the county seat to the Midwest Confidential building. Ms. Roland, Lawrence Otell's secretary, was putting on her coat when I stepped off the elevator into the reception area.

"Quitting time, sorry," she said. "Mr. Otell's busy clearing up some unfinished business."

"So am I. Got a minute?"

"Just about that." She glanced at the watch strapped to the underside of her wrist.

"I guess Mr. Otell's pretty valuable to the company."

"He holds the record for delivering the most policies with the fewest claims. He's the front runner for the president's job when Mr. Silverman retires."

"That's important, huh? I mean about his reporting the fewest claims against the policies he sold."

"Well, yes. For a while it looked like Jeff Knapp had the inside track because he sold more policies, but then he caught a bad break during fire season. It's kind of unfair when you think about it. No one can predict that."

"You don't know your boss as well as you think."

"I'm sorry?"

But I was already going through the door to the private office. Inside, Otell looked up quickly from the paperwork spread across his desk. "Around here we knock," he said.

I said, "Things are a little less formal in Huron. I just spoke with Lloyd Golson."

His square face showed nothing. "Who's that?"

"You'll find him in company files. Midwest Confidential sold a lot of policies around Huron. Several burglary claims were filed. His name came up in four of them as a suspect in the break-ins. He was convicted twice. Is that why you decided to use him, because his name kept showing up in claim cases?"

"Naturally I don't know what you're talking about."

"Sure you do. You've got a shot at the presidency because you've made the company more money from policies than you've lost in claims. That would change if too many customers like Mike Hopper were paid off for their losses in fires. Tampering with the fire scene to make it look like Hopper torched his own house for the insurance would allow the company to reject his claim, preserving your record and your chances for advancement."

He pointed a finger. "Repeat that in front of witnesses and I'll sue you for character assassination."

"I can't kill what you don't have," I said. "Golson talked, Otell. He ratted you out to get a shoplifting charge dropped that would have imprisoned him for five years as a repeat offender. You called him the morning after the fire and offered him five hundred dollars to plant evidence implicating Hopper."

"A man like that would say anything to stay out of jail."

"Maybe. It's enough to make the authorities curious about other aborted claims against policies you sold. A man who would break the law once to improve his statistics would do it again. I'm guessing when they're finished taking a hard look, you'll be facing several counts of interfering in criminal investigations and insurance fraud. You won't like prison any more than Golson. The pinstripes go the wrong way."

He thought about it a second, then opened the top drawer of his desk and brought out a revolver. That disappointed me.

"If you're going to shoot yourself, don't do it in your own office. That joke's too old."

"Who said anything about shooting myself?" He pointed the revolver at me.

Just then Ms. Roland came in. "Larry? Is everything—" She froze when she saw the gun.

Otell didn't. In a second he was on his feet and lunging. He grabbed her arm, pulled her off balance, and swept behind her, grabbing her around the waist and clapping the revolver's muzzle under her chin. "Don't move, Walker!"

"Well, that one's even older," I said. "I thought you didn't go in for blood sports." But I didn't move.

He backed through the open door, bringing her with him. I gave him a beat, then followed.

They were standing in front of the elevator. He took the gun from her throat long enough to push the button with his elbow, then replaced it. His expression was totally alien. The shock of a drop as long as the one from the president's office to the defendant's table affects many different people many different ways.

The doors slid open. He shoved the woman stumbling into the office and backed inside the elevator, swinging the gun from side to side. I stayed where I was. The doors closed and the car started down.

I helped Ms. Roland to her feet. "Are you going to call the police?" she asked.

"No." I went back into Otell's office. The wall behind the desk was made entirely of glass and looked down onto the street before the entrance to the underground garage where the employees parked. The secretary joined me.

"I called the parking attendant earlier," I said. "Otell drives a gray Mercedes?"

"Yes, are the police waiting for him?"

"Not exactly."

A minute later a gray Mercedes nosed out into the street. It was waiting to turn when a battered Dodge pickup swept away from the curb and plowed into the door on the driver's side. After a pause, the passenger's side door popped open and Otell piled out, waving his revolver. Just then a second pickup roared down the lane on that side and screeched to a halt. Both doors swung open and the occupants of the cab leveled shotguns across the tops. By then other pickups had appeared, ringing in the Mercedes and the man who had been driving it. All the drivers and passengers had shotguns except one.

Sergeant Early stepped down from a Ford Ranger, walked up to Otell, and took away his gun without a struggle.

Thomas Sullivan

Thomas Sullivan, who describes himself as ranged if not deranged, has been printed and reprinted in almost every category of fiction here and around the world. Among his seventy-odd publications he is best known for his Pulitzer nominated novel *The Phases of Harry Moon* and for a darker novel, *Born Burning*, recently optioned to Hollywood for film rights. Having lived in a dozen countries, attended thirteen schools, competed internationally in two sports, and lived lifestyles as varied as gambler and city commissioner, it isn't surprising that he maintains "When you don't belong anywhere, in a sense you belong everywhere." Currently the author lives in Lathrup Village, Michigan. Besides writing, "Sully's" passions include playing the tenor sax and cross-country skiing—both nocturnal pursuits, he says.

"The Muse" has a tightly knit style and an aberrant note that rises as insidiously as the hum of a tuning fork. It is dedicated to actor, musician, song-writer and friend Glenn Frey, whose solo career and prominence with the Eagles proves that good guys can be winners.

THE MUSE

by
Thomas Sullivan

He had the voice. He had always had the voice. From the time the adolescent clutch in his throat stopped slipping and puberty was done playing its jokes, he had spoken with a voice marinated in doom. Spoken and sang. It was the singing that showed his range, of course. He could modulate like a violin.

He could sound as mellow as torquing ship's timbers. He could freeze the sweetness of a note in the air like a humming-bird sipping nectar. If sounds had been colors, Teddy Corsica's voice would have been a rainbow.

The trouble was the songs.

The songs were bad. He knew they were bad. Glenn Frey he wasn't. When Frey wrote, the songs marched or soared right off the paper. Whatever Teddy wrote just lay there. You could get someone to write for you, of course. If you had a reputation, you could get just about everybody in the business. But if you were nobody, you couldn't get anybody. Catch-22: you couldn't get a reputation without a writer and you couldn't get a writer without a reputation. The writing was the main thing. Guys like Manilow and Torme made it because of the songs. With a voice like Teddy's, Manilow could have made choir director behind the pearly gates. With a voice like Teddy's, Torme wouldn't sound like a gorilla walking over walnuts every time his voice dipped below middle C. But those guys could write. Teddy Corsica could not. A bird without a song is feathered noise.

So he sang what was history, and the people in the bars

clapped and made requests and when they were drunk enough gave him bills instead of quarters. The voice marinated in doom said thank you, and it was funny, but when it went home and cried it still sounded like marinated doom—or maybe torquing ship's timbers.

He didn't cry a lot. Once a night was his limit. It was the frustration mainly. If he hadn't had such a gift, it would have been easier to hang it up, to push himself away from the piano and sell shoes or bake bread. But such a gift. *Why, God? Why make me half an artist? Is it a joke?*

And he would cry.

And then he would laugh. Because he was like a man with one leg that could run a three-minute mile and another leg that couldn't make it to the end of the block.

And then he wouldn't feel anything.

And then one night the phone rang.

***

"Hello, Teddy."

"Who is this?"

"A fan."

"How did you get my number? It's three a.m."

"You weren't sleeping."

Pause. New tone. "Who is this?"

"Your muse."

"Not funny."

"I know your problem, Teddy."

"Yeah. Who the hell is this?"

"I heard you sing, and I know your problem."

"I don't have a problem."

"Yes you do, Teddy." The voice was a whisper, charged, dramatic. When it tried to speak clearly, it quavered. "Yes you do," it assured him, and the tremolo was evident.

Teddy was alert now. "What do you want?"

"I've got a song for you, Teddy."

Silence.

"Are you ready for it?"

"What makes you think I need your song?"

"Finding a song is your problem, Teddy."

"I don't have a problem! You've got the problem, Mister. I don't know where [*the voice was humming now*] you got my number, but [*quavery, but the song carried its own conviction, a beautiful song, an exquisite song*] don't try to call again, because ... because ..."

Dear God.

It was gorgeous. There at three a.m. through a quavery voice that sounded a million miles away Teddy felt the chill, the haunting runs, the pure passion of the thing. And then the quavery voice switched to words, and the lyrics were fantastic. Soul-stripping words. Neat. Simple.

Teddy stood frozen in the blackness of his apartment. The phone felt like the wing of a butterfly in his hand, a monarch wing, gold and soft and fragile in his own coarse grip. He was afraid now, afraid he would lose the song, would crush the golden wing.

"Is it really yours?" he demanded tightly when it was done.

"It's yours, Teddy! Take it. Sing it. Sing it. It's yours!"

***

He knew in his gut it was original, that the benefactor had given him something wholly free and clear. It had his own resonance all over it. As if it had been written for him. He barely needed the tape recording which the caller had allowed him to make the second time through. By a quarter to four he had it written out and memorized and the super was up pounding on his door because he was playing it on the piano with full chords by then. He took it to the Irish Pub that night, and the patrons wouldn't leave it alone. He lost track of the requests.

"Sing whatchamacallit again."

"'Resurrection,'" he would say.

"Yeah. 'Resurrection.'"

By week's end he had an audience—a genuine I-didn't-come-here-just-to-drink audience. And a month after that the man from Arista records came, and that was Manilow's label.

They wanted to know if he had more where "Resurrection" came from, and he said yes, that he had tons of material, and that was when they offered to fly him to New York for contract talks and an audition. So he went back to his apartment and began to write and pound the piano and write some more. He had inspiration now. He was *resurrected*, and he knew the way. By midnight he had a dozen ideas down and it was all just feathered noise and the super was hammering on his door again.

He put the chain on the jamb. Turned off the lights. Sat. The piano keys seemed to fluoresce in the dark. He was afraid to touch them now. Afraid to find out who he was again, who he wasn't. His hands were sweating like sponges when the phone rang.

***

"How is it going, Teddy?"

"Don't you know?"

"Yes ... I know."

"Then you know it's all going to be over when I get to New York." The marinated doom in his voice had never been fuller.

"Not if you have a repertoire, Teddy."

"You can't possibly have another song like that last one.

Can you?"

"I can. I do." Pause. "More than one actually."

"Who are you?" Teddy demanded suddenly. "What do you want?"

"What does any artist want, Teddy? We want freedom, we want to escape."

"Music is my escape."

"Is it?" The tremor was husky now.

"Isn't it yours? It must be yours."

"You're my escape."

"Listen. Listen. I don't know why you don't market your own stuff—I don't care—but if you want to go through me, that's fine."

"I can't market my stuff, Teddy. I have to express myself through you. I picked you because you have the best voice around. And you can't write worth a damn."

And then they came. Five, six, seven often. Tremendous songs. Bittersweet lines, pulsing rhythms, poignant strains. The state of this man's soul! What cross was he crucified on? Teddy wondered.

***

New York was a piece of cake. The first single was out in six weeks, an album in four months. Within a year he had two more albums and a video. There seemed to be no capping his creative drive. He turned out songs as easily as answering the phone. In the alchemy of Teddy Corsica's career, gold and platinum were base metals.

The gold got into his pockets and for a while that made everything all right in his life. By this time the record moguls were pacing him out in bits and pieces to an eager public. But the less he did the more the money rolled in. He had never dreamed there were so many ways of getting paid. He had an agent, a lawyer and an accountant. He had cars and clothes and apartments. The clothes got frillier, the cars more personalized, and when it seemed he had one of everything from the frivolous to the exorbitant, he began replacing them all with monogrammed duplicates. There were people to tell him he needed these things, people to handle his mail, his clothes, his itineraries, people to pick out carpets and colors and paintings.

For a while the fame was all right, too. Because everyone loved him now, and you could forgive the world all its transgressions when everyone loved you. Forgive and forget.

But in all fables of fame and fortune there is a flaw. And Teddy's was that he was living a lie.

I am not the man the world loves, he told himself. *Half maybe. Half the man they think I am.*

In the end it wasn't enough. And so when Teddy Corsica was done gold-plating the debris of his life, he fired his staff and sat alone in the penthouse cathedral he had built for himself. By the phone. At night. In the dark. And the ring, when it came, was like a scream tearing through the paper walls of his palace.

He picked up the receiver and said: "I'm not happy."

"You have it all, Teddy."

He was looking out a twenty-foot plate glass window and New York twinkled in his lap. But he was shaking. He felt as though he were on both ends of the phone at once, that his insides were stretched like a piece of taffy from one planet to another.

"I don't have it all. *We* have it all."

"You don't owe me."

"That's just the point. I do. This isn't really mine."

"And you feel guilty over that?"

"I don't know. Look ... I want to cut you in on this. Give me a name and an address to send you a check."

"A name? A place? Is that what you want?"

"I just want to square the account."

"No."

"Yes! What's the matter, are you already rich? Then give me the name of your favorite charity, damn it!"

"Stop it, Teddy. It could get a lot worse that way."

"Could it? How?"

"Goodbye, Teddy."

There was a rushing in the line, like a universe passing through, then silence, then a dial tone. It was the last call Teddy got for a while.

He didn't care. There was enough material on hand for the time being. And even after that, he wouldn't care. Because he knew he was coming to an end. There were moments when he thought he would trade it all just to know who was on the other end of that line. What kind of man took vicarious pleasure in Teddy Corsica's spin of the wheel? What kind of artist gave away his soul over the phone? He had given up searching for a special face in the crowd as the audiences grew larger, the stages bigger, but now he was searching again. It would be a face with hidden suffering, inner knowledge, exquisite longing, he knew. Maybe it would be like his own face. The other half of it. But the audience grew more remote, more homogeneous, a clone of themselves with the same handful of rapt expressions. He no longer saw them. They had come to escape into him. And it was already crowded in his soul. He began to wish he could throw someone out.

And finally, one night before New Year's Eve, he made up his mind to do what he must do.

It was no surprise to him when the phone rang.

**

"What are you up to, Teddy?"

"Resurrection," he said.

"It's been a great year. You don't need resurrecting."

"I've made a couple of New Year's resolutions."

"I shouldn't ask."

"The first is not to ask you who you are anymore."

"And the second?"

"To find out who I am."

"You're you."

"I've always been half a man. I was a singer who couldn't write my own songs, and I still am. I think I want to be half a man all by myself again."

"Maybe you did write those songs. Maybe you just think these phone calls exist."

"Sure. Half of me is a genius."

"Could be. Schizophrenics do that kind of thing, I think. It happens all the time."

"Why are you messing with my mind?"

"Believe me, delusions happen."

"In other words I'm talking to myself."

"More or less."

"Get off it."

"What are you going to do, Teddy?"

"Tomorrow night I'm appearing on ABC's New Year's Eve special. I'm going to tell them the truth."

"*Them?*"

"The world."

"Now that's certifiably insane."

"I have to."

"Teddy." A great trembling sigh. "Oh, Teddy, the time has come for me to make you a whole person. You want that, don't you? You really want that?"

"I've always wanted it. But you can't do anything about it."

"Yes. Yes, I can. This wanting to be the real you, that's a healthy sign, Teddy. You're in good shape. Believe me. You can have it all now. And you don't have to give up your reputation."

"I don't want any more of your songs."

"But I can teach you to write them, Teddy. You. Yourself. I can give you what I have."

The long silence of hope filled the line. Could it be, Teddy Corsica thought. Could you actually acquire that kind of insight?

"I learned it, Teddy."

"And what's in it for you if you show me? You said I was your escape. I'm telling you now that one way or the other I want to be free of you. If you show me, I won't be your escape anymore."

"Well ... then I'll retire. Fair enough?"

"Come see me."

"No. You come to me."

***

Joey Wilson. He had a voice that could tame lions, soften granite and make a sphinx cry. But he couldn't write worth a damn. There hadn't been a voice like his since Teddy Corsica's. When he got really depressed, that was what Joey thought about. Corsica and how he had suddenly just left fandom in the lurch and bought himself a private island—or so the tabloids claimed. If only he could write like that, Joey thought.

And then one night the phone rang, and a voice that trembled but still sounded a little like marinated doom said:

"Hello, Joey ..."

Helen Esper Olmsted

HELEN ESPER OLMSTED is an active member and past board member of the Mystery Writers of America. She is also an active member of Sisters in Crime. Olmsted has a certificate in Mass Media and regularly writes mystery news and reviews for the Little Professor newsletter, *Mysterious Ink*. Her feature stories, book and drama reviews have appeared in the *Birmingham Eccentric, Livingston County Press, Detroit MarketPlace Magazine* and others. Her essay on Loren Estleman's fictional PI Amos Walker appeared in the Anthony (World Mystery) Award-winning *100 Great Detectives*, first published in Great Britain and later in the United States by Carroll & Graf. Olmsted received the Laddie Award for Literary Distinction from the Livingston County Council of the Arts in 1994.

Olmsted is the author of "The Chocolate Mouse" and "The Reindeer's New Boots." Olmsted has also been a script writer and co-producer for Homicide Host Productions since 1982. Her interactive mysteries have been produced for dinner theater and mystery weekends for leading hotels, corporations and conventions throughout Michigan, Illinois, Ohio and Ontario, Canada. Segments of her productions have appeared on ABC and NBC in the Detroit area. She has been a guest on Meet the Author—WAAM Radio, the Warren Pierce Show, WJR, and others. Olmsted has done workshops for the Livingston County Writers Club and panels for the Mystery Writers Conventions in Omaha, Nebraska.

Olmsted lives with her husband, Don, in Howell, Michigan. There her eleven grandchildren visit and play with the numerous pets she and Don have adopted over the years.

The Corpse Was Clean-Shaven

By

Helen Esper Olmsted

Homicide Detective Lieutenant Georgi Raconni took the squeal at home. Her partner, detective Howard Blanchard, had been hanging around the squad room; he was close to the crime scene so she'd meet him there.

Georgi ran a comb through her black, feathered hair, and touched a powder puff to her slightly shiny pug nose. She strapped a shoulder holster on, covered it with her suit jacket and gave her Golden Retriever and two German Shepherds a pat on their heads. Lord, she was going to have to find a home for them. The neighbors had been damn decent; however, if she was going to pick up strays, what she needed was a home in the country.

She went out to her unmarked car and slapped a bubble on top of it; she was ready to go full speed ahead. She kept the siren on as she wove her way through the early morning traffic from the extreme north side of Ann Arbor to the west side.

Catching an address on one of the buildings, Georgi abruptly cut off a dark blue Dodge Spirit just entering the parking structure next to Sherri Lynn Publications Ltd., causing the motorist to lean on her horn.

Georgi jumped from her car. "Lieutenant Georgina Raconni, Homicide," she said, using her more formal name, and showing her badge. "Do you work in this building?"

"Did you say homicide?" The girl blanched as the big H-word registered. "Who's been murdered?"

"Mr. Brian Miller; do you know him, by any chance?"

The young lady cleared her throat a couple of times, parked her car, and got out, before replying. "He is, er, *was* our Editor in Chief."

"You work for Sherri Lynn Publications?"

"Well, yes. My name is Joan Best and I'm an associate editor."

"Did you know Miller well?"

"Brian and I worked very closely at times, if that's what you mean," Joan said.

"What type of material does Sherri Lynn publish?"

"We publish children's educational books," the girl replied.

"Do you have any idea who might want to kill Brian Miller?" Georgi inquired.

"Well, no. He had his share of enemies—uh, maybe enemies is too strong a word. He had business disagreements just like anybody else." She shook her head as if trying to rid herself of some unpleasant memory.

"What is it, Miss Best? Did you think of something?" Georgi asked, not unkindly.

"Well, it's only that I noticed Brian's office light was still on and the door was slightly ajar, when I left last night. I thought it was rather strange because Brian usually leaves around five o'clock, which is our normal quitting time. I stayed late because I was waiting for one of our new authors to fax a bio. I wanted to receive it personally because it's close to deadline for his book."

"You didn't check out Mr. Miller's office to see what was happening?"

"Well, no, I was going to stick my head in and see who was in the office, but then I heard the computer going on and the sound of a disk being put in. I thought Brian had stayed to do some last minute work and that I'd better not disturb him. Oh, no." Joan's face went whiter than it had been a minute before.

"What?" Georgi asked.

"It—it's just that, if only I'd checked the office, Brian might still be alive," Joan moaned.

"Or you might be dead right along with him and what good would that have done anyone?" Georgi commented cynically. "Besides, Miller could have already been dead when you passed by his office last night; if you had gone in, you might have surprised a killer in Miller's office. You shouldn't blame yourself," she added kindly. "Come on, let's go inside."

"I'd just as soon not go in. Nobody will be working today and I don't feel very well. I'd rather go home if it's all the same to you."

"Sorry, I'm afraid you will have to go in," Georgi declared.

A few minutes later, Georgi, with Joan Best still protesting mildly beside her, entered the elevator. On the way up to the fifth floor, where the publisher's offices were housed, Georgi explained, "A Maude Blunt found the body early this morning and called nine-one-one. Do you know Blunt?"

"Yes, this is a small publishing house and we all know each other. Maude is a temporary secretary called in when the work load gets heavy, otherwise we share Brian's secretary except when it's time for the spring and fall releases. Then we have a computer pool. Maude usually comes in early on the days she works. That way, she can get an early start and will have time to handle any changes that may come up during the day."

Arriving on the fifth floor, Raconni found the door to the publishing offices in easy proximity to where she and Joan stepped off the elevator.

As the lieutenant opened the door, she was nearly knocked down by a buxom redhead, who greeted her effusively. "You must be Lieutenant Raconni. We heard you'd be here. I mean, what we need here really is a homicide officer with some authority."

"Ah, yes, you must be Maude Blunt. My partner, Detective Blanchard, is generally in charge when I'm not around," Georgi said. "Where's the body, Howard?" she asked, nodding briefly in the direction of a well-built blonde-haired man, who, though in his late thirties, had retained his boyish good looks.

"In the office down the hall, third door on the left," Howard explained. "The forensic team is in there now. I think the doc's about through with the prelim exam and they should be finished with the pictures and evidence-gathering soon. I've got all the employees but a Miss Joan Best here for interrogation, and it looks like you've corralled Miss Best yourself."

"Yes; keep an eye on her and the others, while I take a quick peek at the body."

Georgi headed down the hall. As she pushed open the door to Brian Miller's office, she was met with strobes going off in all directions. The police photographer was just finishing the scene-of-the-crime pictures.

"What have you got on the cause and time of death?" Georgi asked Doctor Pointer, the grumpy ME assigned to the case.

"Come on, Raconni, you know better than to try to pin me down to the time of death at this early stage." Though the doctor was almost dwarf size, there was nothing diminutive about his voice. "As for cause, the victim probably died as the result of being hit over the head with a blunt instrument. Take a look."

As Georgi knelt to look at the victim's bald, blood-encrusted head, she noticed several brownish stains on the blue carpet. She wondered if the stains were the victim's blood, already dried.

As if reading her mind, Pointer cautioned, "Be careful not to smear any of those stains. We may have gotten lucky and those could be samples of our killer's blood."

"It doesn't look as if there was much of a struggle," Georgi noted, glancing around the immaculate, well-appointed office. There was another door besides the one leading to the corridor. It must be a bathroom, Georgi thought. Just as she was getting up from the floor, she noticed a new laser printer sitting on the carved oak desk.

Pointer shrugged, "You never know. The killer could have cut himself on the weapon or something." He shrugged again.

"Let's hope so, but come on, Doc," Georgi wheedled, "what's your best guess as to the time of death?"

"The best I can do until after the autopsy is somewhere between five and six o'clock last night. I could be a little off, depending on the degree of cooling in the office after the heat was turned down for the night."

"All right, if that's the best you can do," Raconni shrugged. "You can have the body removed when you're done here. I assume the meat wagon is out back." Pointer nodded an affirmative. "And by the way, Doc, if there's a bathroom through that door, have forensics check it out."

"It is a bathroom and the forensic team has already been in there. They recovered particles of bristles in the sink. We figure the color matches the slight fringe of hair around the victim's head; in case you haven't noticed, the corpse is clean-shaven."

"Thanks, Doc." Georgi left to interrogate the employees, herding them into Joan Best's office (which was as Spartan as

Brian Miller's was luxurious) so they wouldn't see the body bag when Miller was carried out.

When everyone was settled in, Georgi began, "Joan, what time did you say you left the office last night?"

"I didn't, but it must have been close to six. It took longer to get the fax than I had anticipated."

"All right. Now, Miss Blunt—you're a temporary secretary, is that right?"

"Yes, I'm a call girl, er—I mean I'm a secretary on call. I was working here yesterday, April twenty-seventh and it was Secretary's Day. Do you know what that creep Miller did?"

"No," Georgi looked interested. "Why don't you tell me?"

"He knew I was going to be in yesterday and he didn't include me when the goodies were passed out. He pretended he'd forgotten. No flowers or anything for the good old temp. Not only that, but he promised me a bonus months ago, for being so efficient. I still haven't seen a penny of it."

Georgi asked, "So you had a good reason to dislike the victim?"

"Well, sure, but not enough to kill him, if that's what you're driving at," Maude replied indignantly.

Georgi noticed a heavy-set man about six feet tall, with graying hair and a mustache to match, who had been standing away from the rest of the group. He came forward and Georgie wondered briefly why he was in coveralls, but she decided to let the action play itself out.

"Geez, Maude, why don't you just shut up? You're going to get yourself in trouble." The heavy-set man frowned.

"Well, I never," Maude exclaimed angrily.

"Yeah, I know you never, but maybe you should have," came the rejoinder.

"Knock it off," Georgi commented mildly. "Now, before we go any further, I'd like to know what your function here is, Mr.–?"

"Jason," the man in coveralls supplied. "And I don't really have a function with the company, as such. I'm employed by the We Clean It All service. They're contracted to service this building. In fact, I picked up this contract through Maude, who's my next door neighbor," he finished proudly. "And before you ask, yes, I was working here yesterday."

"Fine." Georgi looked in the direction of a sexy, giggly, blonde girl. The type the gang at the cop shop called a "bubblehead." The girl was talking to a suave, good-looking, dark-haired man, probably in his early forties. He was standing in a relaxed position, hands in the pockets of his fashionable, double-breasted, light blue suit.

"I haven't spoken with either of you yet," she said. "I'd like your names and positions with the firm. You first, Miss, and I'd like to know what's so funny."

"I'm Dee Danson. I was Mr. Miller's secretary. And there is nothing funny about any of this. I guess I'm a little hysterical," the girl replied nervously. "Mr. Miller was not an easy man to work for, but I never wanted to see him dead."

"She's right about that," Joan said. "Why, the clutter that poor girl had to clean off Brian's desk some days just because he got impatient when looking for things—well, all I can say is, she had to be a saint to work for him."

Georgi nodded. Then, the gentleman, who had been talking to Dee Danson said, "I'm Arthur Wheat, Lieutenant, and I'm rather new at the firm; I do a great deal of the editing. I'm also in charge of book layout. I came from a bigger house because Brian was my friend, and he needed my help with a job he was inexperienced at. Say, can you at least tell us how Brian was murdered?"

"Yeah," Georgi replied. "I guess it can't hurt anything. He was killed with the proverbial blunt instrument."

"Well, I must say it couldn't have happened to a more deserving person," Maude offered her opinion.

"I'd watch my mouth if I were you," warned Joan Best. "With Brian's death, I expect that the board of directors will promote me to Editor-in-Chief at the next meeting, and *I* don't appreciate the way you're talking about a man who's no longer here to defend himself."

"Look who's talking," sneered Jason. "Rumors abound that the board is rather fed up with your willingness to walk over everybody in order to get ahead. Now that Miller, your champion, is dead, they're likely to hire an Editor-in-Chief from an outside house, whereas Maude is invaluable even on a part-time basis."

"You're only sticking up for Maude because you've been sleeping with her," Joan scoffed.

"I wouldn't talk about sleeping around if I were you. Maybe you'd better look to your own bedroom habits."

"Gee, isn't anything sacred around here? I don't think it's anyone's business who's sleeping with whom," Dee Danson tittered.

Lips slightly pursed in amusement, Georgi said, "Well, I don't think there's much more to be done here today, but I'll expect all of you to be at police headquarters, one hundred North Fifth Street at nine-thirty tomorrow morning. There will be someone there to take your statements and you can sign them. And one more thing—none of you will be able to return to work for a few days. There will be scene-of-the-crime tape around the office door and it cannot be broken," Georgi admonished.

Just as everyone was leaving, Dee Danson approached Howard and asked coquettishly, "You don't really think one of us is a murderer, do you?"

"Well, *I* don't really think it's an inside job, but the lieutenant always has her own ideas. Just hang loose for a couple of days while we gather more evidence. In the meantime, I'll see you at headquarters in the morning."

"Just in case you have some free time." Danson batted her eyelashes at Howard as she slipped him her card.

"Geez," Georgi exclaimed, disgustedly. "Let's go, Howard. Oh," she threw over her shoulder as if it had just occurred to her, "as Mr. Miller's secretary, would you happen to know why he shaved last night when he was ready to leave the office? Did he have an appointment with someone after hours?"

"No appointment," chirped Danson. "Mr. Miller was in the habit of shaving before he left for home. He has—er, *had*— an awful five o'clock shadow and always shaved twice a day."

***

Back at police headquarters, Georgi put in a hurried call to the Medical Examiner's office; the chief medical examiner for Washtenaw County was in. After chatting with her friend and colleague for a few minutes, she told her the purpose of her call.

Hanging up the receiver, she turned to her partner, who was sitting at the desk just opposite hers and said, "Doctor Blaine said we should be able to pick up the autopsy report on Brian Miller along with all his personal effects by seven p.m. this evening. She promised to call the pathologist on duty and put a rush on it. We'll at least get the essential information even if we have to wait on some of the lab work. I'd appreciate it if you'd pick everything up for me. I've got a date tonight that I'd like to keep."

"Sure, no problem, Lieutenant," the detective said good-naturedly.

"I have one more call to make to the Department of Sanitation. Then I'm out of here."

At a quarter of twelve that evening, just as Georgi was coming in from her date, the phone rang. She picked up the receiver reluctantly. It wasn't Howard as she had expected, but when she heard what the caller had to say, she snatched her coat from the closet and headed for the door, receiving yet another pout from the dogs as she let them out into the yard.

***

It was with grim determination that Georgi met with the employees of Sherri Lynn Publications the next morning at headquarters. As she shuffled them into one of the interrogation rooms, she said, "My partner's in the hospital with a shoulder wound, and I'll be damned if any of you will get away with it."

"Whatever are you talking about, Lieutenant?" Dee Danson's voice sounded loud in the hush that followed Georgi's statement.

"One of you already knows what I'm talking about, but I'll fill in for the rest of you," Georgi said. "I sent my partner down to the morgue last night to pick up the victim's effects and some pertinent information, and someone shot at him, wounding him in the shoulder. He was lucky another officer had just come out the door, and although he didn't get the license number of the car, he got off a couple of shots, which scared the perp away, otherwise he might have finished off my detective."

"I don't know what you're getting at, Lieutenant. You're acting like one of *us* shot him. Why would we want to do that? We're not savages, you know," expostulated Arthur Wheat.

"Yeah, well, I'm not so sure of that," Georgi said. "At least one of you was pretty sure there was something on the victim that he or she couldn't afford for the police to find. That same someone first broke the scene-of-the-crime tape and searched Miller's office. When the intruder didn't find what he was looking for, he parked near the morgue and waited for someone to show up. He, or she, waited until they saw my partner come out with a plastic sack and they shot at him."

"Wait a minute! You're telling us that someone waited to waylay your partner just on the off chance that he or someone else might show up at the morgue for the victim's things? That's incredible," said Dee Danson.

"Maybe not so incredible and not so chancy, either," Georgi answered.

"When are you going to start speaking English and explain whatever it is you're rambling on about?" Maude asked.

"I'll explain all that in a minute, but first let's talk about the clues Howard and I have uncovered that will tell us who killed Mr. Brian Miller. I'll start with the murder weapon, which, incidentally, was recovered from a recycling bin behind an office building a few doors from the publisher's," Georgi began.

"Don't tell me a sexy, good-looking broad like you went trash-picking, fer chrissakes. You wouldn't even catch me doing that and I'm in the cleaning business. But then, I could never understand why women wanted to be cops; you gals must get off on doing dirty work, Lieutenant," Jason chuckled.

"Well, let's just say it's a dirty job, but somebody's got to do it." Georgi replied sweetly. "However, in this case I was not the one to recover the weapon. In fact, it didn't occur to me what the most probable, as well as most available weapon, was until my partner and I stopped back at the office for a few minutes to go over the case. As soon as it hit me, I gave the Department of Sanitation a call. Fortunately, pick-up in that neighborhood wasn't slated until this morning and the supervisor sent somebody right out to take a look for a discarded laser printer.

"I noticed a new one in Mr. Miller's office yesterday; the old printer must have still been there the day before yesterday. When Miller discovered someone in his office, that person panicked, picked up the printer and smashed Miller over the head with it, and then threw it into the trash when he left. We're not, however, relying too much on any fingerprints the lab recovers from the weapon because it can be assumed that all of you could have handled it one time or another."

"So what's the point? What are you trying to tell us?" Maude demanded.

"That I have another piece of evidence I'm relying heavily on to point the finger at the murderer."

"Aren't you going about this backwards, Lieutenant?" Joan asked. "I always thought detectives looked for a motive first because that would lead them to the murderer."

"We already have the motive," said Georgi.

"Geez, maybe we should call our lawyers," Dee said.

"Suit yourself," Georgi shrugged. "I haven't accused anyone yet."

"And that's another thing," Jason bellowed. "You can't hold us here without a warrant or something." Then he looked vague.

"Oh yes, I can. I can hold any or all of you for twenty-four hours. After that, if you haven't been arraigned, you're free to go. Now, if you'll please just give your statements about what you were doing between the hours of five p.m. and six p.m. April twenty-seventh to the sergeant over there," she indicated a uniform sitting at a nearby desk, trying not to look bored, "he will get someone to type them up and you can sign them. In the meantime, I will be in the office waiting to hear from the lab."

The prime suspects in the murder of Brian Miller went over to give the sergeant their statements, muttering as they did so, while Georgi retreated to the quiet of her office, a small alcove off the main squad room. She felt depressed as she stared at the garish green walls that seemed grimmer than usual with her partner's absence from the scarred desk with its numerous cigarette burns, opposite her own. She thought of her father, the retired Captain Alfredo Raconni, who had always encouraged her to be a detective with the Ann Arbor Police Department. God, how had he survived thirty years of this? She wondered how many times he'd worried over his fellow detectives. On impulse she reached for the phone. It was time for a pep talk from dear old Dad.

Her father was at home and it wasn't long before he had her back on track again. She had barely hung up the phone when it rang. It was the lab reporting their findings.

"Hello, Lieutenant. We put a rush on the analysis of that note you gave us because it was a fellow officer who got shot. We not only have the brand name and manufacturer of the stationery, but we also got a good set of prints. We'll send it all over for you in about ten minutes."

***

Georgi was grinning broadly when she met with the suspects again, their statements in hand. As she riffled through them she said, "Now that I have all of your signatures, I'll be able to prove just who the guilty party is."

"What's she talking about?" Maude looked confused.

"I have here," Georgi dragged the words out, savoring them, "a blackmail note found in the victim's pocket. Want to hear it?" Not waiting for an answer, Georgi went on, "It says, 'Brian, I have an offer from another publisher and if you don't talk to the board about making me an equal partner in the firm, I will leave and take all the authors I have brought in, along with some of yours.' Now, who do you suppose wrote this note?"

"Well, it wasn't me," Danson said. She suddenly looked stunned. "Do you mean that whoever wrote the note killed Brian?"

"Exactly. Mr. Wheat, I'm sure that you're not surprised to learn that your handwriting matches the writing on the note." She then looked at the assembled group, and spoke to them. "Brian Miller caught Arthur Wheat in his office and Wheat killed him."

"But—but how did Arthur get Brian's password to get into the computer? I thought I was the only one who had it, other than Brian, that is," said Joan Best.

"Yesterday, there were some accusations flying around about sleeping around, which was okay as far as it went. The only problem is that you had the wrong people playing bedroom games," Georgi said. "Dee Danson was sleeping with Brian and so he trusted her with his password, which she promptly passed on to Arthur Wheat, her real love, or so she thought."

Wheat looked angry as the sergeant moved in closer and he found himself blocked off by both the sergeant and the lieutenant.

"You can't prove any of this," Dee Danson blubbered.

"Oh, I don't think I'll have a problem with that," Georgi replied. "You see, when I visited my partner in the hospital last night, he told me he'd taken you up on the invitation you'd more or less extended him, when you gave him your card. Howard has always been a sucker for a pretty girl. Unfortunately, he didn't realize you were pumping him for information when you played on his ego by asking him about his police work, in particular this case, and he let it slip that he was making a trip to the morgue that evening and that's why it had to be an early date. You took this information and passed it on to Wheat, who had been using you all along. We already knew that Mr. Miller must have been killed by someone he knew, because there were no signs of a struggle. After what my partner told me at the hospital, I put two and two together and came up with you and Arthur Wheat. You see, Wheat was the only one with a real motive."

"What's that supposed to mean?" Wheat snarled.

"You were the only one whose job could easily be dispensed with once Brian got your ideas. As Brian became more knowledgeable in his position, you suddenly realized what a tentative hold you had in the firm. You began making demands on Brian. When he didn't satisfy those demands, you went to his office when you thought he was already gone for the day, with the intention of stealing pertinent information—authors' names, addresses, income and future potential—from the computer.

"Brian was in his private bathroom. Forensics discovered evidence of him recently shaving—bristles in the sink—which were carefully bagged for evidence. While he was in the bathroom, he must have heard someone in his office. He came out to confront the intruder. You panicked and hit him over the head with the nearest thing handy, an old laser printer. Then you went to work on his computer. That's what Miss Best heard when she went by the office that night."

"It's all a mistake," Dee Danson wailed. "Nobody was supposed to get hurt."

"I believe you," Georgi said, "and if you turn state's evidence, you'll no doubt get a lighter sentence. Not so with Mr. Arthur Wheat, the mastermind behind the plan. Take him away, sergeant."

As Arthur Wheat was led away by a uniform reading him his rights, Georgi called after them, "Just to tidy things up, sergeant, have DNA get a blood sample to try to match with the bloodstains found on the weapon and the carpet near the corpse. I think if you look at his hands, you'll find some cuts from the weapon—a man who keeps his hands in his pockets all the time must have something to hide."

Bill Kienzle

WILLIAM X. KIENZLE, author of 18 best-selling mysteries, was ordained to the priesthood in 1954 and spent twenty years as a parish priest. For twelve years he was the editor-in-chief of the *Michigan Catholic* newspaper. After leaving the priesthood, he became editor of MPLS magazine in Minneapolis. He then moved to Michigan, where he was associate director of the Center for Contemplative Studies at Western Michigan University in Kalamazoo. Later he moved to Texas, where he was director of the Center for Contemplative Studies at the University of Dallas. Kienzle and his wife, Javan, presently live in Detroit, where he enjoys playing the piano as a diversion from his writing. His first mystery, *The Rosary Murders*, was released in 1987 as a motion picture, starring Donald Sutherland as Father Koesler.

EXIT LAUGHING
by
William X. Kienzle

"**W**ould no one rid me of this troublesome priest?"

"That's from something, isn't it?"

"It was Henry the Second," the bishop grumbled. "The king wanted to get rid of Becket. And I would like nothing better than to have someone rid me of Father Walsh!"

"Excuse me, Bishop," Monsignor Bell said, smiling, "but didn't they murder Becket? You didn't have that in mind?"

The bishop worked his lips for a few moments. "No," he said, finally. "Not murder. But there must be a way of getting him off my back. He calls practically every day. And he writes on the days he doesn't call."

Silence.

"Maybe," the bishop said, "if I made him a monsignor ..."

"He'd like that. But he'd still want an assistant. And he'd still keep bugging you about it."

"Dammit!" The bishop's palm hit his desk. "We haven't got anybody to send him. When old Tom Black retired last month that wiped out my bench. We're closing parishes, clustering parishes. Parishes that used to have four priests are lucky to have two, now. And, in a little while, it'll be one. Why does everybody seem to grasp that except Vince Walsh?"

"Actually," Bell said, "I think I may just have a solution—at least in this particular case."

"Oh?" With his scrawny neck and bald pate, the bishop resembled a rarely successful raptor.

"It's a young priest—one of the four you ordained last week. Gunther Hildebrand."

The bishop had a name, but couldn't come up with a face. He tried to recall the new priest. "Who the hell is Gunther Hildebrand?"

Bell might have been surprised—even shocked—that the bishop couldn't remember a man he'd ordained to the priesthood only days before. But Bell was not surprised. Over years of close association, he had come to know the bishop well. If someone had made a significant financial contribution, there would have been no hesitation on the bishop's part.

"You know ..." Bell prodded. "The young man who spilled the wine? Dropped the hosts ..."

"No ... no ..."

"After the prostration, the one who stepped on his alb ... and tore it? Damn near ruined it. We had to get him another one."

"Oh ... oh ... yes. Wasn't he just nervous?"

"I checked with the rector at the seminary. Bungling and clumsiness are Hildebrand's cruising speed." Bell spread a series of reports on the desk. "Look at these grades, will you?"

The bishop looked. "Good heavens! Unbelievable! How could we have ordained someone like this?"

Bell overlooked the "we." The bishop had ordained the man. Granted, the seminary recommended ordination, but the bishop did it.

"You know we've had to compromise on standards," Bell said. "That doesn't mean we're not getting some excellent men. But they're simply not enough ... though Hildebrand is about as rock bottom as we've accepted."

The bishop shook his head. "So how does this solve my problem with Vince Walsh?"

"We send Hildebrand to Walsh. A straight player trade. No cash involved."

"He'll never take him!"

"He'll have to take him. Hildebrand is a warm body. He can handle weddings and funerals and daily Mass and help on weekends. He can do all the dirty jobs. Walsh may not comprehend just how desperate the priest shortage is. But, after all this time, he'll know that if he doesn't accept Hildebrand, he'll have a hundred percent of nothing."

The bishop massaged his closely shaven chin. "It might work. It just might. We haven't already assigned this ... Hildebrand ... to a parish?"

"No. I've been over this with the assignment board. All they know is that the Hildebrand assignment has been put on hold. We await your decision."

"Hmmm. Well, let's get a look at this creature. Have him come in. My earliest opening."

Monsignor Bell shifted his weight. "The sooner we settle this, the quicker you'll be rid of Vince Walsh. I took the liberty of having Hildebrand come in. He's waiting in the foyer."

The bishop looked at Bell wordlessly.

"If you'd prefer," Bell said, "we'll have the kid come back later. I just thought ... Vince Walsh ..?"

"All right. All right."

As soon as the bishop saw him, it all came back. Trotsky, the early Communist leader. Hildebrand resembled him even more so this morning. So small, so skinny ... almost emaciated. Dark hair that looked as if he'd combed it with an eggbeater. Yup, short of the beard and mustache—Trotsky. Even to the thick, wire-framed glasses.

The bishop stepped around his desk and extended his hand. Hildebrand took it, turned it over, genuflected and attempted to kiss the bishop's ring. The bishop tried to pull his hand away, but Hildebrand was holding it so tightly that he ended up getting a sharp crack on the nose with the ring.

"Sorry," said the bishop. "We don't do that sort of thing anymore."

The priest's nose was bleeding, not profusely, but bleeding.

Small children sometimes call a handkerchief a snotrag. An inelegant term, but one that graphically described the cloth that Hildebrand partially stuffed up his left nostril. At least it stopped the bleeding.

They all sat down. The bishop informed Hildebrand that he was about to begin his priestly ministry at Holy Innocents parish. The bishop waxed eloquent, if somewhat inaccurately, about the parish, its proud record, how it always reached its goal in the diocesan fund drive, the fine attendance at weekend Mass, the number of organizations run by the parish, and so on.

The bishop then spoke of the pastor, Father Vincent Walsh, and his long years of service. The bishop did not dwell at any length on the pastor, as Father Walsh's history of dealing with priest assistants had not been marked by joyful camaraderie. In the days when, with greater numbers to play with, priests simply went where they were sent, it was a given that no one went to Holy Innocents willingly.

All through the exposition, Hildebrand was lost in endless distractions. The bishop really didn't need to describe life at Holy Innocents in such detail. Vince Walsh, among his peers, was notorious. Nor was he admired by many of his parishioners. Other priests could be openly critical; parishioners—those still faithful—realized it was Walsh or perhaps nobody.

The bishop was winding up. His tone of finality called Hildebrand back to the present.

"Necessarily," the bishop said, "this is only a sketchy description of Holy Innocents parish. But it will at least introduce you to your first parochial assignment, Father."

"My friends call me Hildy."

"I'm glad you told me that. Well, Father, if you have no questions, we will consider this meeting concluded. Monsignor Bell will send you official notice of your assignment, along with your faculties for priestly function in this diocese. Your assignment, Father, will take effect on Monday of next week."

Still not paying close attention, Hildebrand was aware that something was wrong. But he couldn't quite pin it down.

The bishop rose from his chair. As did Hildebrand.

The young priest, hand extended, moved toward the bishop, who stepped back so suddenly he almost fell. "No, no," the bishop said. "That won't be necessary. Just leave."

Hildebrand smiled broadly and departed.

"I'm whacked," the bishop exclaimed. "Whatinhell are we doing to Holy Mother Church?"

"Remember, Bishop, vocations are God's problem. He's calling good Catholic boys, but they're not responding." This rationalization usually soothed the bishop's all too realistic fear of the future.

"How about an early lunch?" the bishop proposed. "I could use a drink right about now."

"Excellent suggestion, Excellency."

It was only then that Bell noticed a pool of liquid at the front corner of the chair Hildebrand had occupied.

Bell was embarrassed. He managed to steer the bishop out the door before he could become aware of the indiscretion. The bishop was troubled enough.

As the bishop preceded him through the outer office, Bell managed to whisper to the secretary. "Our guest had a little accident. I don't want the bishop to know. Could you clean it up and ... something ... you know, spray the place ..?"

The secretary nodded. If the diocese ever published an honest and comprehensive job description for the post of secretary to the bishop, they'd have to recruit ducks.

Meanwhile, Father Hildebrand, en route out of the city, suddenly identified what had been making him uncomfortable. His pant leg was wet. With a disgusted expression, he carefully removed a squirt gun from his pants pocket. Somehow it had fired its full load of water.

Sadly, if the opportunity for a practical joke were to arise, his gun was empty.

MONDAY

Woody Woodpecker! My God, he looks like Woody the Woodpecker! Except instead of a crest he's got all that hair that sort of goes straight up. A long thin nose just like a beak. Woody Woodpecker! They sent me Woody the Woodpecker!

His new assistant had been scheduled to check in Monday morning. Father Vincent Walsh had begun his vigil at 8:00 AM, watching from behind the curtains at the large living room window. He checked his always-correct watch: 11:58. With any luck he'd get to the rectory door by noon.

Walsh had not counted on bad luck. As Father Hildebrand eased a large suitcase out of the car's trunk, the lock gave way and the suitcase flew open, its contents spilling onto the street.

Walsh might have helped, but he was too occupied in studying his new assistant.

He did not look promising.

Walsh had tried to get some idea of what to expect as soon as he'd gotten the man's name. But the cronies he hung with neither knew—nor cared—about the recent crop of clergy.

Finally, Hildebrand got the clothes collected and crammed back into the suitcase and the case closed and latched—barely; segments of clothing hung from the suitcase like mouse tails from an owl's mouth.

The doorbell rang.

Walsh sat very still, waiting for two full minutes to pass. Good to be casual at the first meeting. Don't give the impression you're anxious. Just another day ... another assistant. Never mind that it had been over a year since the previous assistant's departure.

During this two-minute drill, the bell did not sound again. Was he still there, waiting? Walsh, large in every direction, hurried, panting, toward the door. Under his heavy dark hair, his face looked as if it had been hit too often in football or boxing.

Since it was now just past noon, Walsh led his new assistant directly to the dining room, where Hildebrand was introduced to Sophie, the housekeeper.

"My friends call me Hildy."

"That's nice," Sophie acknowledged. "Will you want coffee with your lunch, Father?"

"No, thanks."

"After lunch, Father, I'll show you around," Walsh said.

"My friends call me Hildy."

"For now, Father, I'll just give you a list of what you'll be in charge of."

"Is it okay if I call you Vince?"

"'Father' will do." Walsh passed over several sheets of paper. Hildebrand, holding the paper in one hand, an egg salad sandwich in the other, began to read. Egg salad dripped onto the plate, onto the table, onto Hildebrand's suit.

Fearing the salad would shortly hit the floor, the walls, or possibly even the ceiling, Walsh retrieved the papers. "I'll just read you the names of the organizations. The descriptions you can read later."

Hildebrand did slightly better with his sandwich using both hands.

"Here we go," Walsh began. "Adult Convert Class; Legion of Mary; Boy Scouts; Girl Scouts; Senior Citizens; Ushers; Altar Boys; Catholic Youth Organization; Men's Club; Women's Guild; Youth Group; Lectures; Ministers of the Eucharist; St. Vincent de Paul Society; and Bingo."

Hildebrand had stopped in midlist in midbite.

"As I said, Father, you can read the descriptions of these organizations later. Any questions?"

"I think this was very generous of you, Father—entrusting all these groups to me, I mean."

Walsh studied him through narrowed eyes. Sarcasm? For the moment he'd give the young man the benefit of the doubt. "One more thing, Father: You will find on the desk in your office several boxes of collection envelopes for our parishioners. They're ready to go; just bring them to the post office. Now ... let's get to work!"

TWO WEEKS LATER

For the first time in their relationship, Father Walsh invited Father Hildebrand into the pastor's private study. Hildebrand could not think of a reason for this. Did this bode well? He shrugged; he would know soon enough.

The pastor was seated behind his desk. A modest, straight-back chair stood against the wall. Hildebrand, adapting the Biblical admonition to take a low position in hopes of being invited higher, headed for the simple chair. As he lowered himself into it, the pastor shouted, "Don't sit in that ch—"

Hildebrand and the delicate chair collapsed as one.

"—air!" Walsh buried his face in his hands. "It is ... was ... an ... an antique ..."

"Sorry, Father. It looked like a chair."

Walsh could say no word more. Nothing seemed adequate. He waved his assistant to the chair on the other side of the desk. There was silence as Walsh mourned his loss and Hildebrand kept his own counsel.

Finally, Walsh recovered sufficiently to get to the business at hand. "Father, when you first arrived two weeks ago, I gave you the collection envelopes to take to the post office. Yesterday, the first Sunday the old envelopes ran out, there were no envelopes in the collection. Nor was there much cash. Have you an explanation?"

"Envelopes? Envelopes ... You're going to laugh: I believe they're still in the trunk. I forgot all about them."

"In the trunk! You didn't mail them?"

"I'll do it this afternoon."

"Yes, you will! But not through the mail. You will get in your car and deliver them, each one, personally. It's the only way you'll learn."

"Yes, Father." It appeared to be an improbable task. But "Yes, Father" seemed the appropriate response.

As he ran a line through the word "envelopes" on the agenda sheet, Walsh became aware that his hand was trembling. He shook his head as if that would halt the tremor. "Now, Father, we come to the matter of your assault on Mrs. Canavan."

"Assault?"

"Three evenings ago. Your first appearance at a Women's Guild meeting. During your closing remarks ... well, as it was told to me, during your closing remarks, you grabbed—the word 'clutched' was also used—Mrs. Canavan's left breast. Can you explain that?"

Hildebrand responded without hesitation. "That's not the way it was at all ... well, that is the way it was, but not quite. See, I was making a gesture. My right arm swung out—like this." His arm hit the desk lamp, knocking it to the floor. "Sorry," he said, hesitating only a moment before continuing. "I didn't plan on hitting anything. But then I felt something. Let me tell you, Father, I was as surprised as anyone. It was, to be sure, Mrs. Canavan's breast. If I had been standing just a couple of inches to the left, this wouldn't have happened."

Walsh's fingers were tapping the table. "That's where the word 'clutched' came in. According to the responsible source who told me, you ... uh ... squeezed—squeezed, I say—!"

"Put yourself in my shoes, Father. Imagine it: Here I was, making an innocent gesture—a totally innocent gesture—when I find myself holding something. Something soft, yet firm. Instinctively, I tried to ascertain whatinhell it was. So, I—instinctively, mind you—I felt it. I must admit, it felt good. So, maybe I felt it a little longer than necessary. But, I swear, I didn't know it was a breast until I turned and saw for myself. It was an accident at worst, Father. But I'll tell you this: If Mrs. Canavan's right is as good as her left, she has one terrific set of boobs. I mean that in all innocence," he added.

Walsh had the unmistakable onset of a dirty thought. Before he entertained it or it entertained him, he moved on.

"Finally ... I mean, this could go on for hours, but I'm holding it to a minimum ... there's the matter of baptismal stipends."

"Your pardon?"

"Baptismal stipends. The money parents or godparents offer at the time of baptism. You've had baptisms two Sundays now. Didn't anybody offer anything?"

"Oh, yes. They were quite generous."

"And?"

"And?"

"What did you do with the money?"

"I told them to keep it. Matthew Ten Eight: *'Freely have you received, freely give.'*"

Father Walsh almost choked. "Father, that's how we eat!"

"That wasn't covered in the seminary."

"From now on," Father Walsh managed to get his breath, "bring the stipends to me. *And deliver those collection envelopes!*"

TWO WEEKS LATER

"Have you delivered all the collection envelopes yet? The collections haven't improved very much."

"I'm up to the L's," Hildebrand said brightly.

Walsh's mouth hung open. With effort, he managed to speak. "Father, do you know how many S's there are?"

"Well, this one wants her house blessed. And that one claims no priest has ever visited. What with one thing and another ..."

"Never mind! Make this the very first item on your agenda. If this deficit keeps up, I don't know how we can continue."

"Are you feeling all right, Father? Your color ... uh, your face seems florid."

"Never mind! There are more important things to consider. We must do something about these daily Masses with the children." *I never thought I'd have to say that.* "What happened during your sermon last week?"

Hildebrand, eyes raised, tried to recall. "Oh, you must mean when I asked what does a bishop do? And Tommy Sloan said, 'Moves diagonally.'"

"You didn't correct him?"

"I thought it was quite clever. Besides, at least as far as chess goes, Tommy was right."

"Never mind that!" Walsh was increasingly aware that both his hands had been trembling quite often lately—especially when he had to deal with his assistant. He made an effort to still the shaking. "Besides, that wasn't the sermon that was reported to me. I'm talking about the one, Father, about the Pentecost event."

"Oh, that one. Well, I was trying to get the children to consider the force of the Holy Spirit when He came to the Apostles in a great wind. I asked the children if they'd ever heard of a hurricane or a tornado. Almost every hand went up. Then I asked if any of them had lived through a tornado.

Little Henry Watkins raised his hand. So, I asked him to tell us about it ..." Hildebrand hesitated.

"And?"

"And Henry said, 'It blew the fuckin' roof off the house, Father.' The children seemed to think that was quite humorous."

"Well, I don't. And neither did the Sisters and the teachers. I must insist, Father, that you cease your dialogue sermons with the children. You are proving how dangerous that can be.

"Now, quickly, let's clear up a few other things. Two nights ago, there was a fire in the Dumpster by the church. Did a call come in from a reporter?"

"Yes."

"And your comment?"

"Holy smoke!" Hildebrand chuckled.

"It wasn't all that funny in the paper." Walsh seemed near apoplectic. "And while we're at it, when answering the rectory phone, do you always accurately identify this parish?"

"Not always. Sometimes I say, 'Holy Ignorance.'"

"That, too, is *not* funny. It must cease. Immediately! Now, get on with those collection envelopes!"

"You really ought to see a doctor, Father."

TWO WEEKS LATER

"Father, I'm worried about you. Your color is not good. And there's a vein pulsating in your forehead."

Indeed, Vince Walsh did not appear healthy. Those who had known him longer than the past six weeks might well have trouble recognizing him. Once the master of his fate, he now seemed a beaten man.

But, waving aside his assistant's observation, Walsh launched directly into his agenda. "Those collection envelopes: Where are you in their delivery?"

"Up to the S's." Hildebrand beamed.

"Mail the rest of them."

"But I've been making—"

"Mail them!"

Hildebrand had accomplished what no previous assistant to Walsh had done: won.

"Now, Father," Walsh continued, "I want to know why the bishop is not talking to me."

"He isn't? But how would I know—?"

"It couldn't have been your sermon yesterday. He's probably just now hearing about how you made fun of the Diocesan Development Fund." Walsh's tone was almost pleading. "Why did you do that?"

"I didn't intend to. But I just got out of the seminary and I know there's practically nobody there. The money goes to light, heat, cool, clean and guard a nearly empty building. And as for social services, I think government agencies do a better job than we do. I didn't really want to say all that. But—" Hildebrand extended his hands in a gesture of helplessness. "—the chancery directive said we should talk about the DDF."

Walsh's breathing was labored. "Father, this parish ... has always ... met its DDF quota. But ... this year ... and these weeks with no ... collection envelopes ... Still, that doesn't explain ... why His Excellency won't talk to me."

"But, I—"

"It happened—" Walsh seemed to have regained his wind, at least temporarily. "—last Wednesday at our Confirmation ceremony. Everything was going well, as usual. Our priest guests, and the bishop, arrived in plenty of time. We all enjoyed our preprandial drinks. Dinner went well. The Women's Guild prepared an excellent meal." He paused a moment. "Madam

President, even if she hasn't forgotten, at least seems to have forgiven you.

"Then," he returned to the main subject, "we had the confirmation of the children. After which the bishop pointedly refused to speak to me. Instead, he and Monsignor Bell left as soon as they got their vestments off. I've been thinking about it, and I keep coming back to you. What did you do?"

"Really, I don't know why ..."

"*What* did you do?"

"Well ..." Hildebrand was lost in recollection. "It must've been the stick business."

"The 'stick' business?"

"Yes, Father. You know, the stick that a bishop carries ..."

"It's not a 'stick.' It's a shepherd's crook," Walsh clarified. "It's called a *crosier*, by heaven!"

"Did you know it comes in three pieces?"

"Of course! How is it going to be transported? On a ski rack on top of a car?"

"Well ..." Hildebrand was fidgeting. "I never put one of them together before."

"My God in heaven! They let you play with the *crosier*!"

"Actually, it wasn't hard to figure out how it fits together. There's a bottom piece that screws into the middle piece, which screws into the top—where the crook is. I got the bottom and the middle part together without trouble. But when it came to the middle and the top part ... well, that was another matter entirely. They just wouldn't go together. Personally, I think the threads were stripped. I kept trying, but it just wasn't working. I want you to know, Father, I was feeling a lot of pressure—"

"What happened!" Walsh was almost shouting ... and near wheezing at the same time.

"Well, the children had all marched into the church. And the bishop was drumming his fingers on the vestment case."

"And?"

"Well, I figured the most important part of the stick is the top. So I handed the top part to the bishop and suggested that he go out on his knees and pretend he was Toulouse-Lautrec."

"You said that to the bishop?"

"But he didn't do it. He just went out without any part of the stick at all."

Hildebrand had never witnessed a heart attack in person. From what he'd seen on TV and in the movies, the victim always seemed to pitch forward. In the case of Vince Walsh, his eyes rolled back as he sort of slid under the desk.

FOUR DAYS LATER

"He looks pretty good, eh?" said Father Cook.

Father Tracy nodded. "Never saw him so much at peace."

"He went awfully fast," Cook observed.

"Lucky bastard," Tracy said.

The late Father Vincent Walsh lay in state in front of the altar in Holy Innocents church. In a little while, most of the clergy, together with the bishop, would gather here. This used to be called simply a funeral; now the correct ecclesial term is Mass of Resurrection. Or the Mass of Christian Burial.

Father Walsh looked as if he were resting before taking his place with the other clergy. He wore all the vestments necessary for participation.

A group from the Knights of Columbus stood at attention in their medieval uniforms and swords. The median age of these gentlemen appeared to be about 103.

Nearing the church was a sparkling clean Lincoln Town

car driven by Monsignor Bell. The lone passenger was the bishop.

"I can't believe," the bishop mused, "that I actually said that I wanted someone to rid me of Father Walsh."

"It was just a figure of speech," Bell suggested. More and more his responsibility seemed to be to soothe the bishop's troubled conscience. "Anyone would understand that what you really meant was that you wanted Father Walsh to stop nagging you."

There was no response. The bishop was lost in thought. "My *crosier*," he said finally. "There was nothing wrong with it?"

Bell shook his head. "I had no trouble assembling it."

"Strange. You know, I only ... experienced ... Hildebrand for a very short time—in the office and in the sacristy at the parish. But I found that it doesn't take long for him to reach you."

"That must be true."

"Because you're appointing him pastor of Holy Innocents parish. It's a big job and he will be, by far, the youngest pastor in the diocese."

"He wanted it."

"Vince Wade wanted an assistant."

"What could I do? I can make exceptions to chronological order anytime I please. I can't discipline him. He's done nothing canonically wrong. And I can't have him as an assistant hurrying other pastors to an early heavenly reward." He smiled, but it was a shallow expression.

"Extortion," Bell muttered behind clenched teeth.

"What was that?"

"Exceptional," Bell articulated.

Holy Innocents church was filling. There were fewer parishioners than might have been expected. But the turnout of priests was gratifying.

The bishop had arrived. It was time to close the casket.

"They're going to close the casket, Harry," Father Tracy said. "You want to take one last look at Vince?"

"I don't think so, Arnold. It's too depressing," Father Cook replied. "Look: There—coming into the sanctuary now. It's the kid, Hildebrand. He's got a lot of nerve. They say he killed poor Vince—metaphorically, that is."

"Funny, he doesn't look much like those pictures in the paper and on TV."

And indeed, he did not. His hair had been cut and shaped stylishly. His tailor-made cassock was spotless. His shoes were highly polished. His roman collar was linen—not plastic—and starched.

Hildebrand joined those helping to close the casket. Unseen, just as the lid was lowered, he slipped something into the casket alongside the body. It was a squirt gun.

Hildebrand took an immaculate, pressed handkerchief and touched it to his forehead.

The undertaker looked around the church. A good crowd, but not nearly enough to fill the pews. "You never know exactly what to expect, do you, Father?" he said to Hildebrand.

"I don't know," Hildebrand replied. "Sometimes things turn out exactly as planned." He covered his mouth with the handkerchief and lowered his head as his shoulders shook. He might have been weeping.

Then again, maybe not.